Praise for *A Show for Two*

'You'll fall head-over-heels in love with these characters while they fall in love with each other. Tashie Bhuiyan is a force to be reckoned with."
—Chloe Gong, #1 *New York Times* bestselling author of *These Violent Delights* and *Our Violent Ends*

"Tender and bittersweet, *A Show for Two* is an honest, clear-eyed look at the inevitability of pain even in the ferocious pursuit of happiness."
—Tahereh Mafi, #1 *New York Times* bestselling author of *Shatter Me*

"An endearing story of rediscovery that brings out tears of both laughter and heartbreak."
—*Kirkus Reviews*

Praise for *Counting Down with You*

"A witty, romantic, deeply insightful debut that steals your heart from start to finish."
—Emma Lord, *New York Times* bestselling author of *You Have a Match*

"I'm completely heart-eyed over this book."
—Rachel Lynn Solomon, *New York Times* bestselling author of *Today Tonight Tomorrow*

'I. Love. This. Book."
—Mark Oshiro, award-winning author of *Anger Is a Gift* and *Each of Us a Desert*

'Tashie Bhuiyan has done an excellent job of portraying the conflicts faced by many South Asian diaspora kids in this debut."
—Sabina Khan, author of *Zara Hossain Is Here* and *The Love & Lies of Rukhsana Ali*

'A brisk and buoyant YA romance anchored by well-drawn family dynamics and anxiety issues."
—Jenn Bennett, author of *Alex, Approximately*

'Hand to fans of Netflix hit *Never Have I Ever*."
—*Booklist*

Books by Tashie Bhuiyan
available from Inkyard Press

Counting Down with You
A Show for Two
Stay with My Heart

TASHIE BHUIYAN

STAY

with my

HEART

inkyard
PRESS

Recycling programs
for this product may
not exist in your area.

ISBN-13: 978-1-335-01003-2

Stay with My Heart
Copyright © 2024 by Tashie Bhuiyan

"Ba Ram (Levanter)"
© 2019 JYP Publishing & Interpark
All rights administered by Sony Music Publishing (US) LLC, 424 Church Street,
Suite 1200, Nashville, TN 37219. All rights reserved. Used by permission.

For questions and comments about the quality of this book, please contact us at
CustomerService@Harlequin.com.

TM is a trademark of Harlequin Enterprises ULC.

Inkyard Press
22 Adelaide St. West, 41st Floor
Toronto, Ontario M5H 4E3, Canada
www.InkyardPress.com

Printed in U.S.A.

For Chloe Gong,
who has always stood by me.

I let my dreams tie me down
Is it too late, can I break out?
They say it's darkest of all before the dawn

•••

I wanna be myself
Yeah, I gotta be myself
And now that your weight's come off my shoulders
I realize that I can fly
I needed to find me
Now I know the key was inside of me all along
I'm listening to my heart, let it guide me
I feel the light, I feel the light

—Stray Kids, "Levanter"

AUTHOR NOTE

Dear Reader,

In all honesty, writing *Stay with My Heart* was one of the most difficult things I've ever done in my life. A large part of that is down to the fact that my grandmother unexpectedly passed away while I was still working on revisions for it. If any of you have read my debut novel, *Counting Down with You*, you might have an idea of how much my Dadu means to me. Within my family, she has always been my biggest supporter. She won't be here to see the publication of this book or any of the future ones to come, but I hope they all make her proud. When I started drafting this book, I had no idea I would come to identify with the main character, Liana, as much as I did by the end. It was like rediscovering the story all over again. All this to say, Liana struggles with mental health, complicated familial relationships, and grief in a way that's similar to a lot of us.

Despite all of that, this is a story about hope, like all of my books before it. Throughout my life, I've loved so many songs. I can't even start writing a book without creating a playlist for it first. It seemed inevitable that one of these days I'd write one inspired by my love for music. But more than that, I wanted to write a book about the way music can bring people together and give you a family, hence Liana and the relationship she has with Third Eye. I've met so many of my best friends because of our shared interest in the same artists (admittedly, mostly because of One Direction), and I wouldn't trade that experience for the world. A very serious part of me believes that music—and the friendships that come from it—can save your life, and I'm certain it saved both mine and Liana's.

If you've ever listened to a song and felt an immediate, intense connection to it, this book might be for you. If you've ever become a fan of an artist and met your best friends in the entire world through your love for them, this book might be for you. If you've ever attended a concert, and felt a sense of home in the community around you, this book might be for you. If you love music and found family and strong-willed girls who find a way to survive despite it all, this book might be for you.

No matter what the world throws at us, I hope we all continue to find a safe haven in the music we love.

All the love,
Tashie

PART ONE

I had this picture in my head
Of all the promises you made
But you turned them into dust

—Stray Kids, "Levanter"

1

BRUTAL—OLIVIA RODRIGO

I'm late to my own graduation.

With a quiet grunt, I scuttle past the people sitting in the last row and sit in the first empty seat I see, trying not to make eye contact with anyone in the process. This is definitely not my designated seat or even my designated row, but it'll have to do for the time being.

Somewhere near the front of the room, my best friend is most certainly staring me down for an explanation, but there's no way to explain my late arrival across a crowded auditorium. Instead, as soon as I'm settled, I take my phone out and go to shoot her a text, only to realize there's *six* already waiting for me.

Evie Khodabux: bro where are you

Evie Khodabux: you know graduation started *checks watch* uhhhh ten minutes ago right

Evie Khodabux: LIANAAAAAAA WHERE ARE YOUUUUU

Evie Khodabux: liana bibi sarkar,,,,,,

Evie Khodabux: I swear to god if you don't text me back,,, the next time I see you will be at your funeral <3

Evie Khodabux: are you seriously going to ditch graduation??? YOU SHOULD HAVE TOLD ME??? I WOULD HAVE DITCHED WITH YOU WTF

Me: omg STOP I DIDN'T SEE THESE I'M SORRY I'M NOT DITCH-ING SFKLJSFKLJ

Me: DON'T KILL ME IT WASN'T MY FAULT MY DAD DID IT

Me: tldr: as always his job comes first at all times, up to and in-cluding the day of his only child's graduation l o l

I tuck my phone under my thigh and resist the urge to sigh. I don't know what I even expected. My dad's never on time these days, but I thought today might be the *one* day he would at least try.

My fingers snag in the purple material of my graduation gown, and the guy beside me casts a wary look in my direc-tion before scooting over for good measure. He's kind of fa-miliar but also not. He might have been in my AP Psych class during junior year. Who knows.

It's not like any of this matters. It's been three years since my mother died—and three years since my father and I picked up everything and moved from New York to Los Angeles. So even though I'm friendly with a lot of the people in my high school, the only person I really latched on to enough to call my friend since moving—my very best friend—is Evie, and I wouldn't have it any other way. She's the only one whose opinion of me will still matter once this ceremony ends.

If Evie were beside me, she'd remind me a good percentage of our classmates are going to UCLA in the fall like I am, so I'll probably run into them at some point or another. I'd stick my tongue out at her in response.

But she's not here. She's all the way across the room, holding her diploma, and I'm in the back, all alone, wondering if they'll even call my name to walk across the stage.

Ugh.

I somehow muster up the nerve to nudge the guy beside me. "Hey, do you know if they've already finished *S* last names?"

He shrugs. I try not to wrinkle my nose at the overbearing smell of weed coming off his graduation gown. "Probably."

"Great," I mutter, leaning back in my seat. I might as well have not shown up at all.

A part of me is itching to call my father and yell at him, but the rest of me knows it wouldn't faze him. He doesn't care what I have to say. He never has.

I glance up toward the balcony to see if I can spot him among the sea of parents. I can't help but notice how many of them are in happy tears, recording the ceremony with their phones, holding flowers and balloons in celebration.

When I finally find Baba, he's standing off to the side, his phone held to his ear, looking away from the stage. Probably talking to someone from work. I scowl and look away before

I give in to the urge to throw a temper tantrum right here in the middle of the auditorium.

I'm seventeen years old. I'm too old to start screaming and throwing things. I *know* this, but Jesus, am I tempted.

It's in my old age that I've realized why children cry so much. It's so hard to say *look at me, look at me, just look at me. See me the way I want to be seen. Hear me the way I want to be heard.* It's a lot easier to start sobbing in a demand for attention.

I wouldn't have to if Ma were still here. But it's been a long time since I've seen her smile or felt the warmth of her love and support.

She should've been here. To see me walk across the stage and receive my diploma. To start a new chapter of my life. *She should've been here.*

My lower lip trembles without my permission and I suck it into my mouth, biting hard enough to nearly break through the skin.

I will not cry. Not today.

"When can we leave?" I ask the guy beside me. He seems like he'd rather be anywhere but here, listening to our principal drone on, so he probably knows when this is supposed to end. My voice is slightly gruff when I speak, but he doesn't seem to notice or care.

"Not soon enough," he mutters, checking his phone for the third time. Then he gives me a brief once-over. "Are you about to have a mental breakdown or what? Your hands are shaking. Do you want a hit?"

"I—no, no, I'm fine," I say, tucking my hands under my thighs. Good God. I need to get it together. For the most part, I tend to have high-functioning anxiety, allowing me to *appear* like I'm holding it together even when I'm not, but today clearly isn't my day.

He raises his eyebrows, but thankfully doesn't push. Instead, he says, "Liana, right? AP Lit?"

"I think it was AP Psych," I say, though I'm even less sure that's right than I was two minutes ago.

He blinks slowly, his eyes growing distant for a moment, like he's searching through his memories for me. But then he shrugs. "Cool, whatever. I'm David."

"I would say nice to meet you, but I'm probably never going to see you again so…" I offer him a thin smile.

"Well, we'll see each other tonight, at least," David says, a touch too confidently, considering I don't even know what my plans are for tonight yet. "You're going to Sophia's grad party, aren't you?"

Oh shit. I completely forgot about that.

Sophia is the most popular girl at Wexford High School, and probably the friendliest, too. We were in the same Spanish class sophomore year, and to this day, she always says hi to me whenever we pass each other in the hallways. Earlier this month, she sent out a mass invite to the entire senior class inviting them to a grad blowout at her house tonight.

If I were on my own, I probably wouldn't go, but Evie mentioned wanting to attend and I can never say no to her— especially not tonight, since it's her last day in California, before she flies out to New York City for some pre-college summer program at Columbia.

I've been trying not to think too much about how lonely I'll be without her for the entire summer, stuck with only my father to keep me company (or *not* keep me company, as it is), but it hasn't been going well. At least I'll have my part-time job at my uncle's record shop and my internship at Ripple Records to distract me.

"Yeah, I'll be there," I say to David wearily. He gives me a thumbs-up and turns his attention back to the stage.

I try to do the same, but I'm too jittery to focus.

Something underneath my skin is *boiling* with anxious irritation at the fact I'm letting my dad ruin this day for me. I wish I didn't care so much, that I could pretend he doesn't exist, that none of this is happening, but he's all I have left.

This isn't what Ma would have wanted for us, but it's not like that matters much these days.

The room suddenly bursts into noise and graduation caps fly into the air, startling me half to death. I'm not even sure how long I zoned out for.

"Congratulations!" the principal yells. "To the class of 2024!"

I toss my cap half-heartedly and watch as it flops pathetically at my feet.

Happy graduation to me, I guess.

2

MATILDA—HARRY STYLES

Los Angeles traffic is the bane of my existence. Second only to my father refusing to listen to me.

"Did you really have to go back to get these CDs?" I grumble, staring out the window instead of at him.

If Evie's car hadn't been packed to the brim with her family, I would've caught a ride with them instead. Then I wouldn't be late *again*.

At least it's more fashionable to be late to a party than your own graduation.

But still, each moment I sit here in traffic is another moment I could have spent with Evie.

Usually long drives help with my anxiety, letting the world around me slow down for once, but today it's only heightening it, making me more tense.

If only my dad didn't make a pit stop at his office to pick up a cardboard box full of CDs from his assistant. Then maybe

I'd be at this party already, dramatically holding Evie in my arms and reminiscing on all our high school memories.

My dad isn't a huge fan of the new digital age of music, so he always manually burns demos onto CDs instead of downloading them onto his phone like any normal person would. Usually, I wouldn't care, since I also like the physical feel of holding a CD in my hands, but right now, it's a huge inconvenience.

"I had to, Bibi," my dad says, replacing the current CD with a new one. "It's for work."

Work. It's always *work*. He's an A&R coordinator at Ripple Records, a prestigious record label whose headquarters are located in downtown LA. His job is recruiting new talent for the company, and once upon a time, I thought it was the coolest thing ever.

Even if I won't say it aloud, a part of me still finds it insanely cool. Despite how I feel about my dad, he gave me my love for music, and that's something I wouldn't trade for the world. Things were easier when Ma was still alive—when music was something we all shared. Singing at the top of our lungs in the car. Dancing in the kitchen. But after she passed away, music became an almost selfish thing. Baba's music is his music. My music is my music. They no longer overlap.

And it's not like I haven't been trying. I'm going to UCLA to study music management. I work part-time at a record shop. I'm interning at his company this summer. I go to local shows, concerts, festivals, all in an attempt to connect with him somehow. To remember this thing that we once shared *together*.

"You could have gotten them after you dropped me off," I say under my breath.

"Then I'd have less time to listen," Baba says, replacing yet another CD. He barely even played the one he's taking out. I can't help but feel bad for—I glance at the CD case in his hand—Phantasma.

"You know Evie is leaving first thing in the morning," I say, trying not to let the frustration bleed into my voice. "I won't see her for *months*. This is our last night together."

"You two are on the phone all the time, anyway," he says, like that's remotely the same thing. "You'll be fine."

Why do I even bother?

"She's going to Columbia, Baba. In *New York*." *Our old home*, I don't say. I don't like to think too much about New York if I can help it. It's like poking at an old bruise that refuses to heal over. "She might not even come back to California before starting her fall semester."

He gives me a sideways glance before looking back at the traffic. "No one was stopping you from going to college in New York with her if that's what you wanted. I told you I'd move back to the NYC office if you needed me to."

"That's not—I don't want to move back to New York," I say through gritted teeth.

Ma and Baba always promised they'd follow me wherever I went for college, and I used to be so happy, so grateful for that. But now I know that no matter where we go, Baba will still be like this—distant, neglectful, *unseeing*. And being in New York, where Ma's ghost haunts the city, would only make it worse.

"What do you want then, Bibi?" my father asks, as if *I'm* the one being unreasonable.

I throw my hands up. "I just want to be able to see my best friend. Surely that isn't too much to ask."

"And you'll see her. It's not like I'm stopping you from going to this party," Baba says loftily.

I open my mouth to snap back but fall short when I see him switch out yet another CD—but this time I recognize the cover art. It's a highly minimalistic depiction of an eye with huge block letters spelling out *THIRD EYE* underneath it.

I know this band. Or at least I know *of* this band.

One of the members goes to Wexford High School. I think he's in the year underneath me. I remember seeing him play the drums in our school talent show.

What was his name? Uhhhh—*Ethan*. The image of a bright-faced blond boy comes to mind and the memory clicks into place.

I grab the CD case out of my dad's hand, flipping it over to the back to skim the credits. Baba gives me a surprised look but doesn't complain.

Members: Skyler Moon, Thomas Smith, Mohammed Anwar, Ethan Mitchell, Vincent Alvarez.

Track list: Flying, Soda Pop, Triple Down, Genesis, Spitfire.

"They're not bad," Baba says, drawing my attention. He's humming along to the first song, his fingers tapping against his steering wheel. "The lead singer is a little raw, though. Definitely needs more vocal training."

He can expertly analyze a song within seconds of hearing it, and yet still has trouble understanding me when I say the most straightforward things. I stare at his fingers for a moment too long, watching them match the song beat for beat before making a face, tossing the CD case back into the box. "Were you even listening to anything I was saying before? About Evie?"

"This again?" Baba asks with a sigh. "We're almost there, okay, Bibi? Stop the whining, please."

I scoff in disbelief, but it's mostly to cover up the fact there's a lump growing in the back of my throat. He wouldn't be this casually cruel if Ma were still around. "You can't be serious, Baba. This is important to me. You're not even looking at me when I'm talking to you—"

"I'm *driving*," he reminds, gesturing at the windshield. "Come on, Bibi. Act your age for once."

"Driving doesn't stop you from working, but it stops you from paying attention to me, is that right?" I ask, shaking my head. My eyes threaten to leak in the corners and I rub at them before they can expose me. I can't be in here anymore. I can't do this. "You know what? Just drop me off here. I'll walk."

"Bibi—"

"I said I'll walk," I repeat thickly, refusing to meet his gaze.

Baba pinches the bridge of his nose with one hand but doesn't bother saying anything else, pulling over on the side of the street and unlocking the doors. I can't help but grow even more resentful at his lack of protest. He's not even going to try to convince me to stay in the car? To let him drop me off?

God. Whatever.

I quickly wipe my eyes again before I gather my stuff and throw open the passenger door. I don't even bother to say goodbye.

"Be home before ten," Baba says before I can leave, and I

suck in a harsh breath. It's not like he'll be home by ten o'clock to even know if I'm there or not.

"Whatever you want," I say with a thin smile, and slam the door in his face.

3

BLUE FLAME—LE SSERAFIM

"Liana! Are you sure you don't want a drink?"

I turn around from where I'm watching a rather pathetic attempt at beer pong and smile helplessly when I see Evie holding out a White Claw. "I'm good, Evie. Thanks, though."

She shrugs. "Hold the extra for me, though, will you? I'll have it when I finish this one." She opens her can with a satisfying pop. "There we go."

"You have a flight at eight in the morning," I remind her, gently patting her hand, but after a moment, I give in, holding the extra White Claw for her. "Go easy, will you?"

She harrumphs but lowers her can. "It's fine. God knows I'll be too busy learning astrophysics to drink all summer. Let me have this while I can."

"No one told you to study rocket science," I say and laugh under my breath when she pouts, nudging her elbow into my side.

"It would be easier if someone had," Evie admits, her words

a little softer. The decision to go to college in NYC has been rough on her. She's never really left California, much less been to the East Coast. Part of it is being the eldest daughter—something I've never been able to relate to as an only child—and part of it is the fact Evie's father is out of the picture. She basically helped her mother raise her younger siblings. Leaving them behind, even if it's for something she's genuinely excited about, is hard.

"Hey, it'll be good for you," I say, soothing her as best as I can, running my hand up and down her arm. "NYC is a whirlwind. Are you sure you don't want me to put you in touch with my cousins? I'm sure Karina or Mina would be happy to show you around."

"It's okay," Evie says and finishes the rest of her White Claw in a matter of seconds. I wince but don't say anything. She pulls a hair tie off her wrist and ties her red dreadlocks into a large bun at the back of her head before grabbing the extra can from me. "I'll figure it out on my own."

"But the point is you don't have to," I say, pressing my chin into her shoulder once she's settled again. "I know you're used to taking care of everyone, but it's okay to let other people take care of you sometimes."

"I guess," she mutters, but she leans her head against mine. Despite the actual weight of her head, my body feels lighter when I'm around Evie. It's comfortable and easy to breathe in her presence. I have no idea what I'm going to do without her for the entire summer. I already know there's going to be endless FaceTime calls between us.

"Don't make that face," Evie says, flicking my nose. "Listen. New rule: no being sad. Either of us. Let's snap out of it. We're here to have fun, right?"

I blow out a long breath and nod. "Right. Let's go have fun, then."

Evie grins and tugs my hand, pulling me through Sophia's house. The place is overcrowded and smells entirely too much of sweaty teenagers. There are definitely people here I've never seen before in my life, and I'm pretty sure I overheard someone say that they're a student from our rival high school. Sophia's popularity seems to know no bounds, and I'm not even remotely shocked.

Eventually, Evie and I find a couch without too many stains to sit on, and I flop down, resting my head in her lap. "I feel like I could fit in your carry-on if I bent myself correctly. I've been doing yoga for my anxiety lately and I'm much more flexible—"

"You're so weird," Evie says, but she's grinning and running her fingers through my dark hair. We've always been rather tactile—it's why Evie's mother thought we were dating junior year of high school. It didn't help that Evie came out as a lesbian just a few months beforehand.

I smile at the memory of her mother introducing me to Evie's extended family from Guyana as her daughter-in-law at their family reunion before Evie had to jump in and incredulously explain we were best friends and nothing more.

"What are you thinking about?" Evie asks, poking at my freshly threaded eyebrows. "You're smiling a little too much."

"Hey!" I say, smacking her arm. "I smile."

"You could stand to smile more," Evie says, but squeezes my arm to soften the blow. "Promise me you'll have so much fun without me this summer." I squirm and she points a stern finger at me. "No—I'm serious. Promise me."

I roll my eyes. "How am I supposed to have fun without you?"

"Find a way," Evie says, and it's the most pleasant threat I've ever heard. "This better be the best summer of your life thus far. I don't like how serious you've gotten these last few months. It's always UCLA this or UCLA that. You start your internship at Ripple Records next week, don't you? Be a little excited for once and focus on yourself."

"If I'm left alone with my own thoughts for more than five minutes, I might lose my shit," I say, and it's more honest than I intend for it to be.

Evie gives me a sad smile. "Hey. It's going to be a good summer, okay? For both of us. We're doing big things! And we'll FaceTime at least once a week to catch each other up on everything."

"You're too much of an optimist," I say but muster up a smile for her in return. "Yeah. Okay. I promise."

She holds out her pinky and I take it with mine, twining them securely. Before we can separate, Evie's phone buzzes.

I shift out of the way, giving her space to take it out of her pocket. While she taps at the screen, I glance at the rest of the party from the corner of my eye. It's thinned out since I first arrived, which is a relief.

"Shit," Evie says.

I look back at her and something pangs uncertainly in my chest. "What? What's wrong?"

Evie doesn't say anything, clicking rapidly on her phone, her eyes darting up and down her screen. I worry my lip between my teeth and watch her silently, my anxiety building slowly under my skin.

"Fuck," Evie says, leaning her head against the back of the couch.

"What, Evie?" I ask. She slumps farther into her seat, groaning, and I shake her arm. *"What?"*

"My flight just got canceled. American Airlines is asking me to pick a new one, but basically all of the ones for tomorrow are booked," Evie says, and looks at me with panicked brown eyes. "I have to be on campus by tomorrow night and the only flight I can take that will get me there in time departs at five a.m. Like—in *eight hours.* I haven't started—"

"—packing," I realize and sit up straight. "Oh my God. You have to leave now, then."

Evie worries her bottom lip between her teeth, looking between her phone and me. "But I made you come to this party. I can't just leave you here—"

"I'll come with you," I offer helplessly, but I know it's not an option. Her mother is lovely but she still has her limits. There's no way she would let me hang out at their house until three in the morning.

Evie's face falls, confirming my thoughts. "I'm so sorry, it was supposed to be our last night—"

"Hey, don't apologize to *me*," I say, quickly pulling her into my arms. "If this is anyone's fault, it's American Airlines. Who even cancels a flight this late? Which genius thought of that?"

"Liana," Evie mumbles in my ear, holding me closer. "I'm sorry. Really."

"It's *fine*, because you're going to FaceTime me tomorrow night from New York and we'll just drink White Claws together on opposite sides of the country, okay?"

Evie makes a sniffling noise that's concerning, but I don't

pull back. If I see her crying, I'll start crying, and it'll be bad for both of us. "I'm going to miss you."

"I'm going to miss you, too, but a long-distance friendship will hardly be the thing to break us. We're going to have fun this summer, remember? You made me promise!"

Evie takes in a deep breath and finally lets go of me. I pretend not to see when she carefully rubs at her eyes, neatly avoiding her makeup as she wipes away her tears. "Right. Yes. Okay." She takes a deep breath. "Love you, Liana."

"Love you, Evie," I say, and I wish it didn't sound so much like goodbye.

4

STYLE—TAYLOR SWIFT

If it weren't for the promise I made Evie, I'd leave the party at the same time as her. Instead, I force myself to stay for another half hour and try to enjoy myself, to make sure I'm at least *trying* to have a *summer of fun*.

But the more time I spend at the party, the more jittery and irritable I become. Today's my graduation. One of the most important days in my life. And yet it could not be going *worse*.

At one point, I even run into David from earlier, who's so out of it that I feel like I'm getting a contact high just by looking at him. Even though he's so far gone it's laughable, he looks like he's having fun, which is more than I can say.

I sigh and take a sip of my soda, glancing around the room without much interest. I might as well call it a night and request an Uber. I unstick myself from the wall, moving for the kitchen to throw out my drink. Halfway there, I stop in my tracks.

There's a boy leaning against the island, surrounded by

half a dozen girls, and he's wearing a tank top with—with a minimalist eye design?

I blink, trying to recall the design from the THIRD EYE album cover. It's near identical to the boy's tank top, except the background on the cover was black and his tank top is dark green.

I give him another once-over, this time cataloguing his features. He's obviously not Ethan, given the fact he's neither blond nor white. His black hair is messy, curling near his neck, and his eyes are dark, overbrimming with amusement as one of the girls nearby lays a hand on his arm. There are half a dozen rings spread across his fingers and a silver earring stud in his left ear. I think he might be wearing makeup—he turns his face toward me slightly and I can tell he definitely has eyeliner on. He has a few visible tattoos, all too small for me to make out except for the—leaves?—flowers?—vines?—on his neck. It only heightens my suspicions that he's one of the band members.

My theory is confirmed a moment later when one of the girls says, "It's so cool that you started your own band." She's beautiful—too beautiful to be fawning over a silly boy at a party, but it's not exactly my business.

"Thanks," the boy says, and his cheeks are flushed now, a pretty pink color that I've only heard about in songs.

Started the band, huh? The leader, then.

I lean against the fridge, taking another sip of my soda and trying to remember the member names on the back of the CD. It's going to bug me until I do. One of them was definitely Mohammed, I remember that, but I doubt this is him, unless he's mixed. He looks East Asian, but there's no way for me to know without asking him his specific ethnicity, and I have no interest in doing that.

One of the girls giggles so loudly I nearly drop my soda in surprise. Lord. I doubt whatever he said was *that* funny.

I can't help but step closer, eavesdropping despite myself.

"I'll buy your album, I swear," another girl says, wrapping her arms around his neck. He doesn't react other than to laugh, gently removing himself from her reach.

"You're not going to remember this conversation tomorrow," he says, tapping her nose. I furrow my brows at the slight condescension in his voice. It isn't inherently obvious, but I've been around enough of his type to see right through them.

The giggling girl shoves her way past her friend to stand unsteadily in front of him. "Sky, tell us about your first show."

Sky. Skyler Moon. There we go.

Satisfied with myself, I throw away the rest of my drink and move to leave the kitchen, leaving him to tell his spectators about his first show. I pause only to grab a water bottle when I hear Sky say, "If you can name three of my songs, I'll take you out on a date. Cross my heart and swear to die."

A chorus of complaints come from the girls and I slowly turn back to face them. Name three of his songs? He's not even *famous*. If he's so desperate to get these girls off his back, there are other ways to do it that don't involve stroking his ego.

"Um, Spitfire?" a girl says, scratching her head. "That's one, right?"

I can't help but make a face at how entertained Sky looks by the lack of response from the rest of them. Boys are so stupid.

"Come on. Weren't all of you begging for tickets to my next show earlier? Surely, you can name a few of my songs," he says, raising an eyebrow.

"Spitfire is definitely one," the first girl says, firming her expression. "Is another... Double Down? Is that right?"

Sky shrugs, a smirk on the edge of his mouth. "I don't know. You tell me."

I narrow my eyes at him. He's really going to keep this going until someone names three of his songs? And keep humiliating these girls in the process? I'm not even a part of their conversation and I'm anxious at the thought of having to keep guessing as an attempt to satisfy this guy's whims.

"Anyone?" Sky asks, picking up his drink. When only silence greets him, he chuckles, shaking his head. "I didn't think so."

He moves to take a sip of his drink when someone says, "Soda Pop, Triple Down, Genesis."

Everyone turns to look at me, surprised, and belatedly, I realize it was me who spoke.

Oh shit.

Sky's expression is slack in disbelief but his eyes are so bright it hurts to look at him. "Seems like we have a winner. Who are you?"

"No one," I say, taking an uneven step back. Stupid, stupid, *stupid*. I shouldn't have offered myself up on a platter to save those girls. I don't even know them.

"No, tell me your name," Sky says, a full-blown grin coming to life on his lips. "I need to know who I'm taking out on a date."

I scoff, unable to help myself. "Thanks, but no thanks."

Without another word, I turn on my heel and exit the kitchen, desperate to put as much space between me and him as possible. Skyler Moon is someone I have no desire to run into again.

5

FOOLS—TROYE SIVAN

As soon as I make it into the hall, I bump directly into someone, nearly falling into their arms. I look up in shock, opening my mouth to apologize, but the boy shakes his head, helping me stand upright.

"Sorry about that," he says easily, a small smile spreading across his face.

The tension in my shoulders ease. His smile is disarming, warm like his brown eyes. My stomach can't help but flip at the sight of it. Maybe Evie was right. This summer is already looking up. "No, it was all me. Sorry, I wasn't looking where I was going."

He laughs, shaking his head again. His brown hair is floppy, falling into his eyes. "No, I didn't mean—well, I'm sorry for that, too. But I meant for Sky. I know he can be kind of obnoxious."

I blink, trying to make sense of the words. It's hard to focus when a cute boy is staring me down. Once I sort it out in my head, I gesture back to the kitchen in surprise. "You know him?"

The boy's smile widens and he holds his hand out. "Yeah, I'm in Third Eye. His—his band. I'm Thomas."

I take his hand, shaking it slowly. Thomas Smith, then. I'm attracting Third Eye band members like moths to a flame tonight. "Liana."

"Nice to meet you, Liana," he says, tucking his hands into his jean pockets when I let go. "But, yeah. Sorry about him. The small-town fame is getting to his head." Thomas rolls his eyes, and I can't help but join in. "I'd say he gets better with time, but..."

I laugh despite myself. "Why'd you join the band, then?"

Thomas shrugs, and takes a few steps back to avoid a swarm of seniors rushing past him. I follow him until we're both leaning against one of the walls in the living room. "I was young," he says. "Dumb."

"You're still young," I say with a raised brow.

He smirks. "And still dumb."

"Yet to be determined," I say, waving him off, but a part of me is undeniably pleased. It's rare to meet a guy who actually acknowledges how dumb teenage boys can be. "So, what, you and the rest of the members just put up with Sky's ego, then? No one calls him out on it?"

"He wouldn't listen if we did," Thomas says, and then glances over my shoulder, eyes scanning the room before leaning closer. "If I'm being honest, I don't even think the others notice."

"Rose-tinted glasses," I surmise and tilt my head, moving closer to him.

"Exactly," he says, matching my energy by leaning forward until we're only a few inches apart.

"*You* notice, though," I say, poking his shoulder. It's a little more flirty than I would usually be, but Thomas doesn't seem to mind and Evie told me to have a summer of fun. "Why don't you say anything?"

He makes a face, his nose scrunching up. "I think they'd kick me out of the band if I tried."

My mouth falls slightly open. "Are you being serious?"

He sighs, running a hand through his hair. "Yeah. It's just not worth it. At the end of the day, the music is what matters."

I frown at him. "Thomas, that's awful. I'm sorry."

"It is what it is," he says, offering me a thin smile. "But hey—you knew our songs? Have you been to one of our shows?"

"Oh, I—" I falter, unsure how to proceed. I can't tell him about my dad, not when I barely know him. Baba would have a fit and lecture me once again about how people could use me to get to him, and I'm not in the mood to deal with that. He's been even more adamant now that I'm going to be interning at his record label.

"Yeah?" Thomas asks, watching me so closely that my cheeks flush with warmth. It doesn't help that he's conventionally attractive, with a beach tan, soft eyes, and even softer-looking hair curling around his ears.

"I—I've seen Ethan Mitchell around," I say finally, licking my lips. "So I've checked out Third Eye's SoundCloud page before." A lie, since I've never heard their music outside of Baba's car, but I doubt they have a Spotify page at this stage of their career—SoundCloud is the most reasonable conclusion, but if I'm wrong, I might have to dig my own grave and crawl into it.

"Oh, that's cool," Thomas says, and I resist the urge to visibly deflate in relief. "Well, you should come to one of our shows sometime."

I perk up. An invitation. That's a good sign. "Really?"

"Really," he says, bumping his shoulder into mine. "I can let you know the next time we book a gig?"

I nod immediately. I've always loved attending concerts, whether they're in huge stadiums or small clubs. Even better when I'm personally invited by one of the band members and he has a sweet smile that makes me feel like the sun. "Yeah, I'd like that."

"Pass me your phone, then," he says, holding his hand out, and I easily oblige, taking his iPhone when he returns the favor. "There. I'll let you know, then."

I grin at my phone, where he saved *Thomas from Third Eye* in my contacts. "Sounds like a plan."

Thomas from Third Eye: hey it's thomas smith from 3E

Thomas from Third Eye: from the grad party?

Me: oh hey!! :)

Me: how are youuuu

Me: how was the partyyy

Thomas Smith: it was good aside from sky lol

Thomas Smith: I wish you didn't leave early

Thomas Smith: it would've been cool to hang out for longer

Me: I guess then we gotta hang out sometime in the future to make up for it hahaha

Thomas Smith: I'm down

Thomas Smith: what are you up to this summer?

Thomas Smith: can you make time for me in your schedule? ;)

Me: lmao I don't think it'll be a problem

Me: I just have an internship and part-time job

Me: otherwise I'm as free as a beeeeee

Thomas Smith: that's rad

Thomas Smith: where are you interning/working?

Me: I work at Ahmed's Record Shop :)

Me: you should stop by sometime

Me: we have the coolest vinyls

Me: we also have basically any album you need

Thomas Smith: any recs?

Me: oh so many

Me: but I'll limit it to one for today

Me: Communion by Years & Years

Me: their debut album is one of the best I've ever heard

Thomas Smith: I'll come by and check it out then :)

Me: I look forward to it :)

6

LOVE LIES—KHALID, NORMANI

Thomas starts texting me rather frequently after that. I can't find it in me to complain, not when talking to him makes the long summer days so much more interesting. Evie is absolutely delighted by this development.

He tells me about Third Eye and their endless rehearsals at Thomas' parents' house, and I tell him about my days working away at Ahmed's Record Shop, accompanied by my cousin Riya, who's also my manager. I'm careful not to mention anything about my internship, skirting around it in our conversations.

I also don't tell him about how despondent I've felt lately. Ever since my graduation, I haven't been able to stop thinking about how my mom is going to miss every single important event I ever have in my life. My high school graduation, my college graduation, my first job, my first long-term relationship—all of it.

But that's too much baggage to put on anyone aside from a

therapist, so I've spared Thomas the sob story. We talk about lighter, easier things. I prefer it that way.

Thomas Smith: what's ur fav ice cream flavor?

Me: coffee maybe? idk hahaha

Me: I'm also partial to cookies n cream but it can be a little too sweet sometimes

Thomas Smith: still not as sweet as you

"Put your phone away," Riya says, smacking my arm lightly as she passes the counter. Her black curls hang down her back, almost past her waist. I have no idea how she handles it. I impulsively chop my hair every year, and right now it's just below my shoulders, which is already a nuisance.

I pout at her. "There aren't any customers right now, Riya Apu."

"You're still on the clock," Riya says as she picks up one of the discarded records in the aisle and sets it back in its rightful spot.

"You're on your phone half the time," I complain, but tuck my phone back into the pocket of my pants, sitting down on the stool behind the counter.

"When you're the manager, you can do what you want," Riya says, but I catch a hint of a smile in the corner of her mouth before she turns away to reorganize another display shelf.

"When Biptu Uncle fires you, then you'll realize," I say under my breath and ignore her huff of amusement.

It's a slow day today. We had a few customers come in when

we first opened, but it's midafternoon now and it's awfully quiet aside from the faint music over the speakers. It's one of my playlists on shuffle, and right now "Eye in the Sky" by The Alan Parsons Project is playing.

If it weren't for Thomas' texts, I fear I may have already died of boredom. When my phone buzzes again, Riya shoots me a pointed look before I can reach for it, and I scowl at her.

"You're so annoying," I say and slump in my seat, leaning my elbows against the glass counter.

Riya laughs and disappears into the back room. Despite our bickering, seeing Riya is one of the reasons I like this job as much as I do. When I first moved from New York, I didn't know anyone here, and Riya was quick to show me the best places around the city and offered me a job at the shop when I complained about homesickness. Uncle Biptu talked to Baba, and it was a done deal before I even really had a chance to think about it.

I don't regret it, though. Being surrounded by music has always been my happy place, especially during the more difficult times in my life. While I'm tone-deaf and can't play an instrument to save my life, I love listening to music anyway, love breaking it down and analyzing it, until only the bare bones remain. It's always been a part of me, and I doubt I could carve it out even if I tried.

The small bell in front of the door rings as someone enters the record shop, and I look up, pasting on my customer-service smile. "Hi, welcome to Ahmed's Record Shop, how can I—Thomas?"

Thomas grins at me, walking up to the counter. His hair is sweaty, like he ran all the way here, but his smile is as warm as ever. "Liana! Hey. Glad I caught you."

"I—I wasn't expecting you," I say, and my hands go to my hair instinctively, sorting out my curtain bangs the best I can without a mirror in front of me. Thomas doesn't seem to notice, taking a look around the shop before turning his attention back to me.

"Me and the boys stopped in to get some ice cream down the road," he says, hitching a thumb out the window. He must mean at Dacu Creamery, the ice-cream shop Riya and I go to sometimes during our breaks. It's only then that I notice the small container in his free hand, which he sets on the counter when he catches me looking. "Coffee-flavored, as requested."

"You didn't have to do that," I say, unbelievably giddy at how thoughtful the gesture is. There are nervous butterflies in the pit of my stomach, and I try not to think about them too hard. "Did you run here?"

He shrugs, still grinning. "Didn't want it to melt. Also, remember how I told you I'd let you know about our next gig?"

I nod and he pulls out a stack of flyers from his back pocket, rolled up to fit. "Is that—?"

He nods, handing me one of the sheets and uncurling it for me to read.

Next Level Club Presents
THIRD EYE
Live Show
May 24th, 2024
Entry: $5 | Doors open: 7:00 p.m. | Free Parking

My eyes zero in on the picture of them. I recognize the laughing blond boy immediately—Ethan Mitchell. Next to him is Thomas, who's staring rather seriously into the camera.

In the center is none other than Skyler Moon, wearing a flirty smile. I roll my eyes, and move on to the last two members—neither of whom I recognize, but I can easily guess which one is Mohammed, which leaves the other as Vincent. Vincent has an easygoing, relaxed expression, whereas Mohammed looks a little more nervous, but enthusiastic all the same.

"Are you supposed to be the brooding bad boy?"

"Your marketing major is showing," Thomas says, but dips his head in a nod of agreement. "I think the band has a little something for everyone."

"Not a marketing major yet," I say, but smile anyway. He remembered something as small as what I plan to study at UCLA in the fall. I may have neglected to mention that I'm double-majoring with music management, but that's neither here nor there. "Who's the fan favorite, anyway?"

Thomas makes a show of rolling his eyes, and I already know the answer before he says it. "Sky. But a decent amount also are obsessed with Ethan."

"I promise to stay loyal to you," I say with a playful salute and he laughs. "Next Level Club, huh? Have you guys performed there before?"

Thomas shakes his head. "It'll be our first time."

"Juan is great," I say, giving Thomas' hand a light pat. "I'm sure he'll make sure it goes smoothly."

"You know Juan?" Thomas says, raising a brow.

I falter, finally registering my slipup. The reason I know the event coordinator at Next Level Club is because I go there every now and then to watch shows, and I make a point of introducing myself to everyone there as Jhilmil Sarkar's daughter. Usually, I'd hold that fact close my chest, wary of being taken advantage of, but when it comes to other professionals in the music industry, it's a way to establish my credibility. Half the reason I attend these shows is to network and build up my career, so I'd be remiss if I didn't properly introduce myself.

"Uh—yeah, he's been to the store a couple of times," I say eventually. "He's really nice. He really loves Imagine Dragons, so mentioning them will get you some brownie points."

"We leave the bookings to Mohammed," Thomas says, pointing him out on the poster like I wouldn't immediately be able to spot the one and only brown boy in the group. "I'll be sure to mention it to him."

"You guys don't have a manager or anything?" I ask curiously. Even if artists aren't signed to labels, a lot of the time someone else will step in as their manager, to deal with all the ongoings and bookings. With a band this young, I'm surprised one of their parents hasn't taken up the position.

"Sky wants to keep it within the band," Thomas says, and again, I sense the note of derision. "But it's fine, it's worked for us so far."

I hum, not offering my opinion either way. "Well, make sure to post this online, too, alright? I don't know which one of you handles social media, but that's honestly your best bet for drawing a crowd these days."

"Vincent," Thomas says, pointing him out, too, confirming my conclusion from earlier. "But Sky prefers the old-fashioned way, hence these." He makes a point to wave the flyers in his hand.

"Sounds like Sky has a lot of sway," I say, giving Thomas a pointed look. "What do you do in the band? Does he let you handle anything?"

Thomas opens his mouth to say something, but then there's a knock on the door. I glance out to see Vincent gesturing for Thomas to come outside, clearly irritated.

"Speak of the devil," Thomas says, snorting before squeezing my hand. "I'll see you around, Liana."

"For sure," I say, trying not to glare at Vincent for cutting our conversation short. "Feel free to come by anytime."

Thomas grins. "I'll take you up on that."

Before he goes, he gives me another flyer and points at our bulletin board. I nod, already reaching for one of the pins under the counter, and wave as I watch him leave.

"Bye, Liana!" he calls as the door shuts. With a faint smile on my face, I pin the flyer to the bulletin board and return to work. I haven't had a lot of good days lately, but this is definitely one of them.

7

PINK IN THE NIGHT—MITSKI

It becomes a ritual for Thomas to come visit me whenever he and his friends are in the area. We talk about nothing and everything, and I learn more about Third Eye than I expect to. It's been a while since I've had a crush but I can feel it burgeoning the more we spend time together, even if it's never outside the store or our texts.

It's comforting to have a distraction from the inexplicable sadness that's been haunting my every step for the last few days. I know I'm having a depressive episode—or at least I'm pretty sure that's what it is. I've been feeling listless and exhausted, barely looking forward to my days interning at Ripple Records, even though it's all I've talked about for the last few months.

I spent a lot of my teenage years wondering what the hell was wrong with me, and eventually turned to the internet for an explanation. Most of my symptoms align with anxiety and depression, and while I haven't had a medical professional confirm it *yet*, I know it's inevitable.

Which is why it's nice to pretend I'm neurotypical every now and then, ignoring the myriad of things going wrong in my brain in favor of indulging in this silly little crush.

"He's in love with you," Evie says firmly. I groan, rolling over and stuffing my face in my pillow. We're on FaceTime, and it's three hours later for Evie, almost midnight. Both of us are in our pajamas, committed to our sleepover once a week, and with every single thing I say about Thomas, Evie seems to be more and more convinced that he's halfway to in-love-with-me.

"It's been like three weeks," I say, but the words are muffled. Evie must make them out anyway because she scoffs loudly.

"Okay, fine, he's not in love with you. Frankly, it would be weird if he was, now that I think about it. That's way too soon, especially since he hasn't asked you out yet. But he definitely *likes* you."

I turn on my side, facing my MacBook again. "Maybe it's just like—a friend thing. It doesn't sound like he's close with the members of Third Eye. It must be nice for him to talk about music with someone that won't judge him."

"I'm sure it is nice for him. And that's *why* he likes you. You're pretty, you're cool, and you're into the same stuff as him. What more can he ask for?"

I throw my hands up. "I don't know. I just don't want to misread the signals."

"He's a *boy*," Evie points out. "Most of them have two brain cells in their heads, if that. If it was a queer girl, sure, I could buy that. God knows it's impossible to figure out the line between friendly and flirting with them. But as far as we know, Thomas is a straight boy, so I really don't think he could be any clearer."

"He could ask me out," I grumble.

Evie pauses, and then nods, conceding. "Okay, fine. If you want to wait for him to make the first move, *fine*. But it's just a matter of time. Why else would he visit you at work so often? Didn't you say he brought you a pastry last time?"

"He was just being nice!"

"Shut up," Evie groans, throwing her pillow at her laptop, but it just bounces off harmlessly. "You're so dumb."

"You love me," I say instinctively, and my heart warms when Evie's face softens.

"Yeah, I do. But you're still dumb."

I stick my tongue out at her and she does it back, even more exaggerated, until we both burst into giggles.

"Tell me about your love life," I say instead, lying back in my pillows. "What's new?"

"Absolutely nothing," Evie says with a dramatic sigh. "The girl in the dorm across the hall is gorgeous, but I have no idea which way she swings, so I'm just stuck pining miserably."

"Be serious," I say, shaking my head. "Go ask her for like—an eyelash curler or something. Say you lost yours."

Evie gives me a surprised look. "That's not a half-bad idea."

"I have my moments," I say dryly.

She waves me off. "How's Willow?"

I glance off-camera at my black cat, lying at the end of bed and half-heartedly licking her paws. "The usual. Ignoring me."

"She probably misses Aunt Evie," she says, and starts cooing. "Willow, Willow, come here."

At the sudden high-pitched sound, my cat looks at the laptop with interest. I hold my arm out, offering her the back of my hand, and Willow lazily gets to her feet, stretching her limbs out. Slowly, she limbers over to me, rubbing her cheek against my hand before coming to my laptop, pawing at the screen. Evie laughs in delight, and I let out an exasperated breath, but I can't help but smile, too.

We got Willow shortly after Ma passed away, from the same animal shelter that she used to work at. It was the only thing I could think of at the time that would at least distract from the endless ache in my chest. I'm pretty sure the sole reason my father agreed was because it meant I'd be too invested in my cat to bother him.

I press a kiss to Willow's head while she's preoccupied and settle back in my spot. Willow eventually retreats to the foot of the bed, and I return my attention to Evie who's watching me with a knowing look.

"So I've been seeing your tweets," she starts and I immediately groan, covering my face with my hands. "Are you sure you can't start going to therapy any sooner? Because, quite frankly, you need it."

"You're preaching to the choir," I say under my breath. "It's fine. UCLA has school resources for mental health, so I'll just meet with one of their counselors starting in the fall. I'm already on the waitlist."

"That's still like three months away," Evie says, shaking her head. "There has to be some way you can go sooner."

"I can't, Evie," I say with a sigh. "I wish I could. But I'd have to use my dad's health insurance and I can't do that. At UCLA, it's through the school, so I won't have to deal with all that."

Evie scrunches her nose. "I know, but it's just... I worry about you. Without even addressing all the tweets about wanting to scream into a void, you've also been retweeting a *lot* of Mitski lyrics. It seems dire."

"Maybe I just like Mitski's music."

"Yeah, *okay*. Sure. And I'm the long lost Princess of Genovia."

I scowl at her and Evie rolls her eyes.

"Just take care of yourself, okay? I wish I could help you more," Evie says after a moment, and all my defensiveness falls off like a second skin. "I'm always here if you need anything."

"I know," I say softly. Evie has always been too giving. "I'm also here if you need anything. I've been seeing your tweets, too. Have you been able to talk to your mom today?"

"I just miss her, it's no big deal," Evie says dismissively, but it's the kind of lie where we both know what the truth is. "But that's not the point. What I'm *trying* to say is you deserve good things, Liana."

I smile, but it's sadder than I want it to be. I know a change of topic when I see one. "So do you, Evie."

8

GIVES YOU HELL—
THE ALL-AMERICAN REJECTS

"…and then my dad realized I wasn't in my room, and he freaked out. My phone was dead, so every time he tried to call me, it went through to voice mail, and you can *imagine* how that went down. So I'm sitting there, completely clueless—"

Thomas cuts off mid-sentence when the door to the record shop slams open. My head snaps up in alarm, unused to someone coming in *that* loudly. Riya is downstairs in the basement doing inventory, which means whatever the ruckus is, I'll have to handle it by myself.

"What—?" I start to ask and falter when I realize it's Skyler Moon. And more than that, it's *all* of Third Eye.

"So this is what you've been doing," Sky says, his voice flat. The door shuts behind him with a resounding thud. "*Flirting* with the random record shop girl? Are you kidding me?"

I make a concentrated effort not to splutter in disbelief. *Random record shop girl?*

Thomas' face, which was bright with enthusiasm just moments before, is blank now. My stomach stirs with uncertainty at the unfamiliar expression on his face, even as my chest flares with anger at the way Skyler is talking to him. "Am I not allowed to talk to people now? Was that a new band rule that you forgot to tell me about?"

Mohammed scoffs, trading a look with Vincent who's pinching the bridge of his nose.

Sky is visibly grinding his teeth. "You know that's not what I meant."

Thomas raises an eyebrow. "And what did you mean, my liege?"

"Don't talk to him that way," Ethan says, his cheeks flushed with anger. It throws me for a loop, because I've never seen Ethan anything but smiling.

Thomas' eyes narrow and he turns to Ethan, but before he can say anything, Sky slips in between them, his jaw set with determination.

"You need to cut this shit out," Sky says, his voice low. "I've told you like three times already. I don't know why you're not taking me seriously."

"Maybe because you don't know what the fuck you're talking about," Thomas says sharply.

"I don't know what the fuck I'm talking about?" Sky lets out an incredulous laugh.

He looks like he's gearing up to keep going, so I try to de-escalate, waving my hand in between them. "Can you guys chill out? This is hardly—"

"Don't bother," Thomas says to me before I can finish my sentence.

Sky finally looks over at me, and I can see the moment recognition from the party flickers in, because his gaze turns even more accusatory when he turns back to Thomas. "You have to be fucking kidding me, dude. What's *wrong* with you?"

"What's wrong with *me*?" Thomas asks in disbelief. He's glaring at Sky now, sharp daggers that would intimidate anyone. Sky doesn't seem ruffled, though, meeting Thomas' stare without flinching. "I work harder than anyone in this band, but you're always on my ass. Why is that?"

Ethan's mouth drops open behind Sky, and Vincent wraps his arms around Mohammed's waist before he can take a step forward, beyond incensed.

"Are you serious?" Sky asks, clearly at a loss. "We're wasting practice time right now because of *you*."

"Then go practice," Thomas says, gesturing toward the exit. "The door is right there."

"You're a real piece of work, you know that?" Vincent asks, shaking his head. "What happened to you, man?"

"I woke up," Thomas says flatly. "And you should, too."

The bell above the door rings again as another customer comes in. Some of the fog in my head clears and I stand up straighter. "Welcome to Ahmed's Record Shop," I say to the elderly woman. She gives me a smile before wandering deeper into the shop.

When I'm sure her back is turned, I shoot a glare at all of Third Eye. "Please leave if you're not going to buy something."

Ethan mutters an apology and starts herding them out, lightly nudging Sky's back when he refuses to move from where he's still staring at Thomas.

"Sky, come on," Ethan murmurs, squeezing his arm, and Sky looks down in surprise. "It's not worth it. Let's just go."

Sky sighs and nods, looping his arm with Ethan's and Vincent's, before leaving the store, not bothering to look back at Thomas.

"Jesus Christ," I mutter once they've all left. "What was that?"

Thomas shakes his head, running his fingers through his hair. "They're always like that. I can't do anything right these days."

I frown, watching through the storefront windows as their figures become tinier in the distance. Something about this feels off, but I can't put my finger on what. "Are you late to practice right now? Should you go before you get in more trouble?"

"No, it's fine," Thomas says before turning a beautiful smile on me. "Do you want to go on a date?"

If I were drinking something, I would've spit it out. As it is, I nearly choke on the air in my lungs. "A date?"

He nods, still smiling. "Saturday night?"

"I—yes," I say, slightly dazed. That was the last thing I was expecting. My heart is pounding like a drum inside my ears. "I'd love to."

"Perfect." Thomas leans across the counter and I nearly squeak when he brushes his lips against my cheek. "I'll pick you up at eight."

Before I can process any of that, he leaves, the bell above the door signaling his departure.

My fingers reach up to touch my face, warm where he kissed it. "Holy shit," I say to myself.

And then I immediately scramble for my phone to text Evie.

9

COMFORTABLY NUMB—PINK FLOYD

Later that day, with less than an hour left before closing, the door to the shop opens. I look up with a practiced smile. "Welcome to Ahmed's Record Shop."

Belatedly, I realize it's Skyler Moon again, but this time he's alone. I blink twice to make sure I'm not seeing things. But it's undeniably him. The plaid shirt he was wearing before is gone, and his black tank top leaves his arms bare, which means the small tattoos on the inside of his arm are visible, even if I can't quite make them out. If that weren't enough, his neck tattoo gives him away beyond question. Now that he's closer, it becomes obvious that they're a few different types of flowers, all climbing up the side of his neck.

I look away before he can catch me staring, meeting his gaze instead. "Can I help you?" I ask, losing my customer-service voice completely.

Sky sighs, absently scratching the back of his neck. "I don't know if you remember me from the party a few weeks back, but—"

"Oh, I remember you," I say coldly, recalling all too well how easily he got under my skin.

"Right," he says, his voice hesitant. It's a far cry from the confident dickhead he was being at the graduation party. "I, uh, wanted to apologize for earlier today. We didn't mean to cause a scene. We should've handled the matter on our own time somewhere else. I swear I'm usually more aware of these things, but I just—well, it doesn't matter. But I'm sorry."

I stare at him for a long moment, trying to figure out how much of this is genuine and how much of this is to prevent me going on the internet and wailing about how awful the leader of Third Eye is, effectively ruining their career before it even starts.

Maybe I'm being paranoid, but having a parent in the entertainment industry and wanting to major in music management, my brain is hardwired to consider all angles, especially when it comes to public figures. Even if he isn't *quite* a public figure yet.

"If you're not a paying customer, you need to leave," I say finally, crossing my arms and cocking my head at the door.

Sky frowns but nods. I expect him to turn on his heel and disappear, but instead he wanders deeper into the store.

Do you even own a record player? I'm tempted to ask, but the last thing I want is to initiate another conversation with him.

I tap restlessly against the counter as I watch him wander through the store. There's no reason for him to still be here.

Naturally, he peruses the aisles for a while. Much longer than is necessary, considering he's probably just loitering and doesn't plan to buy anything. Fifteen minutes to closing, I open my mouth to tell him to *leave* already, but then I notice that he's carrying a record, even as he continues to glance through the rest of the store.

I grumble under my breath, knowing Riya will beat my ass if I kick an actual customer out of the store.

When Sky finally comes to the counter, he's still holding the same record. He sets it on the counter and offers me a timid smile.

I don't return it. Instead, I stare down at *The Wall* by Pink Floyd in a mixture of shock and incredulity. It's one of my favorite albums by one of my favorite bands, one I've played countless times on repeat in the store. Of all albums, why would Skyler Moon pick this one to buy?

"What's your favorite song on the album?" I ask almost robotically. I don't mean to ask it, but I *need* to know. Does he really like this album? Did he just pick one at random?

"Comfortably Numb," Sky says, giving me a curious look. "What's yours?"

A long silence.

"Mine, too," I say slowly and then immediately ring the vinyl up, wanting to be far, far away from Skyler Moon.

He doesn't say anything as he pays, but I can feel his stare on the side of my face as I bag his record and pass it back over the counter.

"Sorry again," he says, lingering even still. My fingers curl into fists and I hide them beneath the counter, resting against my thighs instead. "I hope you have a good night."

I nod shortly and don't meet his eyes as he leaves the store. When I'm sure he's gone, I slump against the wall in disbelief.

The lyrics to "Comfortably Numb" are close to my heart—so close that the idea of someone like him perceiving them makes me slightly nauseous.

It reminds me far too much of the inside of my brain. My anxiety might be high-functioning, but my depression feels debilitating at times. It's like the world turns off around me, until everything is gray and bleak and meaningless. Comfortably numb.

And no matter what I do, I can't find the motivation to keep going, to take another step. I'm so detached to it all and the world just passes me by while I'm at a standstill.

My depressive episode right now isn't quite that bad. During the day, I can force myself through the motions, and I have tiny distractions to keep me going, but at night, I'm alone with my own thoughts and it's a lot harder. In fact, just last night, I listened to "Comfortably Numb" and felt the heaviness of the song settle like a stone in my chest.

I hate the idea of Sky knowing the song, of him *liking* it, maybe as much as I do. I expected him to say "Another Brick in the Wall" at *best*, if he even knew the album at all. It's not that "Comfortably Numb" is unpopular—in fact, it's the opposite. But I just can't make sense of any of this in my head. How can he know the song? Why does he know the song? What's going *on*?

"I think I'm turning into one of those annoying music snobs," I say to Riya in distress when she passes by, sweeping through the store with an old broom. "Can I gatekeep Pink Floyd?"

"I think that ship sailed a *long* time ago," Riya says with a snort and hands me a rag to wipe down the counter. "If our dads listened to them in Bangladesh in the '70s, I think it's safe to say they have a worldwide impact. I don't think anyone, much less you, can gatekeep them."

"I can try," I say, but it's weak even to my own ears. It's not even like I actually want to—the amount of times I've tried to get Evie into the same bands and artists as me is immeasurable. Usually, I love sharing my playlists. Enjoying music with people who *get it* is one of my favorite parts of the music industry.

But something about sharing "Comfortably Numb" with Skyler Moon is driving me up the wall. No pun intended.

10

SUPER SHY—NEWJEANS

When I hear a car pull up down the road at 7:59 p.m., I wave Evie a quick goodbye on FaceTime. "Thank you for helping me get ready," I say, quick but sincere. "I'll text you all about it after."

"You better," Evie says and waves back as I end the call. I glance in the mirror one last time, fixing the bobby pins in my hair. I pinch the skin beneath my wrist once to make sure this is all real and I haven't fallen into one of the love songs I adore so much.

But sure enough, the pinch hurts, and that's what gives me the confidence to run downstairs when I hear the doorbell ring. I take a deep breath before unlocking the door, pulling it wide open to see Thomas standing there, smiling at me. For a brief moment, I forget how to breathe, and only remember when I need to talk.

Thomas is holding out a bouquet of red roses, and it's all so endearing that I have half a mind to shut the door right there because I can't even *cope* with how sweet it is. Somehow, I manage to say, "Thank you."

He waves me off, but it's clear he's pleased by my reaction. "It's nothing."

I take the roses and set them on the table in the foyer. I'll probably be home before Baba, but even then, I doubt he'd notice or care if there were roses in the hallway. It's like there's a ghost living in this house with me.

When I turn back, Thomas is holding an arm out, as if he wants me to loop mine through it.

I raise my eyebrows, but Thomas just grins at me. I pretend to consider it, stroking my chin for emphasis.

"Well?" he asks, tilting his head. His eyes are shining brighter than I've ever seen them, and I can't find it in myself to even pretend to say no.

I loop my arm through his and nod at the door. "Lead the way."

We end up on a boardwalk at Venice Beach, slowly trailing along the path to the sound of the waves brushing up against the shore. Thomas keeps kicking a pebble as we walk, a strange look on his face.

"What are you thinking about?" I ask, nudging his side with my elbow. I'm not much of a beach girl, but the boardwalk is nice enough. It's even nicer with the company by my side.

"Isn't that the question of the century," Thomas says before nudging me back. I don't know how he's not warm in his button-up shirt and slacks, since I'm sweating in my sundress, but the last thing I want to do is bring attention to it. "I don't know. I was just thinking about the future."

"Oh God," I say with a groan, shaking my head. "Why would you ever willingly be thinking about that?"

Thomas shrugs. "I don't know. I've just been thinking about…" He laughs nervously, scratching the back of his head. His hair is growing out, something close to a mullet but not quite. "Maybe leaving Third Eye? I don't know."

My brows rise so high on my forehead I'm afraid they're going to disappear into my bangs. "Oh?"

"I don't know," he says, laughing again. "Forget I said anything. What do you see when you think about the future?"

"Me eating ramen?" I say, half joking. "I don't know. Going to college, I guess. Figuring my shit out. Finding a therapist. Definitely that one."

"All admirable goals," Thomas says, a soft smile on his face. "What about after that?"

I lick my lips, unsure how to even really talk about this. "I mean, I'd like to work in the music industry…maybe in marketing? Public relations? Something like that. I feel like that's right up my alley."

"Yeah?" he asks, giving me a curious look. "I bet you'd be great at it."

"I think so, too, since I'm chronically online," I say, rolling my eyes.

When Thomas grabs my hand, I nearly jolt in surprise, but eventually relax, intertwining my fingers with his.

"Who isn't chronically online these days?" Thomas asks with a chuckle.

I snort, returning my attention to our conversation. "Fair.

It's kind of hard not to be. Although, Third Eye's socials could use some work. You said Vincent's in charge, right?"

"Yup," he says, popping the *p*. The derision is obvious in his voice. "But forget Vincent. I wanna talk about *you*. Why do you wanna work in the music industry?"

My cheeks warm without my permission at his undivided attention. It's been a long time since someone aside from Evie has looked at me with such focus, giving importance to each word that comes out of my mouth.

"I've always loved music," I say honestly. "It kind of runs in the family. I grew up with it, so it seemed obvious that it was going to be my future."

There's more to it that feels too personal to share just yet. What I really want is to be an advocate for people, to support them as they chase their dreams, to take them to new levels of fame. It's important to me, especially since within in the music industry, most of the employees tend to be white more often than not. I've seen the halls of Ripple Records, and Baba is one of the few people of color around. Maybe someone like me can help make a change for the better in the music industry.

"You don't talk about your family much," Thomas says, giving me a side-glance, pulling me from my thoughts.

I swallow past the sudden lump in my throat. It's fine. I can talk about Ma. It's *fine*. "Yeah, well. My mom passed away a few years ago," I say, trying and failing to smile. "My dad's still around but it's...a strange relationship. We don't really get along that well. It's fine, though. I'm making my peace with it." A blatant lie, but I don't need Thomas to go running for the hills once he realizes exactly how bad my daddy issues are.

"I get that," Thomas says, squeezing my hand. "It's hard to navigate tricky relationships like that. Especially when you're reliant on them."

"Exactly," I say with a sigh before giving him a cursory glance. "Are your parents—?"

"No, no," Thomas says, shaking his head. "They're really supportive."

"Oh." I look around awkwardly, unsure what to say to that. It's true that Baba *is* supportive of my dreams but…it's because we have the same dream. I knew what I was doing when I chose my career path, and as much as it's for myself, a large part of it is because I *knew* there was no way my parents could stop me, not when Baba had already made the same decision.

A sigh builds in my chest, but I hold it in. This is hardly the time to be thinking about all that. I'm on a date with a cute boy who's holding my hand and asking about my life. If there was ever a moment to fully live in, this is it.

"I was talking about Skyler."

I look up in confusion. There's a light breeze now, making the overhead sun more bearable. "Hm?"

"My tricky relationship," Thomas says, keeping his gaze focused on the ground, his foot kicking out every now and then to connect with the pebble. "It's with Skyler."

My brows furrow. He's evaded talking about his band twice already tonight, but he's the one bringing it up now. I'm uncertain whether to ask—whether that's overstepping. "Do—do you want to talk about it?"

Thomas' nostrils flare as he exhales loudly before he stops in the middle of the boardwalk. I stop with him but make sure to tug us to the side so people can walk around us easier.

I stare at him, biting my bottom lip uncertainly. Maybe I shouldn't have said anything.

"Let's sit," Thomas says finally, gesturing to one of the benches that faces the beach. I nod, following him. I falter only to pick up the pebble he'd been kicking, offering it to him once we sit down. It's shiny and blue, probably carried in by the ocean.

He smiles faintly at it and wraps his fingers around it, letting it sit in his palm. "Thank you, Liana."

"It's nothing," I say, squeezing his arm.

There's another long silence, but I don't press. Instead, I sit quietly, playing with a loose thread in my dress, and letting the cool sea breeze keep me company.

"Sky and I started the band freshman year of high school," Thomas says, and I meet his gaze. "And I thought this was it, you know? We'd been friends our entire lives and we shared the same dream. There's no reason it shouldn't have worked out."

I nod, staying quiet and allowing him the space to tell the story at his pace.

Thomas shoots me a grateful smile. "But as we started adding members, it seemed like Sky was losing sight of why we started in the first place. Everything was about him, and the other members were all too happy to cater to his whims. It felt like I was the only one who could really see what was happening."

"That must have been very lonely," I say quietly.

"It was," Thomas says, shaking his head. "I would've quit earlier but—I write all the songs for the band. If I left, they wouldn't have anything. I didn't want to ruin it for everyone."

"I didn't know you wrote all the songs," I say in surprise. In all our conversations, Thomas has yet to mention anything about songwriting.

"I don't really like to talk about it," Thomas says sheepishly, but then his expression grows darker. "Sky takes all the credit for them, so there wouldn't be any point."

My mouth falls open. "Sky takes credit for the songs *you* write? Are you joking?"

"I wish," Thomas says, his fingers curling tighter around the blue pebble. "He's been doing it for years, and I've been letting him. I barely get any lines in the song these days, even though I'm the one who wrote them. They've been letting Vincent sing them instead, and sometimes Ethan, and I—I don't know how to break the cycle. I've wanted to go solo for ages now, but I have no idea if I'll be able to succeed on my own, and I'd feel so bad leaving the band, but it's like they *want* me to be their enemy. I can't do anything without them pointing fingers at me."

"What the hell?" I ask, shaking my head. "That's—holy shit, that's so fucked up. You can't let Sky do that, Thomas. I know you're used to being with the band and you pictured a future with them, but this isn't—this isn't okay."

"I know, but I don't know if I'm ready to take that leap of faith in myself. There's no guarantee I'll make it, and the band would hate me, and—"

"Stop, stop, stop," I interrupt, putting my hand on his. "I—I might know someone. If you have a demo or something, I can give it to them. You deserve to give yourself a chance, okay?"

"You know someone?" Thomas repeats, turning toward me with wide eyes. "Who?"

I bite the inside of my cheek and look away from his piercing gaze. Baba will kill me if I name drop him in an attempt to help someone get a record deal. "I'll tell you if it works out. Let's not jinx anything, right?"

"Are you superstitious?" Thomas asks, but his voice is teasing, which makes my shoulders less tense. Okay. Okay. I can work this out.

"A little," I say with a light laugh. "So, demo? Yes? No?"

"Yes," Thomas says, nodding. His grin is growing wider by the second. "I actually have a flash drive in my car right now, if you want it?"

I return his smile easily. "That'd be perfect."

11

I'LL BE GOOD—JAYMES YOUNG

Sometimes it feels like preparing to talk to my father is like preparing for war. I can't sleep at all the night before, tossing and turning until daylight breaks through my window.

I sigh, louder than I intend, causing Willow to sit up on my windowsill, blinking her green eyes at me in bemusement.

"Sorry," I whisper.

Willow stretches and meanders over to me, laying herself down on my chest. I smile faintly, scratching behind her ears, and watching as she goes back to sleep right there and then. Oh, how I wish it were that easy for me.

I haven't seen Baba in three days. It's like this more often than not, the two of us operating on schedules that rarely cause our paths to cross. Sometimes I think Baba tells Uncle Biptu to schedule me at the record shop according to *his* schedule to ensure I'm never home when he is.

The only time we've spent together this summer is when I've joined Baba at his office. Twice a week, I've been going to my internship with him, where I shadow different people at Ripple Records to get an understanding of what the day-to-day is like at a record label. Even then, I don't really see *Baba* so much as the people he works with.

Today is one of the days I come with him, and I'm determined to give him Thomas' demo.

But a large part of me is terrified he'll listen to it and hate it, and then judge me for even bringing it to him.

The other part of me is terrified if I don't, then *Thomas* will hate me for even suggesting that I could maybe make his dreams come true. If I were in his shoes, I would definitely resent me.

Then again, I don't know if that's saying much, considering I don't like myself most days.

I wring my hands nervously, waking up Willow again. She makes a snuffling sound and climbs off me, going to sit at the foot of my bed. At the sight of her swinging tail, I close my eyes and blow out a deep breath.

It's going to be fine. It has to be.

I don't say anything to Baba the entire car ride there, but I follow him to his office when we get to Ripple Records. He gives me a cursory glance but doesn't attempt any conversation, tapping away at his keyboard.

I sit in the seat across from him for a few awkward beats, trying to work up the courage to just do what needs to be done. It shouldn't be this hard.

"Can you stop that?" Baba asks.

I look away from the pictures of Ma lined up along the cabinet beside me. "What?"

"Your leg," Baba says, his gaze pointed.

Belatedly, I realize I'm bouncing it incessantly. "Oh. Sorry."

"Just say whatever it is, Bibi," he says tiredly, leaning back in his chair. "It shouldn't take this long for you to spit out a sentence."

The words feel like tiny needles against my skin, and I force myself to ignore it. "Right. I—I heard a really great demo recently, and I wanted to show it to you."

Baba raises his eyebrows. "And how exactly did you come across it?"

I firm my lips, trying to look older, taller, stronger, so he'll take me more seriously. "I heard the songs at a local coffee shop. The one on Ventura Boulevard."

I'm half expecting him to kick me out of his office. I've tried to offer him my opinions on music before and he usually brushes them off, especially in recent years.

So it comes as a surprise when he holds his hand out.

In slight disbelief, I take out the USB from my pocket. When Thomas handed it to me, his eyes were bright, full of hopes and dreams.

And Baba might ruin them in the next ten minutes.

I listened to the demo when I got home from my date with Thomas. It had the same vibe as a lot of the Third Eye songs, but this time Thomas' vocals were isolated. I paid more attention to the lyrics this time around, knowing that he'd written them.

The songs were heartbreakingly beautiful. About grief, about loss. About following your dreams, about fearing your own ambitions. About love, about the warmth that comes from choosing your family, rather than being born into it.

I can't stand the idea of my father hating them. Not when so much of it resonates with me, feels true to my own heart.

Baba takes the USB, plugging it into his laptop. He grabs a pair of headphones before I can urge him to play it without them, so I can offer my own insights.

With a sigh, I sit down in the seat across from him and prepare to take whatever verbal lashing is probably coming my way. It feels inevitable that I'll let him down. I always do.

The next few minutes are excruciating. I keep my eyes trained on Baba's face, watching every minute change of his expression. Every slight tic sends my heart racing. If I were religious, I would start praying right now.

When he finally takes his headphones off, he's staring at his screen with a considering look. My spirits lift *slightly* if only because he's not immediately trashing it.

"Well?" I ask, sitting on my hands to keep him from seeing the way my fingers are trembling. "What did you think?"

"It's…"

"It's…?"

"Good."

"Good?" It doesn't register as a real word at first. "Wait, did you say *good*?"

"Don't look so surprised," Baba says, raising his brows. "Where do you think you get your music taste from?"

I mean. I *guess*. If that were the case, one would think he'd listen to my music recommendations more often, but I'm not one to look a gift horse in the mouth.

"You really like it?" I ask instead, clasping my hands together. I'm afraid to let myself get excited, but for Baba to say that it's good feels like a positive sign.

Baba nods, unplugging his headphones from his laptop. Thomas' demo starts to play on the overhead speakers, his voice a soft croon.

"Tell me about him. Who is he?"

I immediately launch into PR mode, listing off the most important information. "Thomas Smith. He's an eighteen-year-old singer-songwriter based in the Valley. He's going to USC in the fall, but his real passion is music. His contact information should all be in a file on the flash drive."

Baba clicks into the aforementioned file, looking through briefly, before returning his attention to me. "He wrote all these songs?"

"Yeah. It's all him."

Baba nods again, but this time a smile spreads across his face. I blink at him in surprise. I don't remember the last time he smiled at me. He's usually so stoic and serious, or exasperated and tired. A happy expression on his face is few and far between.

"You did good, Bibi," he says, and my heart seems to collapse inside my chest. "I'm proud of you."

"Oh," I say, unsure what to even do with myself. Baba is *proud of me*? I didn't even think those words could exist together in a sentence. "Thank...you?"

"I'll get in contact with him soon. Keep up the good work, alright?" Baba says, flashing me a thumbs-up that does little to help me make sense of the situation. This is unfamiliar territory—absolutely unprecedented. Even as I hoped for the best, I expected the worst.

"Right. I—uh—I will." I do some kind of weird bow for

God knows *what* reason, but I don't really know how else to respond. "I'll see you later."

And then I scurry out of the room with a lump in my throat and my cheeks burning red with embarrassment. I lean against the wall outside my dad's office and wonder what kind of relationship he and I have that even a few words of praise leave me reeling like this.

I can't deny that a part of me is pleased. My anxiety has fizzled away momentarily, and only confusion and something that tastes like joy is left behind.

Baba liked Thomas' demo. Baba is proud of me.

Maybe the next few months won't be so bad, after all.

Thomas' jaw hits the ground. "Your father is Jhilmil Sarkar? You didn't—why didn't you say anything? Oh my God, Jhilmil Sarkar heard *my demo?*"

I giggle, squeezing the hand he has on my arm. "Yeah. I'm sorry I didn't tell you sooner. My dad drilled it in me to keep it under wraps, so people don't try to get to him through me. I also didn't wanna get your hopes up in case he didn't like it, so…"

"But he did? He liked it?" Thomas asks, wide-eyed.

I nod, unable to help the wide grin spreading across my face. "He loved it. He thought the songs were really well written and that you have a promising career ahead of you. He said he'd be in contact soon."

"You're kidding!" Thomas wraps his arms around my waist, swaying us back and forth. I break into laughter, snaking my arms around his neck. "That's so incredible, Liana, holy shit."

"I'm so beyond overjoyed for you," I say, dizzy with happiness when we finally come to a standstill. "This is what you deserve."

"I couldn't have done it without you," he says, returning my smile tenfold. "I know you have a tricky relationship with your dad, so the fact you did this for me…"

I shrug, suddenly bashful in the face of how earnest he's being. "I'm glad I could do it for you. And—my dad said he was proud of me." My lips stretch wider and I ignore the wet feeling between my lashes. "It's been a long time since he said that. I didn't think he'd ever say it again. So thank you for that."

Thomas reaches forward, pulling me into a hug. I let myself relax in his hold, resting my head against his shoulder. "I'm glad it all worked out."

"Me, too," I say quietly. "I was really afraid he wouldn't like it. Not because it's not good—it is. But he's such a harsh critic, especially when it comes to me… The idea of letting him down is probably my worst nightmare."

"Well, you didn't," Thomas says, rubbing his hand in circles down my back. It's so easy to sink into him, to forget about my worries. "And you won't. I know it."

12

WICKED GAME—URSINE VULPINE

Befriending the security guards at Ripple Records is an underrated part of interning here. Most of them have seen the wildest things, and they're happy to tell you about it after a few conversations.

My favorite guard, Damon, is working the front desk today and retelling the story of when he met Britney Spears at the American Music Awards for the umpteenth time.

"Microsoft Theater has a really strict bag policy, so I was kind of worried, you know?"

"Naturally," I say with a forced grin. It's mostly real, if you ignore the fact my leg is bouncing up and down rapidly and I keep checking my phone to see if Thomas has texted me back.

It's been days since I've heard from him and I have no idea what changed. We went from talking constantly throughout the day to radio silence, and I've gone over our conversations a hundred times now, looking for something I might've said that scared him off.

Me: omg hozier just dropped tour dates

Me: are you coming by the store anytime soon? :)

Me: do you wanna go to the kelly clarkson show next week? daveed diggs is going to be a guest ahhh

Me: have you heard this song? it's so good!! it reminds me a lot of your demo

Me: I was thinking of going to a show at the troubadour this weekend if you wanna come!! it's always fun to check out some new artists and tickets are like $25 :)

Me: hey is everything okay?

Me: lmk if you need anything

Me: here for you <3

So far, I can't figure out what I did, and my anxiety is gnawing at my insides as I grapple with all the possible things that might have gone wrong between us.

With nothing to distract me from my depression, I've been wallowing. When I'm not at the record shop or my internship, I sit around and do nothing. I tell myself it's fine, I'm already doing so much, I'm allowed to rest—but is it resting? When all I do is sit in my bed and stare at the wall, sad music drifting through the speakers?

<u>for days when existing is harder than it should be:</u>
The Happiest Girl—BLACKPINK

Gemini Feed—Banks

Liability—Lorde

If You Think It's Love—King Princess

Earth—Sleeping At Least

Forget Me Forgotten—Hollow Wood

coney island (feat. The National)—Taylor Swift

Are You With Me—nilu

Stay—Sarah Close

Another Guy (Acoustic)—FLO

Augusta—Gracie Abrams

I've never gotten to the point of self-harm, and I hope I never will, but sometimes I wonder if letting myself sink into a hole like this isn't also a form of hurting myself.

I hate this passive dread I feel at existing, weighing over my head like a storm cloud. It's been like this for as long as I can remember. Even when Ma was alive, this feeling was brewing inside me, though I didn't know how to put a name to it then.

It only worsened after her death, to a degree that was absolutely exhausting. Now it's lessened, but it's still there. Always, no matter what I do. There are certain things that trigger me. Most recently, it's been the quiet devastation I feel at my mother's absence from such a pivotal turning point in my life—the summer before college, before adulthood. But I've learned that my mental health can and will take a downturn even when I'm not triggered.

I've come to accept that my mental illnesses are an inescapable part of me. I'm always going to be anxious, and I'm always going to be depressed, but as I grow older and hopefully wiser, I'll find better ways to manage it, whether it's in the form of therapy, medication, or something else altogether.

Right now, all I can do is try not to isolate too much, texting Evie frequently, wanting updates on how things are going for her in New York. *One* of us should be living our best life.

At least listening to the security guards at Ripple Records recount wild encounters with celebrities serves as a decent pastime. "And then what?" I ask Damon, egging him on.

He gestures wildly. "So I look at her, and I'm like, Miss Spears, I'm sorry but—"

The front doors to Ripple Records slam open, snagging both of our attentions. There's only a few people in the lobby, but all of them are staring at the group of teenage boys who enter the building panting for breath like they ran all the way here.

Is—is that *Third Eye*? What the fuck is going on?

"We—need—Oh my God, I cannot breathe." A rough intake of air from Mohammed. "We need to see Jhilmil Sarkar."

The guard manning the door, Rivus, looks at them in bemusement. "Do you have an appointment?"

"No, but..." Vincent says, glancing uncertainly between his band members, "we *need* to see him. You don't understand."

I stand up without meaning to, leaning over the front desk to see the scene more clearly. I can't help but hope that Thomas is with them. But my heart sinks when I don't spot him.

Great. Not even his band randomly showing up is providing any helpful answers for why he's *ignoring me.*

"I'm sorry, but without an appointment, that won't be possible," Rivus says. "I'm going to have to ask you to politely—"

"You don't understand!" Ethan says, his voice shrill with panic. "We—Sky, tell him, we can't let this happen."

"We need to talk to Mr. Sarkar," Sky insists, squeezing Ethan's shoulder, though it doesn't seem to calm the blond boy at all. "It's extremely important. I know we don't have an appointment, but please, we won't take up any more than ten minutes of his time."

Rivus' face softens with sympathy at Sky's earnest tone. "I'm sorry. There's nothing I can do. Maybe see about emailing his team and securing an appointment first, alright?"

"Are they talking about your father?" Damon asks quietly, jarring me away from the scene.

"I—I *guess*?" I shake my head, clearing any thoughts about Thomas. "I don't know why they would need to meet with him that badly."

"We need to see him *now*," Mohammed says loudly, his face set with determination. He starts to push forward, slipping under Rivus' arm. Damon stands up at once, moving to intercept Mohammed before he can make it to the security turnstiles in front of the elevators.

"Nope," Damon says, grabbing Mohammed's arm and leading him back toward the front doors. "Not today, kid."

"You don't get it! I need to—*Liana*?" Mohammed stops flailing to stare at me in confusion. I blanch under his sudden attention. I didn't even know Mohammed knew my name. I guess between my thing with Thomas and encounters with Sky, it's not completely out of the blue, but *still*.

"Liana?" Sky repeats, equally bewildered.

Damon looks at me with raised brows. "Do you know them?"

"No—I mean, kind of, but." I falter, unable to form a coherent sentence. What is Third Eye even doing here? Why do they want to see my dad? "I—I'll talk to them. Outside."

Damon shrugs, gesturing for me to walk toward the door. I nod, grabbing my ID before following him. He lets go of Mohammed once he's safely deposited outside the building, but not without a warning look directed at the whole group.

I wait until he's out of earshot to turn on the others. "What are you *doing*? Why would you storm into a record label and start making demands? Are you insane?"

"What are *you* doing here?" Mohammed counters, thick eyebrows raised. "Why do the security guards know you?"

"I—I'm an intern here!" I say, hoping to God they don't notice the tremor in my voice. It's not a lie, but it's not exactly the truth, either. "And it doesn't matter why I'm here, anyway. The four of you are acting *deranged*. I bet Thomas told you not to do this, didn't he? That's why he's not here?"

"Thomas isn't here because he's an utter piece of *shit*," Mohammed says acidly. Vincent places a hand on Mohammed's arm to calm him down, but like with Ethan earlier, it doesn't help.

I massage the bridge of my nose to stop the burgeoning headache. "I'm not going to stand here and let you slander Thomas for no reason, so I suggest you get to the point and tell me why you want to see Jhilmil Sarkar so badly."

"For no *reason*—?" Mohammed asks, aghast, only for Vincent to cut him off.

"Chill, Mo, she probably doesn't know."

"Know what?" I ask, narrowing my eyes. A part of me is

suddenly terrified they've murdered Thomas and buried him in some sandy grave, and that's why he hasn't texted me back for the last few days. "Please tell me you didn't kill Thomas."

"I wish," Ethan mutters, which does little to assuage my concerns, especially coming from who I thought was the boy-next-door sweetheart of the band.

I turn to Sky, who's been suspiciously quiet for the last few minutes. There's a pit of anxiety in my stomach, brewing stronger with each passing moment. "Explain. Now."

Skyler grimaces. "We need to speak to Mr. Sarkar regarding a personal issue within our band."

"And how does your band concern Mr. Sarkar?" I ask, casting a cursory look at the rest of the band members. Ethan is scowling, his cheeks bright red. Mohammed has an angry jut to his chin, his jaw set. Vincent is pressing his lips together, gaze skyward as he shakes his head. None of it bodes well.

Sky sighs, scrubbing a hand over his face. There are dark bags under his eyes like he hasn't slept for days. "It's Thomas. Okay? We need to talk to him about Thomas."

"What happened with Thomas?" I ask slowly.

"See. I told you," Vincent says to Mohammed. "She doesn't know."

"Doesn't know *what*?" I ask, irritation bleeding into my voice. The longer they hold out on the issue, the more time my brain has to come up with the worst possible scenario. "Just say it."

"Thomas stole Sky's music," Ethan blurts and all of the members turn to him in disbelief.

Vincent flicks his arm. "Ethan! We're not supposed to tell anyone!"

Mohammed shakes his head. "Come on, dude!"

Ethan pouts at them. "She has a fling with him! Don't you think she deserves to know what an awful person he is?"

"What—what do you mean he stole Sky's music?" I scoff. "You mean Thomas' music? He told me how he writes all of the songs and you all take credit for it. Come on, isn't this going a little far now?"

"He told you that?" Sky asks, his voice deathly quiet.

"That's a lie!" Ethan shouts over him, shaking his head. Vincent places his hands on Ethan's shoulders, holding him back from charging forward in Sky's defense. "It's the opposite. *Skyler* writes all of our songs. He has since the band started. Thomas doesn't even know—"

"Ethan, come on!"

"She's the enemy, Ethan!"

I splutter. "I'm not the enemy. I don't—but it doesn't matter because you're lying. He *told* me you guys always take credit for his songs. Be serious."

"Be *serious*?" Ethan shakes free of Vincent's grip, pulling his phone out of his pocket. "This is *literally* a video of Sky coming up with the hook for 'Triple Down.'"

I frown but look down at Ethan's phone. In the video, all of the boys seem younger, a little softer around the face. Sky is sitting in the middle, sheets of paper splayed out in front of him and a guitar in his lap. Mohammed is lying upside down on a piano bench next to him, spinning a pencil between his fingers, and Vincent is draped across a beanbag, absentmindedly sorting through a Rubik's Cube.

"Wait, I've got it," says Skyler in the video, lightly strumming his guitar. *"No matter what I say, no matter what I do, you don't listen. In one ear, out the other. It's always you, always you. Gotta be right, can never be wrong. You'll double down, triple down, break my heart over and over until I'm nowhere to be found."*

Vincent sits up instantly, eyes bright. "Yes. *Yes.* That's perfect, Sky."

"I love it!" Ethan says, his voice loud from behind the camera.

Mohammed flips over, landing on the ground and using his pencil to write down the lyrics. "I have no idea how you always manage to come up with the perfect chorus, Sky, but I'm not complaining."

Sky laughs, covering his face with his hands.

In the corner of the video, Thomas shows up in the doorway, holding a pizza box. "Are you guys done yet? The food's getting cold."

"Yeah, we'll be there in a minute, just gotta finish the song," Sky says, offering Thomas a small smile.

Thomas shrugs carelessly. "Whatever. I still think we could do cover songs and it would be just as good. All of this feels like a waste of time."

Sky's face falls slightly. "Right. Well, if you have any cover songs you wanna recommend, you know we'll always hear you out."

Thomas turns away without responding to Sky, disappearing back through the door with a faint, "Hurry up."

There's an awkward silence, the rest of the band members looking at each other uncertainly, before Vincent breaks it. "Sing it again, I wanna try it with you."

Skyler's answering smile is blinding. "Let's do it."

It cuts off there. I stand before the four members of Third

Eye, recreating the awkward silence from the video, but infinitely more tense. I'm all too aware of how my heart is beating, reverberating through my body until the pounding is incessant in my eardrums.

Thomas lied to me. Thomas *lied* to me.

He lied to me and I gave my dad his fucking demo of *stolen songs*.

And now he's ignoring me, as if I don't matter to him now that I've served my purpose.

I'm gonna be sick.

Within the span of a second, it becomes crystal clear why Third Eye is here to see my dad. Because their bandmate stole their music, took credit for it, and is on his way to maybe accepting a record deal for it without an ounce of regret.

And it's because of me. Because I let Thomas manipulate me into helping him backstab his band.

"I—" My throat feels painfully dry. What have I *done*? I can't find it in me to look at Skyler. For all I pride myself on being paranoid about telling people who my dad is, clearly I wasn't paranoid enough when it really mattered. "I'm so sorry."

"It's not your fault," Vincent says, pulling Ethan closer to him, squeezing his arms.

But it is, I don't say. *I did this. I destroyed your dreams.*

"Do you think you could get us in to see Jhilmil Sarkar?" Mohammed asks, and I nearly flinch.

My dad can never know about this. If he ever finds out that I brought him a *fake* demo, I'm never going to hear the end of it. For the first time ever, he thought I did something worthwhile. Something for him to be proud of.

Only for me to have made what is inarguably my worst mistake ever.

I resist the urge to sink to my knees and start screaming.

Oh my God, I've fucked up terribly. I can't tell my dad but I also can't let Third Eye's career go down in flames because of *me*. What the fuck am I supposed to do?

"I'm just an intern," I say meekly, shaking my head and backing away from them. "I don't think so."

Mohammed groans and Skyler pulls him into a hug, squeezing the back of his neck.

The others can't see Skyler's face, but I can. The dead look in his eyes is heart-wrenching, and it's even worse knowing I'm responsible for it. The line of his mouth quivers, but then he notices me looking and smooths his entire expression out.

Please don't, I try to say, but can't. I've made such a terrible mistake.

"It's okay, Mo," Skyler says quietly, closing his eyes. "We'll figure something out. I can write more songs."

"That's not the *point*, Sky." Mohammed pulls back, his hands clenched into fists at his side. "You worked so hard on those songs—they *mean* something to you. Thomas shouldn't be able to just take them and get away with it while we sit by twiddling our thumbs. You deserve so much better than that."

"Mo. There's nothing for us to do right now." Sky looks at all of his band members, holding each of their gazes. "It's okay. We'll figure it out, yeah? We always do."

Ethan's face crumples and he rushes toward Sky, pulling him into a hug. Vincent and Mohammed follow suit without hesitating.

I fight the urge to heave as I watch them. This is my fault. I did this. This is *my* fault.

And I have to fix it.

13

EARTH—SLEEPING AT LAST

There's something spiky and sharp sitting in between my lungs, making it hard to breathe. I didn't know Thomas that long—what I felt for him wasn't anything deeper than a crush. Objectively, I know that.

Subjectively, it's a lot harder to ignore how much my heart aches. When I'm in my bed later that night and the tears threaten to come, I don't try to stop them even though I know I'm being dramatic.

If Thomas had just called it off, said he wasn't interested in seeing me anymore, it wouldn't hurt this much. The ghosting would've pissed me off, but I would've lived with it. But to know that he lied to me, that he *used* me, is a lot harder to stomach.

It's clear now that this was always his plan. I don't know when he realized who I am—who my dad is—but it's obvious he did at some point.

Maybe from the start. Maybe he knew the moment he ran

into me at that party and was just waiting for the right moment to sap me and my connections dry for his benefit.

I crawl into bed, pulling my blanket up and burying myself in pillows until I can barely breathe. I don't want to exist
right now.

Some days, I wish I were never born. This is one of those
days.

My sniffles must alert Willow something is wrong because
she wanders over to look at me. I don't say anything, not that
she would understand even if I did.

She noses at my arm and then lies down right on top of
my chest. I let out a shaky breath. Even my cat can see how
miserable I am.

My only solace right now is music. Spotify is running
through a handful of breakup songs, a playlist I made after
my first boyfriend broke up with me in middle school and
have been adding to ever since.

More tears push at my tear ducts and I let them loose, doing
my best to stifle my sobs so Baba won't hear me. I doubt he'd
care either way. I've spent way too many nights crying in my
room only for him to be oblivious down the hall.

Evie called me earlier, offering to talk for as long as I
needed it, or to watch a comfort movie to help distract me. I
declined both, unable to stomach the thought of doing anything besides lying in bed and mourning the loss of something
that was never really mine in the first place.

Maybe that was on me for thinking I could possibly have
a happy ending.

I want to hit something. I want to rip something apart. I
want to do *something*, but there's nothing for me to do.

It's not fair. It's not fair.

But it's not like life has ever really been fair to me before.

I trusted him. I trusted him and he took advantage of it.

Worse, I liked him. I let him do this. I thought he was cute and his smile was swoon-worthy and that he understood me and that for once in my miserable life things were going right.

It isn't even just me that he fucked over in the process. It's his entire band.

And now that's a weight I have to live with, too. He's made me guilty by association.

I'm partially responsible for sabotaging his ex-band, and fully responsible for fixing it.

Coming up with a game plan on how to save Third Eye's career proves to be harder than expected. I don't know enough about their band to make any active moves, and there's no way for me to get to know them at this point without revealing my hand.

After I finally manage to get out of bed and wash up, I scratch my head over it for the entire weekend and resist the urge to scream into the void.

In between spitballing ideas, I text Thomas, demanding explanations. All of my texts go unread, even though I can see him on Instagram, posting stories of getting In-N-Out or going to the movies or *ten million other things* that don't involve replying to me.

He doesn't even regret what he did to me.

The thought makes me so mad I snap the pencil in my hand. What an *asshole*.

If it wouldn't reflect poorly on me, I'd march into my father's room right now and tell him all about Thomas' back-stabbing behavior.

But Thomas knows that I won't. Of course, he does. I *told* him how complicated my relationship with Baba is. How happy I was that Baba was finally proud of me for once.

I flop onto my bed and finally scream into my pillow until I run out of breath. *ASSHOLE.*

"There has to be something I can do," I say to Willow, who stares back at me blankly. *"Something."*

When Willow doesn't reply, I turn back to my phone where Evie and I have been texting back and forth about this situation for the last few days. Her texts consist mostly of detailed threats against Thomas' life, and they make me smile faintly, even in the midst of all this mess.

Evie Khodabux: I mean literally how selfish can you be

Evie Khodabux: I've never been happier to be a lesbian because wtf why are boys LIKE THIS

Evie Khodabux: I can't even imagine how the members of 3rd eye feel

Me: I literally feel so awful just thinking abt it like

Me: I guess it's one thing to do this to me since we've known each other for like a month (still mf shitty but w/e) but to do this to your bandmates who you've known for YEARS????????

Me: I'm gonna kms this is the worst

Evie Khodabux: ok well don't do THAT

Me: death is looking a lot nicer than whatever tf life has going on

Evie Khodabux: you have to stay alive if you want to see me beat the shit out of thomas

Me: ...suddenly my will to live is stronger than ever

Evie Khodabux: so true lemme go buy some brass knuckles

Me: I'll send third eye a group invite to the beatdown<3

Me: but for real. who does that to their friends wtf

Evie Khodabux: it's sociopath behavior and I'll say it

Evie Khodabux: didn't you say they used to rehearse at his house too??

Evie Khodabux: so now they prob have nowhere to practice huh

Evie Khodabux: what an a s s h o l e

Me: I didn't even think about that

Me: bruhhhhh

Me: wait

Me: they have nowhere to practice

Me: riya apu was saying uncle biptu was thinking abt renting out the basement since we've been cleaning it out

Evie Khodabux: omg

Me: what if I got them a rehearsing space? that's a start right?

Evie Khodabux: absolutely bro you gotta do it

Evie Khodabux: it's a great idea

Me: ok ok

Me: thank you you're the best I could not have thought of it without you

Evie Khodabux: ofc ofc that's what besties are for

Evie Khodabux: now go to talk to riya and keep me updated!!!!!

Me: I will!!!!!!!

Riya gives me a flat look. "So, let me get this straight. You want to put half your check every week toward renting out the basement for some random band you don't even know *and* you want me to reach out to them and offer it to them like it's some random charity *and* you want me to swear to not tell them you're paying for it because it's a secret that could ruin your life. Is that right?"

I nod. "Exactly. You get it."

"Tōmār māthā ki khārāp?" she asks, switching languages

to Bangla to emphasize how poorly she thinks of my mental state. "In *what world* does any of this make any sense?"

"Riya Apu, please," I say, clasping my hands together. "I'll never ask you for anything ever again, I swear."

"You know how ridiculous this is, right?" Riya asks, raising an eyebrow. "They're obviously going to find out at some point."

"And I'll deal with that then," I say, unable to keep the whine out of my voice. "Riya Apu, *please.*"

She frowns, staring at me for a long moment. Eventually, she sighs. "Fine. Draft the email yourself, and let me know when you're done so I can look it over. Don't forget to use my bhalo nam instead of my dak nam."

I squeal, hopping around the counter to pull her into a hug. "Of course! I'll use Ayesha, don't worry. You're the best, thank you, thank you!"

"Don't thank me yet!" Riya says, pushing me away to hold me at arm's length. "The basement isn't completely cleared out yet. You'll have to do that for the next few weeks."

"*Weeks?*" I shake my head. "No, no, it's fine. They won't care about the clutter. I'll work on cleaning it, but they have to be able to use the space right away."

Riya gives me an incredulous look before blowing out a resigned breath. "Whatever, Bibi. As long as it gets clean."

"Thank you!" I say, jumping in for a hug again, but she deftly avoids it, disappearing into one of the aisles while muttering under her breath.

I grin after her and turn back to the store's computer after texting Evie an affirmative. I crack my knuckles and get to work without letting another second go to waste.

Dear Ethan Mitchell,

My name is Ayesha Ahmed, and I'm the manager at Ahmed's Record Shop. I heard through the grapevine that your band Third Eye might be looking for a new rehearsal space. As a fan of your music and an alumni from Wexford High School, I wanted to extend a hand and offer the basement at my family's record store. It's currently in the process of being cleaned out, but there's more than enough room for your band to practice if you're interested. The store requires nothing in return as we see it as an investment in an up-and-coming band and want to foster growth in the music industry, so no worries on that front. Let me know your thoughts when you have a chance. I look forward to hearing from you!

Sincerely,
Ayesha

There.

I call Riya back to look it over.

Once she's done, she gives me a thumbs-up and promptly leaves, clearly wanting to wash her hands of this mess. I can't blame her.

I take a deep breath and read over the email again, making sure there aren't any typos. I chose Ethan because it made the most sense for Riya to reach out to him, given that all of us went to the same high school. I briefly thought about addressing it to Sky, but in the end, Ethan won out.

With a deep breath, I click on the mouse.

Sent.

PART TWO

This is the end of the road
I'm holding out for a new hope

—Stray Kids, "Levanter"

14

LANDSLIDE—FLEETWOOD MAC

It takes Ethan three days to reply to the email. It takes another two days after that, emails sent back and forth, before he even shows signs of believing the offer is real.

And still another day until he shows up at the record shop with Vincent in tow.

"Liana, right?" Ethan says as soon as he enters, a set of drumsticks in his hand, and Vincent's arm in the other. "Is Ayesha here?"

I don't know what to say at first. It's been so long that I was beginning to think they wouldn't show up at all. I've been hoping for it, but not counting on it.

"Uh—yes, she is, but she's on her break right now. I can help you with anything you need. Is this about using our basement as a recording space?" I ask, trying to keep my voice neutral.

Ethan nods. Behind him, Vincent is inspecting the shop like he's looking for signs of mold.

"Yeah, were you guys serious about that?" Ethan asks, as if we haven't hashed it out over fifteen emails already.

"Ayesha thinks you guys are really good," I say, trying not to trip over calling my cousin by her government name. It never gets any less weird, no matter how many times I do it. To me, she's always going to be Riya Apu. "She seems pretty dead set on making it happen."

"Can we check it out?" Ethan asks, tapping his drumsticks against the counter. "To see if it'll work."

"Yeah, of course," I say. I almost fall over in my rush to get out from behind the counter and flip the sign on our door to Closed, locking the door afterward for good measure. Riya will probably beat my ass for it, but that's a problem for later. There's no one in the store right now, so it'll be fine. "Come on!"

I lead them through the back door and down the stairs. The hallway is absolutely covered in vinyls, most of them in unlabeled boxes, but there are also a few stacked on the floor in some mishap order. At the end of the hallway, I throw the door open and gesture for them to go ahead first.

"So it's still a little bit of a mess, and I'll be in and out for the next few weeks taking things upstairs as I clean out the room. But what do you think? Is it good enough?"

Vincent immediately launches into action, scoping the space out, and running a finger along the furniture, which isn't much more than two old couches and a large coffee table, as if checking for dust. Ethan stays at my side, but he's also looking around, eyeing the funky green carpet and the "artfully" stained walls.

"It's not great," Vincent says rather bluntly, coming back to stand in front of me. "But if someone can help us carry our instruments down here, I think it would work."

Ethan looks at him in surprise, as if he didn't expect Vincent to agree so readily. A slow smile spreads across his face, growing until it's nearly blinding. "Yeah, what Vinny said."

I smile back helplessly. At least something is working out. It's not perfect and it's not going to make the band famous overnight, but it's *something*.

Before I can feel too fuzzy about the situation, Vincent snags one of Ethan's drumsticks and pokes my arm with it. "So what's your deal? Are you still talking to Thomas? Why would you help us?"

I blink in surprise, but don't let myself hesitate. The last thing I want is to seem unsure in my answer. "First of all, *no*, I'm not talking to Thomas. He basically ghosted me after Ripple Records contacted him and I can't believe what he did to you guys. Second, this has nothing to do with *me*. My cousin is the one who wants to help you guys. I'm just here because I get paid to be."

Vincent narrows his eyes at me like he doesn't *quite* believe me, but he eventually nods. "Alright. How long do you think it'll take to get all this stuff out of here?" he asks, gesturing with a wide hand to all the boxes of vinyls and CDs lined up against the wall.

I shrug. In all honesty, I plan to take as much time as possible, since it'll give me an opportunity to observe them and figure out if they have any weaknesses I can help them shore up. I may not know a lot about creating or playing music, but I know enough about marketing and publicity to do good there.

"I'll have to sort through them and organize before I can

take them out," I say, leaning against the doorway. "So it might take all summer. I'll try not to get in the way if you're practicing."

Vincent looks at Ethan who's still grinning eagerly. At the sight of his smile, the stiffness in Vincent's shoulders eases. "Okay. We'll talk to Sky and Mohammed and let you know where we're at, but it looks good to us."

I keep my expression neutral, but on the inside, I'm jumping for joy. "Sounds good. I'll let Ayesha know."

Vincent and Ethan take one last look around, Vincent snapping a few pictures, before they indicate they're ready to leave. I lead them back upstairs and silently thank any god listening that Riya isn't back from her break yet, because that is one conversation I do not have the spoons to deal with right now.

"Wait, before you go," I say as I grab a notepad and pen off the counter. "Here's my phone number. It'll probably be easier to coordinate with me than Ayesha since she doesn't really check her texts that often. So just let me know what you're thinking and I can pass it on to her."

Vincent quirks an eyebrow at me but Ethan takes the piece of paper with a playful salute. "We'll see you around, then."

"I look forward to it," I say and salute him back.

15

WHY DON'T YOU KNOW—CHUNGHA

The next day, I'm in the middle of putting away a new shipment of albums, stretching on my tiptoes to get them in place on the top shelf because Riya refuses to buy a stool and admit that *both* of us are short brown girls. After I put away the rest of these, I'm going to march over to the closest Target and buy a stepping stool or a ladder or *something*.

I hop slightly to get the handful of CDs left in the box onto the shelf and just barely manage to get them to stick the landing. I smile in satisfaction and dust my hands off.

Someone behind me laughs and I jump, knocking over the cardboard box balancing between me and the shelf. There's a small clatter, meaning there's still at least one CD left. I try not to groan in despair as I reach down to pick it up instead of turning a glare on Riya for nearly giving me a heart attack.

"I thought we talked about sneaking up on me, Riya Apu," I scold before stretching on my toes again, ready to toss the last CD case in, when someone grabs it instead, placing it in the right spot easily.

"Not Riya Apu," the person says and I stop breathing momentarily. That's a boy's voice. How did I even misplace his laugh for Riya's? I slowly turn around to see Sky smiling at me. And he's wearing a fucking *crop top.*

I must be dreaming.

"Oh," I say. That's really all I can manage because I didn't expect Sky to be here so soon, and more than that, I didn't expect him to be this *pretty* up close.

"You're much shorter than I thought," Sky says, clearly self-satisfied as he leans against a shelf of vinyls beside me. He's probably a little less than six feet, but that still gives him over half a foot on me.

I release an indignant noise. "Excuse me?" I ask, only barely refraining from throwing the empty box at his head.

He opens his mouth but I don't wait for an answer as I walk away. There's still one more box of new releases left in the store, but they go in the R&B section, which is lower to ground and shouldn't be as much of a headache.

Behind me, Sky's footsteps follow, and I nearly roll my eyes. *Stay calm*, I remind myself. *He might be a condescending dickhead, but he's a condescending dickhead you owe a life debt to.*

When I bend down to put away the R&B albums, Sky crouches beside me. "You look tired," he says, and his voice is softer, more sympathetic.

"Yeah, well, Willow kept me up all night," I mutter, putting away several CD cases at once. I don't mean for the words to slip out but they do anyway, and it's clear I need to learn to control my mouth.

"Willow?" Sky asks, and when I look over my shoulder, he seems genuinely interested.

"My cat," I say and immediately curse under my breath. I'm not supposed to entertain him.

"What's wrong with it?" Sky asks. He must have heard me talking to myself because from the corner of my eye, I swear I see a hint of a smirk on his face. When I turn around to shoot him an exasperated look, any sign of a smile is gone, and he's fiddling with the hem at the bottom of his shirt instead. I focus very hard on *not* staring at his abs.

"Her," I correct before scrunching up my nose. That's the third time in a row I've replied even after acknowledging that I need to stop talking.

"What's wrong with her?" Sky asks without pause, and I force myself to look back at the shelves because Sky is licking his lips now and my blouse feels too warm and none of this is remotely right.

"Just a bit sick, 's all," I say, bending lower to put away the last of the albums in the box. When I stand back up, Sky is frowning at me as if he actually cares about my cat's health of all things.

"I hope she feels better," Sky says, and I raise my eyebrows but manage to keep my mouth shut. Instead, I move toward the front of the store. There are a few CDs at the front register that still need to be put away, left behind by customers who changed their minds.

I try to ignore the sound of shuffling behind me, but it becomes impossible. I turn around to figure out what in the world Sky is doing only to see him looking through—I squint in disbelief—Taylor Swift albums.

Taylor Swift albums?

I stop what I'm doing to just stare at him. This has to be a simulation.

Don't ask what he's doing, don't ask what he's doing, don't ask what he's doing—"What are you doing?"

Jesus Christ, what's wrong with me?

"I have a few left until my collection's complete," Sky says, picking out *Lover* and glancing at the back.

"Top three tracks," I say and then immediately want to bang my head against the wall. Who cares what Skyler Moon's top three tracks on *Lover* are? Why would I even ask that?

He pauses and gives me a long look. "Okay. 'It's Nice To Have a Friend,' 'Daylight,' and 'Cruel Summer' are probably my top three."

I tilt my head to the side. Nothing about this boy makes sense. "I wouldn't have expected the first one. Is there any reason why it's in your top three?"

Sky shrugs and starts toying with the various rings on his fingers, sliding them up and down over his knuckles. "I guess I think there's something really heartwarming about the parallel between 'school bell rings' and 'church bell rings.' She's really good at creating a story with just a few lines."

I bite the inside of my cheek, trying to stop whatever the hell it is my lips are trying to do. "Fair enough. Mine are 'Afterglow,' 'Cornelia Street,' and 'The Archer'."

A smile slips across Sky's face. "That makes sense."

I shift uncomfortably at the weird twisting in my gut and turn my attention to clearing the counter again. *That makes sense?* What does that even mean?

Quietly, I put away the rest of the miscellaneous albums

where they belong. Sky doesn't move from where he's resting his hip against the front counter, but his eyes follow me around the entire store.

"Is there any reason you're looking at me?" I ask when I finally return to my post behind the cash register.

"Is there any reason you're looking back?" Sky asks, and I try not to immediately scowl at him.

"I asked you first," I say, even though it sounds childish to my own ears.

He smirks a little, like he knows. "And I asked you second."

"But I asked you *first*."

"We can go in circles all day, Liana."

I blow out a deep breath. "I find you very irritating."

Sky grins. "That's alright. So where's this practice room of yours, anyway?"

16

YOUR SONG—ELTON JOHN

Once Sky signs off on using the record shop's basement as a rehearsal space, I feel like I can finally breathe.

It doesn't take long after that for the rest of Third Eye to show up with their instruments in tow. I help them bring their stuff down to the basement, but in one of my trips back and forth, I notice Sky talking to Riya, an earnest look on his face.

I don't catch much of the conversation but he's clearly thanking her for letting them use the basement. I narrow my eyes to cover up how that makes me feel jittery. A few days ago, Riya finally asked why I was helping Third Eye, and I confessed to everything that happened. I don't think she would expose my secrets, but my anxiety isn't known for being rational. On my next trip back, I stop by Riya to interrogate her, but she just looks flushed and pleased, muttering something about what a nice boy Sky is.

"Not you, too," I grumble before making another trip downstairs.

Once everything is moved in, and Vincent has finished dusting the place with a disgusted look on his face, it finally feels like somewhere the band can practice. The walls are soundproofed, something Biptu Uncle did ages ago since he would host karaoke parties down here in the 2000s, so when I shut the door on my way out, not a single sound slips through.

When I come back upstairs, Riya is staring at me, something akin to fondness on her face. "You must know this isn't going to end well."

"It does kind of feel like that, doesn't it?" I ask with a sigh, undoing my ponytail to pick up the flyaway hairs that came loose in the process of hauling instruments downstairs. "But this is my fate. I have to live with it."

"You could be honest," Riya says, reaching forward to tuck a stray lock of hair behind my ear. "Better now than when you inevitably get attached to them."

"Yeah, no," I say but give her a tired smile. "Thanks, though. You can say I told you so if it all goes down in flames."

"Oh, I intend to," Riya says, pinching my cheek and I smack her hand away. "Go call Evie, I know you're dying to."

I grin, blowing my cousin a kiss before I leave the store.

"Five minutes!" she calls after me, and I nod before rounding the corner to where there's shade overhead, courtesy of the block's boba shop.

When I FaceTime Evie, she picks up immediately. She's somewhere off camera, but she shouts, "Well?"

"Well, the plan is officially in motion," I say, leaning against the brick wall behind me. "But now I have to figure out the rest."

"Any word from Thomas?" she asks.

"Nothing," I say darkly. "Why would there be now that he has no use for me?"

Evie sighs, and I can imagine her shaking her head. "He's a dickhead, and you deserve better."

"Yeah, well—" I pick at the dirt underneath my nails "—that's life, I guess. I should've known better than to trust a man."

"I keep telling you to date women," Evie says, and I choke on a laugh. "I'm serious! They're so much better."

"I believe you," I say, smiling despite myself. "If only. However, I've been cursed with my attraction to men, so here we are."

"As long as you know the option is there," Evie says, and this time I laugh freely.

"Yeah, Eve, I know." I close my eyes and just breathe for a moment. Evie doesn't say anything on the other line, but she doesn't need to.

After a minute of silence, Evie breaks it. "It's going to work out, Liana."

"I really hope so," I say softly. "I don't know how I'm going to live with myself otherwise."

"Day by day," she says, equally quiet. "You're a good person. You just made a mistake. It happens to the best of us."

I don't bother disguising the sound of my sniffle, and Evie doesn't bother to cover up her sad sigh.

"I wish I could take it back," I say, wiping the back of my free hand across my eyes. "I honestly feel so awful about it."

"I know," Evie says, finally coming back on camera to give me a sympathetic look. "I'm sorry. But try to remember that

it's not entirely your fault, okay? And you're doing your best
to make up for it."

I nod, blowing out a harsh breath. "Right. Yeah."

"I'm sending hugs from across the coast," Evie says, and
I pretend for a second that I'm in my best friend's arms and
everything is okay.

Then I notice how tired she looks, the dark bags under her
eyes more prominent than usual. For the last few days, she
mentioned being homesick. I should've given it more attention. I'll have to ask her about it later, when I have more time.

"I'm sending hugs back," I say earnestly. "Thank you. Really."

"Always," Evie says, and I know it's a promise. "Now get
back to work before your cousin sends a mob after *me*."

I snort. "Yeah, okay. Love you so much. Miss you so much."

"Love you, miss you," Evie says, blowing me a kiss. "Good
luck!"

I'm going to need it.

I start hanging out at the record shop more often, which
is saying something since I'm already scheduled to work at
least four shifts a week. The other two part-timers, Nivali
and Tiana, give me a strange look when they see me walk in
on one of my days off.

"You're not supposed to be here," Nivali says rather bluntly,
raising her perfect eyebrows at me. "Is there a fire I don't
know about?"

I wave her away, moving toward the back.

Tiana laughs in sudden understanding. "Oh, she's here for
the cute boys downstairs. I see."

I flip her off, but don't bother correcting her. It is true, even if it's not for the reasons they think.

When I get downstairs, only Ethan and Vincent are there. Ethan is perched behind his drum set, scrolling through his phone idly, while Vincent sits near his feet, strumming an acoustic guitar.

I do a double take, certain he's the group's bassist, but no matter how many times I look, it's definitely an acoustic guitar in his hands. Huh. I guess he can play both.

Ethan glances up at my entrance and gives me a cheerful wave before looking back down at his phone, whereas Vincent just nods without pausing his guitar playing.

I leave the door propped open since they're not blowing out the speakers and sit down near the boxes of records. I pretend to occupy myself, but all I'm really doing is trying to figure out what song Vincent is playing. I tap my foot along without meaning to. It feels familiar, so familiar I can taste it on my tongue—and then it clicks. "Your Song" by Elton John.

I hum along, and Vincent gives me a brief glance. When our eyes meet, I quirk an eyebrow, and he raises his back in challenge. He immediately restarts the song from the beginning, the opening notes loud in the silence of the room.

When Vincent starts to sing, my eyes widen in surprise. His voice is *incredible*. There aren't a lot of performance videos on Third Eye's social media platforms, but in the ones I've seen, Thomas is the one singing, with Vincent doing backup vocals every now and then. But I've never heard him belt like this before.

From what I've gleaned thus far, Sky is the band's leader and main guitarist as well as their main songwriter. Ethan is the youngest member and the band's drummer, though he's still learning and gets nervous at times. Mohammed is the pianist, a prodigy since childhood, and he's very dependable. Vincent is the newest member and primarily the band's bassist, which is why his voice comes as a shock to me.

Behind Vincent, Ethan's lips immediately quirk into a smile at the sound of Vincent's voice, though he doesn't look up from his phone.

It probably shouldn't be as shocking as it is when Ethan joins in for a verse, singing at a much lower tone. His voice complements Vincent's perfectly. It's clear Sky knew what he was doing when he chose his band members—of course, he did.

I close my eyes, letting the song wash over me. Less self-conscious without their eyes on me, I join in, though much, much quieter. I'm not a singer, nor do I want to be, but singing along is always a fun pastime. Since I was living in New York at the time, I never attended one of Uncle Biptu's karaoke nights, but me and Ma used to have plenty of our own, just the two of us.

Thinking about her is a little less raw this week. The worst of my depressive episode has passed, my thoughts completely overtaken by my need to fix this situation as soon as possible. Of course, my anxiety is acting up now, but it's not like I can win them all.

Either way, being able to think about my mother without the fear of breaking into tears is always a good thing. Ma used to say karaoke wasn't about being able to sing well. It was about being brave enough to stand in front of someone and put on a silly little performance. I try to muster that same courage now and keep singing, even if both Ethan and Vincent sound legions better than me. Frankly, Vincent sounds better than *Thomas*. He has one of the best vocal tones I've ever heard.

After the pre-chorus passes, I crack an eyelid open to see Ethan beaming at me, joining in wholeheartedly at the chorus.

At the same moment, Mohammed comes inside, a camera around his neck, and a curious glint in his eye. Vincent cocks his head toward the piano bench and Mohammed laughs quietly, taking his seat without preamble. The sound of piano notes join in alongside Mohammed's voice, a gentle croon that's as heartfelt as the song itself.

I open my mouth to sing the chorus again when someone else appears in the doorway, and when I look up, the sight of a flustered Sky, holding a tray of coffee orders, greets me.

He's watching us with an almost stupefied expression on his face.

Vincent keeps strumming but when I don't join in for the next part, he looks up to see what stole my attention. His eyes warm at the sight of his leader, and he breaks into the first genuine smile I've seen from him.

"Sky! Took you long enough."

Ethan looks up from his phone, but this time discards it to the side to hop up from his seat and take the tray of coffees from the leader. "Sky!"

"Hi, Ethan," Sky says with a dimpled smile, reaching up to ruffle the other boy's blond hair. There's a flush to his cheeks as he looks around, and my heart does a stupid twirl when his eyes meet mine. I would pay honest to God money to make this boy less attractive, because it's clearly not good for anyone involved. "You guys sounded good."

I have nothing to say to that, so I don't bother replying, though Ethan is grinning, taking the compliment gracefully. Sky's eyes return to me, curious, prodding, *calculating*. He must see the tight lines of my shoulders, the way I'm biting my lip to keep from saying something I shouldn't. I don't have any filter when it comes to him, so shutting up is my best option.

"Right, well, I brought drinks. Ethan, I got you a strawberry lemonade, because I *cannot* handle you on caffeine today. Matcha for Mohammed and cold brew for Vincent." Sky's gaze cuts back toward me. "Is this going to be a regular thing? Are you going to be here often? Should I put in a coffee order for you, too?"

I shake my head immediately. "Pretend I'm not even here," I say and purposefully turn away from him. Although coffee *does* sound nice right now.

Behind me, I can hear Ethan's pout when he says, "You could've gotten me a caffeinated drink. I would've behaved."

"You definitely would not have," Mohammed says, spinning around in his seat so he can face the rest of his band.

Ethan moves, coming into view, and flicks Mohammed on the forehead. Mohammed squawks in protest, slapping Ethan on the arm.

He slips off his camera, tossing it to Vincent who just barely catches it. "Take pictures, I'm going to file for domestic abuse!" And then he scrambles for Ethan's neck.

Ethan yelps and runs away, Mohammed following after him with far too much gusto.

Sky lets out a loud peal of laughter, throwing his head

back as his bandmates chase each other in the same fashion as Tom and Jerry.

They're such teenage boys—it's laughable. But I can't deny that I have to turn toward the wall to hide the smile on my face.

It's been a long time since I've been surrounded by so much laughter. It's strange.

I don't dislike it.

17

AMSTERDAM—IMAGINE DRAGONS

"Bibi, we're going to be late!" Baba hollers from the doorway.

I quickly grab my Ripple Records lanyard off my door-knob, swinging it around my neck before climbing down the stairs two at a time. "Coming!"

By the time I get to the front door, my dad is already in the car, leaving me to lock up behind me. I slip my feet into some worn Converse and then scramble for the passenger seat.

Baba shakes his head at me but doesn't say anything as he backs out of the driveway.

I try to catch my breath, lowering the window for some fresh air as my dad starts our morning commute to Ripple Records. Usually, I'm downstairs before him, but I was watching one of Third Eye's old performances at a cat café of all things. It was an acoustic set, and Vincent was sufficiently dis-tracted the entire time, but it was adorable. Sweet moments like that are good for their image—I'll have to look into whether the café would be open to having them back again.

"What do you think?"

"Huh?" I turn to look at my dad. "About what?"

"This demo?" he says, gesturing at the console.

I blink, unable to comprehend what he's saying for a solid ten seconds. Then I realize he's asking for my *opinion*, and I have to stop myself from openly gaping at him.

"Oh. Uh. I like her voice. It's very gravelly. Could be good for rock?" I say slowly.

Baba scratches his beard, his gaze focused on the traffic ahead of us. "I could see it. You don't think she's good in this genre?"

"No, she's good!" I rush to say, waving my hands wildly. "I just think her voice would also be well-suited for rock. If she prefers indie pop, then that's fine, but you could always have her feature on some rock songs, too? Even if just for a verse?"

"Interesting," he says, nodding slowly. "Thanks, Bibi."

I almost squeak. "No problem, Baba."

I assume that's the end of that, but over the next week, every time Baba and I are in the car together, he asks me for my thoughts on whatever demo is playing. Thomas may be the worst person on the planet, but this whole mess has given me *one* good thing, at least—Baba is seeking me out more and more often. He's listening to me. It's not the biggest change in the world, but it's more than I've ever been given before.

He even starts giving me attention during *work hours*.

When he calls me into his office on a late Tuesday afternoon, I'm wary, but his expression is placid.

"Yeah, what's up?" I ask, fiddling with my lanyard.

Baba slides over a file on his desk. "I've scheduled a department luncheon at the end of the week for you to give a PowerPoint presentation on a topic of your choice."

I splutter helplessly. *"Me?"*

My dad raises an eyebrow at me. "You may have gotten this internship through nepotism, but I'm hoping you'll keep it through your own hard work, Bibi. Do you have any ideas in mind?"

My brain does a hard reset, working overtime to make sense of the situation. "Uh—well, there's been a recent rise in songs being slowed down and sped up to capitalize on social media trends? I think that could be an interesting topic."

"Fantastic. Here's some background information on members of the department so you can cater your presentation accordingly," Baba says, tapping the folder underneath his hand pointedly. "Don't disappoint me."

I nod like a broken bobblehead and take the folder without another word. A few days later, the presentation goes off without a hitch. I don't think my dad has given me that much undivided attention in years, even if he does make a point to tell me afterward how I could have improved. It's still *something*.

Later in the week, I have the chance to shadow one of Baba's colleagues, a sweet woman named Miya who works on the marketing team and always takes the time to explain things to me when I'm absolutely confused and lost in the sauce.

"I have a meeting with a client, but we can grab lunch next time you're working if you want," she says, standing in the doorway of her office.

I nod, offering her a smile. Miya grins back and disappears behind her door.

Without much else on my itinerary today, I start to wander through the halls, seeing if anyone has their door open and might need a hand.

When I pass my dad's office, I pause, staring at the placard on the door that says *Jhilmil Sarkar*. Unlike some of the other offices here, his walls are solid instead of glass, so I can't see what he's up to.

I stand there for a moment, debating whether it's worth knocking on the door. What if I just annoy him by bothering him while he's working? It's not like I have anything impressive to say right now.

I chew on my bottom lip, trying to decide, when I hear two voices coming down the hall. Not wanting to be caught standing around like an idiot, I bite the bullet and knock on my dad's door.

"Come in!" he calls from inside.

I push the door open, disappearing inside his office before anyone can pass through the hallway.

Baba looks up at me and his gaze is curious, not at all like the frustration I was expecting. "What's up, Bibi?"

Some of my nervous tension fizzles away, and I let myself ask something I've been holding off on for a few days now.

"Hey, I, uh, just wanted to check in. I was wondering how things went with that demo I showed you? Did you end up reaching out?" I ask, standing behind a chair and unevenly balancing my weight on it, as I *pray* he says no.

Baba nods, dashing all my hopes. "I sent him a proposal.

I was actually going to brief you on it during our next one-on-one but I suppose now is as good a time as any. Sit down."

"Oh. Uh, no, it's fine, I'll stand," I say, fingers digging into the fabric of the chair. If I try to move right now, I'm afraid I'll fall over. "So what kind of proposal is it?"

"We're having him come in for a meeting to assess him. Kind of like an audition," my dad says, leaning back in his chair and stretching his arms out idly. "But it's unlikely we'll hand him a record deal right away. You understand, right?"

"Of course," I say, trying not to let the nerves in my stomach rise to my throat. "And what are the next steps after that?"

"We were thinking of having him compete in one of the upcoming music competitions, so we can weigh his talent against others at the same level as he is," Baba says, before sliding something across his desk toward me.

I slowly walk over, snagging the flyer with shaky hands. It's a list of upcoming competitions that Baba will be attending to scout talent, with the soonest slated for *next week*.

"Uh, do you have any idea which one?" I ask, forcing my voice to stay even.

My dad shakes his head. "Not yet. We'll probably decide during our meeting with him. I can't let you attend the first meeting, but if there's a follow-up, I'll see about sending you an invite."

"Fantastic," I say under my breath. Well. Thomas' audition probably won't be next week, given the timing of it all, but that still isn't really helpful information since I can't do anything about it.

"Did you need anything else?" Baba asks, which feels a

little bit like a dismissal. I try not to take it personally. "Or did you have any questions?"

"No," I say, brushing my bangs out of my face. There's something jittery skating across my skin and the way my hair is touching my forehead is making me feel insane. "I—are you going to be home in time for dinner?"

"I have no idea," my dad says, before gesturing to his laptop. "You know it's busy season."

I try to smile in understanding, but it comes out as more of a grimace. "Isn't every season busy season?"

"Exactly, you get it," Baba says, completely missing my point.

I resist the urge to scream. I'm being irrational. It's fine. It's just that I haven't had dinner with him in weeks. But he's busy, and it's nothing for me to be upset over. I'm sure we'll share a meal together at some point soon. I'm being ridiculous.

"I'll see you later, then," I say, and it comes out more stiffly than I intend.

My dad nods, turning his attention back to his screen. "Bye, Bibi."

"Bye, Baba." I slowly fold the flyer he gave me, tucking it in my back pocket before leaving his office, all the while hoping he'll call me back and say we should have dinner together anyway.

He doesn't.

18

SKINNY LOVE—BIRDY

Getting the members of Third Eye alone is harder than I anticipated. I figure if I tackle them one at a time, it'll be easier to convince them to let me help. However, it seems like they always travel in pairs, if not as a whole group of four. The few times I *think* I might catch one of them, Sky swoops in like some protective mama bear keeping me from them.

The only member I ever see alone is Sky, and I've spent more than enough time with him already. No, I need to befriend the others.

Over the course of the last two weeks, I've come to realize that the band is actually insanely talented, and more surprising than that, insanely collaborative. It always feels like they're on the same page, like they move as a unit and function best when they're with each other.

Any time any of them misses a beat, another bandmate is there to pick them up and shore up the edges. In a lot of ways, Third Eye feels like the definition of teamwork. And it's frustrating because it's the exact opposite of what Thomas made it sound like. The more I see their bond and how strong it is, the stupider I feel for believing Thomas' lies.

I have to help them. I have to fix my mistake.

Since it seems impossible to corner one of them, I decide a pair is going to have to be enough. Unsurprisingly, it turns out to be Ethan and Vincent. The two of them spend a *lot* of time together, so it isn't hard to find them after practice one day.

Sky has already left, something about needing to help his sister, and Mo is about to leave, complaining about having a shift.

"Where do you work?" I ask, setting aside a decade's worth of jazz albums.

Mohammed gives me a bewildered look, like he forgot I was there. I can't blame him, since I really do my best to blend into the background and shut up, especially when Sky is around.

"Oh. Hey. I work at my family's restaurant. Dear Paneer."

My lips part in surprise. I know that place—Baba and I have ordered from there more times than I can count, since we do takeout most nights.

Baba doesn't really have time to cook, nor does he care to. I think it's because the first time he tried to cook after Ma passed away, he burned everything. Neither of us have been able to eat khichuri since.

"And they work him to the bone," Vincent says with a shake of his head. "When are you going to tell your parents to give you less shifts?"

"When it won't lead to my funeral," Mohammed replies, sticking out his tongue. "I'll see you tomorrow, yeah?"

"Bye, Mo!" Ethan says, waving with one of his drumsticks. It's rare to see him without them, whether or not he's in front of his drum set. It seems like some kind of security blanket, but I don't think I'm anywhere near close enough to ask about it.

When Mohammed is gone, I turn back to the other two members. "So have you all known each other for a long time?"

Vincent gives me a strange look, but Ethan doesn't hesitate to answer. "I think it's about three years for me now! Vinny is our newest member, and even he joined like, a year ago? So we've been together for a while."

"Oh, wow," I say, blinking. I knew Vinny was the newest member, but I didn't realize it was so recent. Only a year? That's wild if what Thomas said about him and Sky starting the band during their freshman year of high school is true. "How did it all happen?"

"Mohammed can tell you his side of things, but for me—" Ethan pauses, meeting Vincent's gaze. There's a silent conversation that passes between them, something beyond my understanding, but Vincent nods subtly. It's really just a tuck of his chin, but it's enough for Ethan's face to soften. "Right. Yeah, for me, Sky and I met at a Frank Ocean concert."

"And what? You just hit it off?" I ask, adjusting my posture and crossing my legs so I can listen to them more comfortably. A few days ago, I dragged a beanbag chair down here because my ass was getting tired of sitting on the hardwood floor, and Ethan had gasped and looked at Sky immediately with puppy dog eyes. Soon afterward, four more beanbag chairs showed up.

"Sky's really easy to get along with," Ethan says, shrugging.

There are stars in his eyes when he talks about the band's leader. "And I've never met someone as dedicated and passionate about music as he is. He invited me to come to his school talent show, and he and—" A pause. All three of us know that the next word out of his mouth was going to be *Thomas*, but none of us fill the gap. Ethan clears his throat. "Anyway, he performed 'Cry Me a River' by Justin Timberlake, and it was incredible."

"I didn't know Sky could sing," I say, brows furrowed. He's only ever played the guitar in front of me.

"It's not his favorite thing to do," Vincent says, something like steel in his voice. I blink. I wasn't expecting him to get defensive. I didn't think my tone was anything aside from curious, but maybe it came out wrong. "All of us can sing to some degree, but I'm sure you've noticed Sky prefers to stay in the background."

"Oh. Yeah," I say, still a little taken aback. But at least Vincent is talking now. "Right. So…all things considered, are you officially the band's new lead singer?"

Now Vincent is the one who seems startled, like it didn't even occur to him that was an option.

From the band rehearsals I've observed, it's undeniable that Vincent has the best voice among the four. I wasn't entirely sure at first, but the more I've witnessed them singing as a unit, the more confident I am in that judgment.

I think with some vocal training, Vincent could really shine and take this band to the next level. Ethan is also decent at singing, but it's clear his voice is only suited for certain songs where a lower register fits better. Mohammed's soothing voice would be great for backup vocals, to help support Vincent's gaps. I haven't heard Sky's voice for myself, but if he prefers to be in the background…that really only leaves Vincent.

But it seems this isn't a conversation the band has had yet. Maybe because they're still reeling from Thomas' sudden departure. They're not looking at the band critically, not the way I have been for the last few weeks.

"We—we haven't really talked about it," Vincent says, confirming my thoughts. It's the first time he's sounded unsure of himself, and maybe even a little scared.

"For what my opinion is worth, I think you'd be a great lead singer," I say, shrugging a shoulder.

Ethan gives me a measured look, his eyes searching for something I can't pinpoint, but he must find it, because he smiles at me. "I agree with her, Vinny. I know we haven't really discussed it as a group yet, but it makes perfect sense. You've always had the best voice out of all of us." Ethan takes a deep breath before pushing forward. "Better than him, too."

Vincent's eyes widen comically. "Ethan…"

"It's true," Ethan says steadfastly. "And he knew it, too."

My own expression twists with shock, and I turn my gaze to the floor, letting my hair fall into my face to hide it from view. I hadn't considered that Thomas might *know* Vincent is better than him vocally. I don't think Vincent did either given the sharp inhale that follows Ethan's words.

Did Thomas feel threatened by Vincent? Is that why he went off on his own? He couldn't stand to share the spotlight? Couldn't handle the fact that his other bandmates might be more talented than he is?

My nails dig into my palm as my fingers curl into fists. How could I have missed this? Any of this? All of this? How could I have failed to see what a shitty person Thomas was? I just sat by and let him manipulate me, lie to me, make his *band* seem like the bad guys when he was the one who couldn't handle feeling slightly threatened.

And really, given Vincent's reaction, it doesn't seem like it was that big of a threat. I doubt Vincent had even thought about taking over Thomas' position. And from what I know about Sky, I doubt he would have let Vincent do it even if he wanted to.

All of them seem deathly protective of each other, of the bond they have. And this all started with Sky and Thomas, two young boys with a dream bigger than they could handle. Even if I don't care for Sky, I think he would sooner remove himself from the band than try to take another member's spot away from them.

I resist the urge to smack my hand against my forehead. If I ever see Thomas again, I'm going to strangle him, and if I end up in jail, so be it.

Me: would you bail me out of jail

Evie Khodabux: ofc who are we killing

Me: thomas

Me: surprising no one he continues to become a bigger and bigger asshole

Me: the bar is literally in hell

Evie Khodabux: yikes

Evie Khodabux: I'll bring the sledgehammer

19

GOODNIGHT N GO—ARIANA GRANDE

A few days later, I knock on the door to my father's office. I've been debating all morning whether I should bother him, my anxiety insisting it would ruin the progress we've made in our relationship this summer, but eventually, I give in.

I had a dream about Ma this morning. Not just her, but all three of us. We were in the car, on one of our yearly trips to the Poconos. I don't remember how the dream ended, but I can't get rid of the memory of Ma's smile as she belts out the lyrics to "Call Me" by Blondie, off-key and carefree.

If there's anyone in the world who might understand that, it's my dad.

Baba looks up when I walk in, clearly expecting someone else. When he realizes it's me, he waves a hand for me to come in and shut the door behind me. "Bibi."

Well. He doesn't sound excited, but he also doesn't sound actively bothered. I'll take it.

"The one and only," I say, offering him jazz hands.

Baba turns back to his computer screen without any reaction. "Did you need something? I didn't see anything from you in my inbox."

Well. I do, but it's nothing that would require an email.

"Actually, I wanted to ask if you wanted to have lunch—"

"I don't have time," Baba says without looking up.

I fish-mouth for a second, thrown by how abrupt he's being. It's not like I thought him showing interest in my career meant that our father-daughter bond was suddenly going to be repaired, but I did have a little inkling of hope that things were steadily improving.

I wish he would look at me. Just for a minute, meet my gaze, and bridge the gap between us.

We've never been particularly close—I was always my mother's daughter. But we still had a connection of sorts.

He bought me my first record player, accompanied by a copy of Fleetwood Mac's *Rumours*. My favorite song was "Songbird" and his was "Never Going Back Again." It was lucky they were on the same side of the record, because neither of us felt like flipping it over.

On days when Ma was working at the local animal shelter and it was just me and Baba, we'd eat ice cream together and listen to old records like *Rumours* together. I'd have coffee and he'd have mint chocolate chip. He used to tell me about the lore behind all the records, and I'd nod along, completely investing myself within it. I used to tell him about the latest school drama and he'd hum along, pretending to care even when he didn't.

At some point after Ma died, I kept investing myself but he stopped pretending to care, and we've been at something of a stalemate ever since. For a brief moment, I consider telling my dad how badly I've screwed up with Thomas. It would at least make him *look* at me, even if it was in disappointment. It's an irrational desire, because I know I would hate that even more.

"Maybe we could get ice cream instead?" I ask, my voice small. "It shouldn't take too long."

Baba sighs, and I think for a moment that he'll give in, but instead he reaches for his wallet and slides me his credit card. "Here, Bibi. On me, yeah?"

I take the card, my fingers digging into the hard edges. "Yeah. Okay. Thanks."

Later, when I get ice cream, I get mint chocolate chip, think about Ma's smile, and try not to cry.

The upcoming weekend, I lose track of time while I'm on the closing shift. As I'm cleaning up, I realize I saw Sky come in the shop earlier, but I've yet to see him leave. I check the clock on the wall above a display of The Beatles' records, and it says there's only ten minutes to closing.

There's no one in the store that I can see, but I still do a quick jog through the aisles to make sure I haven't missed anyone. Riya is in the back room counting cash, and she shoots me a thumbs-up when I ask if it's okay if I close. I head back to the front of the store, flipping over the open sign and locking the door.

Once I've turned most of the lights off, I make my way downstairs to the basement, trying to figure out what the hell Sky is still doing down here.

I push open the door to the practice room, looking around until my eyes land on Sky.

But he's not looking back at me. No, instead, he's knocked out on the couch, his notebook lying open on the table in front of him. I walk inside, getting closer to make sure he's not faking it, but it seems he really is fast asleep.

I sniff, taking note of the scent of alcohol in the air. That explains the unprecedented nap. There are a few soju bottles lying around, next to Skyler's notebook.

I stand there for a moment, unsure what to do with myself as I look down at him. Sky is really beautiful; it's not hard to see that. His eyelashes are fanning his cheeks and his dark hair falls around his head like a halo. His lips are parted, and the sound of his steady breathing is loud in the quiet of the room. The rise and fall of his chest is calming, settling some frayed nerves I didn't even realize were weighing on me.

I almost don't want to wake him up since he looks so peaceful. But then again, what is even *happening* right now? Why did he get drunk? Is he alright?

I realize I'm staring and look away, cheeks flushing with embarrassment even though Sky isn't awake to catch me. I look down at his notebook and my eyes just barely skim over the words *is that why it's so hard to breathe? is that why I'm drowning? it's true, there's a prickling ocean behind my eyes, an itch I'll never reach. I let you in, I let you in, I let you in. I made a space for you.*

My heart feels heavier for reading the words. It must be about Thomas. No wonder he got drunk. I shouldn't have looked. It wasn't mine to see.

I try to move away from him, but my knee knocks into

the table, and one of the soju bottles on the far edge falls off with a loud thud.

Sky shoots up with a disoriented look, whirling around in alarm, and I'm instantly filled with regret.

"What—?" Sky asks to himself and his voice is drowsy, his eyes blinking blearily. His face is flushed from the alcohol. I hate the part of me that wants to tell him to go back to sleep, to soothe him and tuck him back in.

"You fell asleep," I say instead, and it's a miracle that my voice works at all.

Sky starts at that, as if he didn't notice me standing near the end of the couch until just now. "Oh. *Oh.*" Then he smiles at me sleepily, dimples and all. "You're pretty."

I stare at him blankly, unsure if I'm the one who's asleep and having some kind of insane dream. He must still be tipsy if he's saying things like that.

I don't know what kind of expression I'm making at him but it must be funny given that Sky starts laughing. "I always thought so. Ever since the party. Told Thomas about you afterward." All the mirth disappears from his face. "I should've seen it sooner."

I continue to stare at him, unable to form words, as he stands up and grabs his guitar case. His shoulder bumps into mine as he leaves, heading up the stairs without another word.

He's gone before I can really even make sense of the situation. Told Thomas about me? What does he mean? I sit down on the couch, almost in a trance. A few moments later, a new pair of footsteps come down the stairs, and Riya joins me.

"What's wrong with you?" she asks, poking me in the side.

"He said I'm pretty," I say dazedly before wincing, because

Riya is the last person I should have said that to. She's somehow become a huge Skyler Moon fan in the last month and isn't afraid to loudly broadcast it.

"Did he now?" Riya teases, a grin the size of the continental US stretching across her face. I don't like the way she's looking at me, like she knows more than she should.

"He was drinking, it doesn't count," I mutter, glaring at her. I stand up, leaving Riya on the couch with her stupid smile and stupid knowing looks.

I don't care about Sky, no matter what my cousin says. I might think he's hot, but he's still an anomaly, and one I have no intention of figuring out. And I don't have the time anyway, not when my entire focus right now is finding his weaknesses and fixing them to the best of my ability.

20

TO BUILD A HOME
—THE CINEMATIC ORCHESTRA

Despite my better judgment, I've texted Thomas quite a few times this week. Not because I have any desire to actually talk to him, but because I'd *love* to know what the fuck his game plan is for when he meets with my father. Surprising no one, all of my messages go unread.

It makes me want to tear my hair out. It's not *fair* that he can just do this and not have to pay for it.

"I hate men," I say to Riya, slumping against the counter. A pit of anxiety broils in my stomach, but I ignore it. "They're useless."

Riya snorts. "I've been telling you that for years."

"Yet you're still dating Zian," I say, rolling my eyes.

She reaches over the counter to smack my arm. "Keep your voice down."

"Uncle Biptu is not going to hear me from all the way down in Malibu," I say quieter. "When are the two of you just going to tell your parents that you're dating? It's been like six years."

"When Zian proposes," Riya says frankly. "I don't want to hear the lecture my parents are going to give me otherwise."

"At least he's Bangladeshi," I say, nudging her shoulder. There's a certain level of expectations from our elders, and marrying within our culture is a bigger one than most. "It could be a lot worse."

"The small victories," she says, her voice dry. "I think you could get away with dating whoever you want, though, Bibi."

I snort. "Yeah, only because Baba wouldn't notice if I was dating someone. He has bigger things to worry about."

Riya shoots me a disapproving look, but doesn't refute it, which is proof enough. "Thank your blessings, Bibi."

"Whatever, Riya Apu," I say, waving her off.

When I was younger, Ma read my diary once. We got into a huge fight over it, me complaining she violated my privacy, and her arguing that I shouldn't be hiding secrets from her. Mostly, I was embarrassed about the fact I'd written all about the crush I had on one of the boys in my first grade class.

Once we both cooled down, Ma talked to me about the crush. I expected her to be mad, to tell me to stop it at once, but she only sighed and said to be careful. It wasn't permission to date—far from it, given I was six years old at the time—but it wasn't active discouragement.

Baba was a little more strict, telling me I wasn't allowed to date so long as I lived under his roof, which I just took to mean that I could date the second I moved into my college dorm. I don't think it's what he meant, but I'm going to choose to live in ignorance.

Through high school, I had a few short flirtations, but nothing that panned out. Most of which is my own fault.

Since Ma's death, I feel like I haven't been able to fully just…be myself with anyone. She died so suddenly, a brain hemorrhage that no one saw coming. Between one day and the next, I was irreversibly changed. I don't think I'll ever be able to go back to that old version of myself. This new Liana is here to stay, and so few people truly know her. I thought maybe Thomas could have been the first person I could actually open up to, and look where that got me.

I'm coming to accept that maybe the love that exists in every other song on the radio is entirely made up.

As if on cue, Ed Sheeran comes on over the speakers, and I sigh. I reach for my phone, which is running a SiriusXM radio station, and switch it to one of my playlists.

songs for when all I want to do is lie down on the floor and scream:
this is me trying—Taylor Swift
Memo—Years & Years
Why'd You Only Call Me When You're High?—Arctic Monkeys
Earth—Sleeping at Last
Is There Somewhere—Halsey
what about today?—Lewis Watson
To Build A Home—The Cinematic Orchestra
You Found Me—The Fray
Visions of Gideon—Sufjan Stevens
Falling Apart—Michael Schulte
The Chain—Fleetwood Mac
Stayaway—MUNA
Waiting Room—Phoebe Bridgers

There. That fits the vibe of today.

"This playlist, huh?" Riya asks, giving me a cursory look. I shoot her a dead-eyed stare back and she raises her hands above her head in a general gesture of surrender. "Sorry. Live your best life, Bibi."

"Who's Bibi?"

Both Riya and I startle at the sound of Sky's voice. I turn my glare on him immediately.

"What *is it* with you and showing up out of nowhere?"

Sky blinks at me innocuously. "I came in through the front door. Was I supposed to announce my presence?"

"It would be helpful if you did," I mutter, rubbing absently at my eye. "Don't worry about who Bibi is. The rest of Third Eye is downstairs already."

"Is your name not Liana Ahmed?" Sky asks instead of fucking off like I so clearly wanted him to do.

Then his words register, and I cringe internally. No, that's not my name. Riya and I are cousins on my mom's side, and her dad—Ma's brother—is the one who owns the store. I might be a part of the Ahmed family, but I'm not an Ahmed. I'm a Sarkar.

But he can never know that.

"Don't worry about what my name is," I say instead, ignoring the funny feeling in the back of my throat. Riya gives me a look but doesn't call me out on my evasion.

"Is it like a cultural thing?" Sky asks, because he's never taken a hint in his life. "I have a Korean name, too. It's Si-woo. Only my dad ever uses it, though."

I sigh. It's obvious he's not going to drop the subject. "Fine. Yes, it's a cultural thing. We have something called a dak nam, which is what relatives and family friends call you. And then we have something called a bhalo nam, which is essentially your government name."

"And Liana's dak nam is Bibi," Riya adds unhelpfully. "Mine is Riya."

Skyler offers her a blinding grin. "That's cool. Isn't it weird how we kind of have two separate lives? Like the person we are at home and the person we are outside of it."

Riya nods eagerly, and I resist the urge to smack her upside the head. Surely, twenty-four is too old to be won over by Sky's charms. "Yeah, like how we break up parts of ourselves to be more digestible for those around us."

Skyler snaps his fingers. "Exactly. Sometimes I think we're all so scared of being truly seen for who we are that we hide parts of ourselves on purpose. Maybe it started off as a survival instinct, but now it feels like something bigger than that."

"Aren't you going to be late to practice?" I cut in, gesturing pointedly at the clock. "Or are you going to write a soliloquy about being diaspora?"

Riya shakes her head, but I pretend not to see it. Sky blinks at me, and then blinks at the clock.

"Right. Yeah, I'll get going." He spares me a second look before he heads for the back of the store. Once he's out of sight, I massage the bridge of my nose like it'll get rid of the burgeoning headache.

"Be nicer, Bibi. You're a disaster," Riya says, a little too earnestly for my taste.

"I'm aware of that," I say darkly, turning back to the register. Some days are easier than others. Today just isn't one of them.

21

KABHI KHUSHI KABHIE GHAM
—LATA MANGESHKAR

The first time I manage to get Mohammed alone is when he's leaving practice for his shift at the restaurant around the same time I get off work at the record shop.

"I'll come with you," I say, thinking nothing of it until Mohammed looks at me like I've grown a second head. "I—I need to pick up dinner for me and my dad," I add after a second, realizing how strange that sounded without context.

Mohammed seems uncertain, glancing behind me to where the rest of his band members are. More specifically, at Sky, who's watching us with a frown.

"What, do you need his permission?" I ask, putting my hands on my hips. "Fine, go by yourself, and I guess I'll just take an Uber, even though we're going to the *same place*."

I march off without another word. Mohammed calls after me a few seconds later, jogging to catch up with me, halfway up the stairs.

"Okay, I'll give you a ride," he says, looking incredibly awkward and out of place. "My car is parked around the corner."

I roll my eyes, gesturing to the rest of the stairs with flair. "Lead the way, then."

It doesn't take long to find his car, a beat-up Honda Civic that has definitely seen better days. "This thing works?"

"Enough," Mohammed says with a shrug.

"If you say so," I grumble under my breath and let myself in on the passenger side. It absolutely reeks of AXE body spray inside, and I don't bother hiding my disgust. The seat is reclined so far back that I'm nearly in the back, and there are colorful LED lights lining the car's interior. "Oh my God, you're such a brown dude."

Mohammed shoots me a half-hearted glare. "Do you want a ride or not?"

I sigh. "Okay, fair enough." I pull my seat belt across my chest and adjust my seat so I'm actually sitting up straight instead of halfway to hell. "Ready when you are."

The first five minutes of the car ride are unbearable. There's an uncomfortable silence between us, and it riles my anxiety up with every passing moment. Mohammed isn't any better, tapping against the steering wheel in some strange, offbeat manner.

Finally, I break the silence. "So your parents—they know you're in a band?"

"Kind of," Mohammed says, making a face at the traffic ahead of us. "I mean, yeah. But…no. Yeah."

I stare at him. "That makes absolutely no sense."

"I know," he mutters. "They know I'm in a band. They think it's just a fun hobby."

"Ah," I say, leaning back in my seat. "Right. Brown parents. Let me guess. They want you to study engineering or something?"

"No," Mohammed says, and it's easy to read the defensiveness in his body language. "They're not like that. They want me to do what makes me happy. They don't care what it is."

"Oh?" I say. I can't help but think there's more to it that he isn't telling me. And that's fair—I'm more or less a stranger to him. But still, this doesn't sit right with me.

"Yeah, but—" He sighs, running a hand through his curls. "Well, you know how it is. They came to America from Pakistan so me and my sisters could have better opportunities. I just want to pay them back."

"You don't owe them that," I say, maybe a little too sharply.

Mohammed furrows his brows. "No, I know that. But I want to. I want them to be happy and settled in life. I want to be a good son to them."

I frown. "There's a *but* here, isn't there? Why do they think that your music is a hobby, then? If their love is conditional—"

"It's *not*," Mohammed says immediately. "It's not conditional. I could decide to sell lemonade on the sidewalk for the rest of my life and they'd be happy as long as I'm happy. But I can't—they deserve a son who can provide for them. Making them happy will make me happy. After all they've been through, after all they've done for *me*, it's the least I can do. And right now, Third Eye doesn't pay the bills. So, yeah."

I know there are brown people out there who have parents that love them wholeheartedly, but it's always jarring to hear about it. Putting aside Baba, even Ma's love came with a few terms and conditions, but I was willing to meet them.

While I can say Ma loved me to a solid degree, I know that if she had lived longer, we would have had our fair share of massive blowouts. Whereas Baba doesn't care what I do or who I do it with nowadays, Ma's love was a little stifling. She liked to know everything, and oftentimes put her nose where it didn't belong.

Reading my diary is just one example of my mom being unable to mind her business, but there are countless others. The first time I went to a friend's birthday party in middle school, she waited in her car outside the *entire time* because she didn't trust me on my own. Another time, she confronted me about an offhanded tweet I posted where I called her overbearing, which only served to prove my point. Suffice to say, it was suffocating at times.

But there were more good times than bad, so I could handle it.

What Mohammed's describing, though? It feels foreign and strange. Ma loved me, but it was never unconditional. And Baba's half-hearted love is far from it.

"You'd sacrifice your happiness for theirs?" I ask in disbelief.

"It's not a sacrifice," Mohammed says with a shrug. "And the other members get it. Or, at least, they mostly get it. This is just the way it is."

"None of this makes any sense to me," I say after a long pause. "But I guess if you're...happy."

"I'm guessing your parents are shitty, then," Mohammed

says, more blunt than I expect. I choke on air for a moment, which he clearly takes as confirmation, given his soft, "Ah."

"I—that's not—"

I don't know how to explain that, yes, my parent, *singular*, is shitty sometimes. But he wouldn't be if Ma weren't dead. He wasn't before she died. There was a time when we all used to be happy, minor scuffles aside.

But that time is long gone and I don't want anyone's pity, even if a part of me feels guilty for withholding that information. I hate being seen as the girl with the dead mom.

Mohammed shakes his head. "No, I know I lucked out in the parents department. Even my sisters have it harder than me, just because they're girls. I'm not judging."

I bite my bottom lip, unsure how to even respond to that. Eventually, it turns out I don't have to because we pull up in front of Dear Paneer. Mohammed parks the car and I get out without a word, clutching the strap of my bag tightly and wishing I had a stress ball.

"What's your order, anyway?" Mohammed asks, pushing open the door to the restaurant and waiting for me to pass through. "I'll go and enter it into the system."

"Just—two chicken biryanis," I say and pointedly walk away from him, sitting in the little waiting area with the other people trying to pick up their orders.

It used to be rare for our family to order takeout. Ma loved to cook, especially traditional Bangladeshi food. While Dear Paneer makes an excellent biryani, it's still made in the Pakistani style and very different from my mom's. The closest I've had to hers is when Riya's family invites us over for a daawat, but even that isn't quite the same.

Once Mo disappears into the back, pressing a kiss to a woman's head on his way—undeniably his mother given her age and the way she smiles at him—I sigh heavily.

Mohammed has no idea how much he lucked out. Unconditional love or not, I would do anything to have my mom smile at me one more time. I would do anything to have my dad smile at me, too.

I guess I knew that, though. I wouldn't be in this mess otherwise.

At any rate, I was supposed to be sussing out more on the band. Not getting Mohammed's *life story*.

I've got to get my act together.

22

OUT OF MY SYSTEM—LOUIS TOMLINSON

I'm not sure how, but I get roped into going to one of Third Eye's shows. I probably would have gone secretly, anyway, but after Ethan sweetly asks Riya and me if we'll come to support them, there's no way either of us can say no.

The real problem is that Riya and I rode in the back of their van with them on the way here, and the four of them are *bouncing* with nerves. By the time we're at the venue, I'm considering homicide, and Riya is smirking at me like she knows.

Once we're inside the club, we gravitate toward the back, near the bar. Clearly, that was a mistake, because Ethan is ready to do whatever it takes to somehow get some alcohol, up to and including begging his band members for help with an exaggerated pout.

"Can we—?" Ethan starts only to be cut off immediately.

"I've already bought you *five* drinks," Mohammed says, but he's wearing this fond face that makes it clear he would do anything Ethan asked if he said it nicely enough. "They're not going to serve you anything alcoholic, Ethan."

"Yeah, but Vinny was in the bathroom last time we went, so maybe if we had him, they'd believe we're older!" Ethan says.

I shake my head, keeping my lips sealed. I don't know why none of them turned to Riya to get them drinks—because she definitely would—but I'm not going to be the one to suggest it and deal with their drunk antics.

"Vinny is *still* in the bathroom!" Mohammed says, throwing his hands in the air in indignation.

I snort and cover it up by coughing into my hand when Mohammed throws me a betrayed look. "Don't take his side, Liana. Ethan's ego is big enough as it is—we don't need it growing anymore."

Ethan scoffs. "If we're going to talk about big egos, how about the fact you spent the entire drive here checking yourself out in the rearview mirror?"

"It's not a *crime* to want to look presentable, Ethan! Not that it matters anymore because my hair is just—I would punch you if I didn't know Sky would yell at me for it."

"Oh, what a badass! If you're so tough, then why don't you man up and tell Kate that you're—"

"Excuse me—"

"I'm hungry!" I interrupt loudly, though a part of me is itching to find out what they're talking about. "Can one of you get me some nachos? Or we can all go. Let's all get some nachos!"

I don't wait for an answer before pulling Ethan away, dragging him with me to the other side of the venue where they sell food. Once I'm sure Mohammed isn't following us, I lean in and whisper, "Who's Kate?"

"Sky's sister," Ethan whispers back conspiratorially. He might be my favorite Third Eye member yet. "Mohammed has a huge crush on her but won't admit it, and we're not allowed to talk about it in front of Sky because Sky might kill us *and* Mohammed."

"Got it," I say, nodding.

Ethan eyes the man behind the counter warily. "You don't think—?"

"I'm sorry, sweetie, but you look sixteen," I say, patting his head lightly. "Maybe once you grow into your cheeks."

Ethan sighs, touching his own face. "It's always the cheeks."

I give him a sympathetic smile and order him a lemonade alongside my nachos.

Since we got to the venue, I haven't seen Sky once. He disappeared as soon as we got inside, but all the others seemed used to it, unbothered by him squeezing their shoulders before running off.

"So where did your leader run off to?" I ask as we walk back toward Mohammed, Vincent, and Riya.

Ethan is about to take a sip of his drink but pauses. "Oh, he went to go check on all our stuff. Do a soundcheck, make sure all our instruments are in order, make nice with the people who run the venue, and so on. We always tell him he doesn't have to do it alone but he insists."

"Huh," I say, mostly to myself. "Doesn't it stress him out to do it on his own?"

"I think he'd rather stress himself out than us," Ethan says, a half smile on his face.

Vincent spots us when we're a few feet away, and opens his mouth to say something, but something behind us must catch his eye because he cuts himself short.

I turn around to see what he's looking at and my entire body freezes at the sight of Thomas walking into the venue.

"Ethan," I say, grabbing his shoulder to keep from falling over. "Please tell me my eyes are deceiving me."

"What?" he asks, twisting his head so he can see what I'm looking at. Thomas is now amicably talking to one of the bouncers, laughing like he has no concerns. "Oh shit."

"I'm going to fucking kill him," Mohammed says, loud enough for me to hear it. "Vincent, let me go."

I immediately pull Ethan backward, toward the rest of his band. If I'm within reaching distance of Thomas, I'm going to help Mohammed commit a crime.

Vincent is holding Mohammed by the arm, his fingers digging into Mohammed's skin hard enough to bruise. "Mo, stop it," he hisses.

Ethan immediately goes to Vincent's side, reaching for his free hand.

"You—you know what he did," Mohammed says, so incensed his words are barely coherent. "Just one swing. Come on, Vinny. He deserves it."

"He deserves worse," Vincent agrees. "But he's a white boy who's going to walk away from this without breaking a sweat. If you hit him, you're the one who's going to suffer for it. You *know* that."

"Look at his dumb fucking smile," Mohammed says, his hands curled into fists. "It might be worth it."

I almost agree with him. It would bring me immense joy

to see Mohammed knock the grin off Thomas' face with a swift punch to the face.

"It's not," Sky says, appearing at Ethan's side. He's grimacing and pointedly looking anywhere but at Thomas. "It's not worth it. Please don't do anything stupid, Mohammed."

At the sight of Sky, Mohammed's shoulders droop. Vincent finally lets go of his arm, but his fingers come back a moment later to massage the reddened skin apologetically.

"Sky..." Mohammed whispers.

"I know," Sky says.

I grab Riya's hand, pulling her slightly deeper into the crowd and farther away from the band. "Make sure he doesn't see me," I say quietly.

Riya quirks a brow. "He's barely an ex. You went on *one* date."

"Are you going to be nitpicky or help me, Riya Apu?" I ask with a glare. It's not like I don't know how little time Thomas and I spent together. In fact, I'm all too aware of it and how absolutely fucking stupid it makes me feel.

But this is more about the fact that Thomas *knows* my secret and is apparently a sociopathic asshole that doesn't care if he hurts his friends. The last thing I need is for him to reveal how I accidentally sabotaged Third Eye and send this entire thing into a tailspin.

Riya rolls her eyes but steps in front of me, making more of an effort to hide me with her body.

Predictably, as soon as Thomas catches sight of Third Eye, he wanders over to them with a smirk on his face.

"Hi, guys," he says sweetly. "I didn't know you were performing tonight."

"Yes, you did," Mohammed says darkly. "I'm surprised you even showed up since you blew off our performance last month for a beach date. But I guess when it's not a commitment to the band, you're happy to show up."

A beach date…as in *our* beach date last month? Dear God. I hide farther behind Riya, this time out of shame.

Thomas snorts derisively. "Why would I waste my time playing here when I've already been accepted to perform at the Light The Way music competition?"

All four of the boys go quiet, staring at Thomas in disbelief.

I rack my brain for why those words sound familiar, and then immediately lock in on when my dad gave me a flyer of potential shows for Thomas to perform at. Thomas must've had his initial meeting with Ripple Records, then.

"Auditions don't even open until August," Ethan says, eyes narrowed. "It's June. You're lying."

"Am I?" Thomas asks, grinning.

I take out my phone, quickly looking up the Light The Way music competition. I skim through their website, trying to keep an eye on the conversation simultaneously.

The winner of the competition gets a record deal. It doesn't say with which company, but I can guess.

Briefly, I consider asking Riya to get *me* alcohol to get through the night.

"You're only allowed to perform self-written songs at Light The Way," Mohammed says with a sneer. "Are you actually going to write any or keep using somebody else's like a piece of shit?"

"I have no idea what you're talking about," Thomas says brightly.

Vincent's hand shoots out to hold Mohammed's arm again, but this time with a gentle grasp, contrasting the absolute enraged look on his face. "Walk away, Thomas. No one here wants to hear you run your mouth."

Thomas frowns, but there's a mocking twist to it. "All I wanted was to say hello to old friends."

Skyler lets out a bitter laugh and walks away from the band, brushing past me on his way. The others can't see, but his eyes are glittering with something wet and awful.

I debate following after him, but I can't bring myself to. Not when I'm partially responsible for this.

"Dramatic," Thomas says dryly. "Whatever. I have better things to do, anyway."

He leaves, going in the other direction with a condescending wave of his fingers.

Mohammed starts cursing under his breath. Vincent and Ethan pull him into a hug, but they're all vibrating with barely contained anger.

I can't let Thomas do this to Third Eye. Any of this.

I'm going to make sure Third Eye is able to compete in the Light The Way music competition. More than that, I'm going to make sure they beat Thomas.

I'm going to make sure they win.

23

SHINE—YEARS & YEARS

Before the performance starts, the boys are all amped up with a mixture of anger and adrenaline. A part of me is slightly worried about how they'll perform onstage in that state, but I send them off with a big grin and a clap on the back.

After they disappear backstage, I end up near the bar where Riya is sitting, looking a little bit too curious for my liking.

"Shut up, Riya Apu," I say before she can open her mouth.

"I didn't say anything," she replies, holding her hands up defensively. But she also mutters, "Clownery," under her breath when she thinks I can't hear her.

I glare at her and don't answer, instead taking a seat on the stool beside her and stealing her mojito for a sip, keeping an eye out for Thomas. Last I saw, he was on the opposite side of the room, networking with some of the people who work here.

It gets on my nerves, since that's usually what *I* like to do at these events. The thought of having anything in common with Thomas makes my skin itch.

I'm also nervous to see Third Eye perform, but I'm not going to admit that aloud. It's not like I think they'll be bad or anything—I've seen enough clips of their shows to know they're incredible on stage. But my anxiety is still rearing its head for absolutely no reason, like this performance means life or death.

I cross my fingers and hope they don't let Thomas throw them off.

When the host of Next Level Club gets on the stage, I grab Riya's hand tightly, ignoring the dramatic groan of pain my cousin lets out.

"Right, well, today we have Third Eye here to perform for us. Can I get a little love for them?" the host asks and the crowd cheers, loud whoops and woos.

Third Eye saunters on stage and it feels like a scene out of a movie. Ethan and Mohammed take their seats first, behind the drums and piano respectively. Sky and Vincent come to the front, both of them strapped up with their guitars—Sky's being an electric guitar and Vincent's being a bass guitar.

I don't know if it's because of the lighting or what, but they look like stars. I'm mesmerized by them, and they haven't even started yet. The crowd cheers again and someone up front throws flowers onto the stage.

Sky laughs and taps on one of the microphones lightly. "Hello, everyone." His eyes are bright and I think this is the most charismatic I've ever seen him. "It's nice to meet you all. We're a local band called Third Eye, and we're going to be performing a few songs for you guys if that's alright?"

"More than alright!" someone shouts from the crowd and Sky's cheeks flush red with delight.

"I'm glad," he says, before gesturing to the other band members. "Boys, if you'll introduce yourselves?"

Vincent salutes the crowd before playing a quick riff. "I'm Vincent Alvarez and I'm on bass."

Behind him, Ethan starts playing the drums, ending it off with a hit to the cymbal. He grins brightly at the crowd, waving with one of his sticks. "I'm Ethan Mitchell and I'm on drums."

Mohammed picks up where he left off, running his fingers down the piano keys in quick succession. "I'm Mohammed Anwar and I'm on the keys."

Skyler finally plays a final riff, ending with a wink at the crowd. "And I'm Sky Moon, on lead guitar. Let's get this party started, shall we?"

"*The story starts on a Monday afternoon...*" Vincent sings into the mic and the rest of the band launches into the song.

My nerves dissipate on the spot. I don't even know why I was worried. The music rattles my chest until it feels like my entire body is vibrating, in tune with every word Vincent sings, with every piano note Mo plays, with every beat Ethan hits, and with every strum of Sky's guitar.

The entire crowd is cheering, and I think I see a few people near the front singing along. I move to grab my phone so I can film the performance. Maybe I can edit some of the clips and upload them to 3E's different socials.

"They're good," Riya says, leaning in to shout in my ear. "Vincent is a great singer!"

"Isn't he?" I can't help the pride I feel deep in my chest. "They're killing it!"

When a slower song comes on, the entire crowd falls silent. It's obvious Third Eye was born to be on the stage—and while I knew they were talented, seeing them perform in person is something else entirely.

The crowd starts to sway, hands rising above their heads, their phone flashlights turned on.

My heart continues to swell. They're going to be something big. I can feel it.

When the final song ends, the entire crowd bursts into loud applause, demanding an encore. Sky waves them off, but all of Third Eye is grinning, pleased with the reaction.

I don't expect them to get off the stage and head straight for the bar, making a beeline toward me and Riya. Something in my brain stutters, taken aback, and I realize it's because a part of me is *flustered*. Third Eye are genuinely cool as hell, and I'm allowed to witness their ascent to greatness. I feel strangely honored.

"What did you think?" Ethan asks when he reaches us, bouncing lightly with excitement. "Were we alright?"

I nod despite the fact my brain isn't functioning properly. "Amazing," I breathe. "You were all so good."

Mohammed slings an arm around Ethan's neck, playfully ruffling his hair. "We are pretty good, aren't we?"

It's an understatement if anything.

Before I can continue praising them, Sky comes over with Vincent in tow. Sky's cheeks are bright red and there's sweat dripping down his neck. "Did you like it?"

I stare at him blankly, unable to speak, until Riya whacks

me on the back. Immediately, I clear my throat and look any-where other than the veins on Sky's neck. "Yeah, I filmed some good content if you guys wanna use it. Thanks for in-viting us."

From the corner of my eye, Sky blinks slowly. "Right. Of course. Thanks for thinking about our social media presence."

I smile half-heartedly and down the rest of Riya's drink. There's something off about the way he's saying it, but it's a good point. My priority needs to be helping Third Eye reach their full potential—not swooning over any of the band mem-bers.

But I have a lot more faith in my cause than I did at the beginning of the night. Maybe things will work out, after all.

24

RABBIT HEART (RAISE IT UP)
—FLORENCE AND THE MACHINE

"So did you ever have that meeting with Thomas?" I ask my dad a few days later, tapping along to the beat of "Dreamer" by Supertramp on my thigh.

If I didn't have an appointment with my pediatrician—my last one ever, given my birthday coming up in August—I'm sure he would have told me to just grab an Uber and go by myself. He had to take the morning off from work to drive me and it's obvious he wishes he were there instead of here.

It's just a checkup appointment, which Baba grumbled about for far too long before he finally got ready to take me.

Either way, I haven't been able to secure any one-on-one time with him this week, his schedule booked in its entirety, so this is a chance for me to do some investigating about Thomas. I've already extensively looked into the Light The Way music competition, but there's only so much the internet can tell me.

"Yeah, earlier this week," Baba says, reaching for the volume control and turning it up. "I meant to tell you, but I got caught up in work."

I squint at him and reach over to turn the volume back down. "How was it? The meeting?"

My dad glances at the console briefly before looking at me, but his shoulders ease as he settles into the flow of the conversation. "It was fine. He seems like a nice enough boy. He brought his publicist with him, which was a good sign that he has his head on straight. You did a good job."

A publicist? Thomas has a *publicist*?

I can't even enjoy the compliment from my dad with this new information on hand. The headaches never end.

"Right," I say and lower the window a crack to get some fresh air into the car before I start hyperventilating. "Did you end up deciding which music competition he's going to?"

"Light The Way," Baba says, confirming Thomas was telling the truth. Goddammit. "I'll be attending with Oliver Andrews, and we'll both be on the judging panel, so it seems like a good time to have him perform in front of us."

I choke slightly. "Oliver Andrews? The CEO?"

"He attends one every season," my dad says, like I'm not five minutes from a heart attack. *Why* did it have to be this competition?

"That's cool," I say and resist the urge to bash my head into the window. "Are you looking forward to it?"

"It's work," my dad says with a shrug. "And it's still a while away."

Well. At least my dad isn't bending over backward to sign Thomas. Small victories. Maybe I should take it as a slight that he's not giving Thomas more preferential treatment since I personally recommended him, but in this one case, I'm grateful for it.

Okay. On talent alone, I know Third Eye will beat Thomas any day. It's just a matter of whether my dad—and the rest of the judging panel—will be unfairly biased.

Thomas having a publicist also bodes well for no one. It's clear he's taking this seriously.

I have to stay one step ahead of him for Third Eye's sake. There's only one way for them to win this competition, and it's by being as fierce and calculating as he is.

When my dad leaves the patient room, Dr. Khan pins me with a sharp look. "And how's your mental health been?"

"Well, I'm not actively trying to jump off my roof if that's what you're asking," I deadpan, staring ahead at a poster about recognizing signs of asthma rather than at my doctor.

"No, but that's good," Dr. Khan says with a sigh. "If you would talk to your dad, we could set you up with a therapist sooner rather than later."

"Yeah, I'm not doing that," I say, crossing my arms. "You think that man even knows what anxiety or depression is?"

Dr. Khan frowns at me. "Yes, Liana. I think he does. You're not the only person who lost someone when your mother died."

I blink at her. "That was uncalled for."

Even still, I think Dr. Khan is wrong. My father knows what *grief* is. He understands that. A very specific sadness over losing something.

What he doesn't, and likely won't ever, understand is this

heaviness lingering in my chest, this sadness built into my bones, this buzz that refuses to leave my brain.

Even if things have been better the last few weeks, both of us tied together by our careers, it doesn't erase the years of neglect my dad has put me through.

I'm not going to try to explain my mental health to him, not when I know my words will be tossed aside. Frankly, I don't know that I'd even try to explain it to my mom if she were alive. I already know what both of them would say. *What do you have to be depressed about? What do you have to be anxious about? You have everything you could want in life. A roof over your head. Food on the table. There are people with real problems, Bibi.*

It's frustrating that everyone likes to assume they know what's going on between us from the outside. There's such an ingrained belief in society that your parents must care about you, that they should always get the benefit of the doubt, that even the terrible things they do must be out of love for you. Even when I tell people to their faces that my dad is absent, that he refuses to care about me when it matters, people insist I should give him another chance, that I should give him some breathing room.

Why should I? Why is that *my* responsibility? He signed up to be a father. I didn't sign up to be his daughter. If anyone should be cutting the other slack, it should be him to me.

His wife died, too. And so what? Does that mean he's no longer my father? He's just a grieving husband? I'm some kind of collateral?

It's not fair that people would rather believe he's a good father without even knowing him than believe me about his emotional distance when I'm swearing up and down it's true.

And it's not fair that a part of me feels guilty enough that I keep listening—keep giving him chance after chance in the hope he might one day change.

"Maybe, but I'm concerned about you," Dr. Khan says, shaking her head and forcing me to blink away the wetness between my eyelids. "Are there any stressors in your life you want to tell me about?"

"Nope," I say, but my skin is starting to itch the longer she stares at me, dissecting me apart inch by inch. "I'm good."

Dr. Khan keeps frowning at me, but I don't say anything. There's nothing she can do for me right now.

"You still intend to see a counselor when you start college in the fall?" she asks after a moment.

I nod. "Yeah. I'm on my school's wait list already."

Even in the midst of everything else, I know seeing a mental health professional and getting properly diagnosed is a priority. As soon as I have immediate access at UCLA and I can avoid having to go through my dad, I'm going to immediately book sessions monthly, if not weekly. It'll be free and it won't require his health insurance, so Baba never has to know about it.

It would hurt more to open up to my dad about this and be dismissed than it would to keep suffering in silence. For me, the cons outweigh the pros. If my mental health were worse, I might think differently, but as it is—I'm certain I can hold it together for the next two months. UCLA is so close I can almost taste it.

"I guess that'll have to do," Dr. Khan says, writing something down on her clipboard. "Alright. Well, this is most likely our last meeting, so I want you to take care of yourself, okay?"

"I know, I know," I say, hopping off the patient seat. "Don't worry, I'm fine."

"I wish I believed you," Dr. Khan mutters under her breath. "Make sure you find a primary care physician before you turn eighteen in case you end up getting sick, alright?"

"Will do," I say, saluting her. Halfway to the door, I falter and turn around. "Thank you. Really."

Dr. Khan smiles at me tiredly. "I'll see you around, Liana. And maybe try talking to your father about everything going on in your head, yeah? He might surprise you."

"Not likely," I say, completely certain of that if nothing else, and slip out of the room.

25

SEDATED—HOZIER

When closing comes around and I've yet to see Sky leave the basement, I'm beginning to realize there's a pattern forming. I sigh, walking over to lock the front door of the record shop.

"Going to get lover boy?" Riya asks, mirth visible in the crease of her eyes. I flip her off and hop down the stairs.

I expect to find Sky fast asleep on the couch again, drunk out of his mind, but instead, when I open the door, it's to the sound of music. Sky is sitting on one of the beanbag chairs, an acoustic guitar in his lap. There's a bunch of loose pages on the table in front of him, indecipherable scribbles on them.

He looks up when I come inside, but he doesn't stop strumming his guitar. It's not a tune I've heard before—whether from their demo, from Thomas, or from practice. He must be working on something new.

"It's late," I say for lack of anything better.

Sky cocks his head to the side. "I suppose it is."

"Right." I stand in the doorway awkwardly, unsure what

to do now. I need to talk to him about competing in the Light The Way competition, but I don't know how to bring it up. "Uh, how long do you think—?"

"I'm just finishing up," Sky says, with a thin smile. Ever since we ran into Thomas the other day, he's been more subdued, more focused. It's obvious the others have noticed too, given the way they've been smothering Sky with love every time they see him.

He needs to win this competition. They all do.

"Cool," I say and resist the urge to fiddle with my bangs. "I'll wait, then. Since I have to lock up behind you."

Sky shrugs and returns his attention to his guitar, plucking the strings in a way that looks absentminded but clearly is not.

I grab a water bottle from the pack near the doorway and sit on the couch. Unable to help myself, I glance at the pages closest to me.

Sky doesn't immediately snatch them away, but he does give me a cursory glance that feels a little bit like a warning.

there's blood on my hands / it looks like mine / but it tastes like yours / something inside me aches / a throbbing bruise, a broken rib / are you dead? are you dead? / why am I alive? / the back of my throat is scorched from the pyre I built you / I promised you death but not like this / not like this, please, not like this / together, in one grave, together

"It reads a little bit like a Hozier song," I say offhandedly, and regret the words the instant they leave my mouth.

Sky's head snaps up to stare at me with wide brown eyes. "Excuse me?"

"I—" I push the pages away from me helplessly. "Sorry. I was just—"

"Snooping," Sky says, and I flinch. "And not even subtly."

"I'm sorry," I say, grimacing and leaning back against the couch. I don't have to explain myself, but a part of me feels like I should. Sky's gaze is far too accusing, even if he's not saying anything else. "I've never seen someone actually...create music. I guess my curiosity got the best of me."

"Watch a documentary," Sky suggests, his voice dry. "There's loads of them."

He's never been this curt with me before, and I don't know *why* it's happening now.

Well, I do. I do know, and that makes it even worse.

My teeth dig into my lower lip almost painfully. "It's different. You're actually here."

Sky sighs and rolls his neck in a way that shouldn't be attractive, but it is. "What do you want, Liana?"

"Nothing," I say, but it's the wrong answer. There's no easy way to bring up the competition, but I have to. *I have to.* "I... I don't know. I guess I was just interested in your process."

Dammit, Liana.

"And why should I tell you anything?" Sky asks. He sounds so tired that something inside me aches. "For all I know, you're still talking to Thomas."

"What?" I ask, my mouth falling open. "What the fuck? No, I'm not speaking to Thomas. Why would you even think that?"

Sky peers up at me through his incredibly long lashes. "In case you haven't noticed, Liana, I know absolutely *nothing* about you. So, yeah, I think it's perfectly reasonable that I'd assume you're still talking to the dude you were dating a few weeks ago."

I scowl at him. "Well, I'm not. We went on one date and he more or less dumped me. He's a piece of shit and a liar and he used me, so I'm not harboring any affection for that asshole. Let's leave it at that."

"Join the club," Sky says under his breath.

I pause. The opening is there. I know I shouldn't take it, that I should leave well enough alone but… "What even happened? Why did he leave?"

Skyler fiddles with one of his guitar strings and a rough *twang!* fills the room. "I don't know where to start."

I hesitate but eventually slide off the couch and move to sit on the beanbag chair beside him. "Maybe the beginning?"

He gives me a long look, clearly searching for something in my face. I try to appear as genuine as possible, though I don't know how well that comes across. After a beat, he turns back to what he's playing.

"We've been best friends for years," Sky says, his voice so quiet that I might not have heard it if it weren't just the two of us sitting in silence. "Met in middle school and hit it off the moment we sat next to each other during chorus class."

There's a ghost of a smile on his face, and I can't stand to look at it.

"We live two blocks away from each other, so we'd always go over to each other's houses. Usually his, since he's an only child, and his parents are more chill."

"And you decided to start a band together?" I ask softly.

Skyler nods. "We both loved music so much, it made sense

to come together to make it. I was nervous about my lyrics, but they sounded right when he sang them."

I recall again how the others said Skyler doesn't really like to sing, prefers to be in the background, supporting the others. Hearing this just makes it even more obvious.

"Our music—our band was never supposed to be about being famous," Sky says, absently strumming his guitar again. "It was about having fun and creating something together that we're proud of. I don't know when it shifted to—to *this*."

"It wasn't your dream to perform in front of crowds? To sell hundreds of thousands of albums? To have strangers feel connected to you through your songs?" I ask.

Sky's nose wrinkles. "I mean, I guess. Yeah. But it wasn't the priority. It was Thomas who started pushing us in that direction. The rest of us would have been happy being a garage band, you know?"

"A garage band," I say dryly. "That can't be true."

"You know what I mean," he says.

I don't, actually, but I'm not going to say that. "So, what, his ambitions outgrew yours?"

"No," he says, shaking his head. "I don't think so, anyway. We were happy to go along for the ride, but… I don't know. I guess it wasn't enough. Our friendship wasn't enough."

I grimace. Not being enough is something that resonates a little more than it should.

"And now, none of this matters to him," Sky says, laughing bitterly. Maybe it's because I'm looking so closely, but it's obvious how much this hurts him. How much Thomas hurt him. "He'd rather be a solo act."

I already know the answer, but I ask anyway. "Were you planning to replace him with Vincent?"

Sky gives me an appalled look. "What? No! Of course not."

"Vincent is objectively a better singer," I say, but Sky shakes his head immediately, cutting me off before I can press deeper into the wound.

"It doesn't matter who's a *better* singer." Sky makes air quotes around the word to show exactly how little he thinks of it. "It's about what we agreed on as a team. It's about the promise we made each other."

"And Thomas broke that promise," I say, a muscle twitching in my jaw. "Not to mention, he stole your music and played it off as his own."

It's bad enough that Thomas lied to me in and of itself. But to tell a lie that's *so* far from the truth?

"I don't even care about the music," Sky says, and I shoot him an incredulous look. "Okay, I do care about the music a little," he amends. "But I can write new music. I can't pull a new band member out of thin air. Not that I even *want* to, but you know what I'm saying."

"And he was your best friend," I say and wish I didn't a moment later when Sky flinches at the words. Something dark and red simmers in the pit of my stomach at the dejected look on his face. "You can't let him get away with this. Sky, you can't—you have to do something."

"What, like TP his house?" Sky asks, curling his lip. He finally sets his guitar down and lies back, closing his eyes. "There's nothing for me to do. It is what it is."

"No!" I say, reaching over to shake his arm. "This can't be it. Forget TPing his house, that's beyond stupid and childish.

I'm talking about doing something worthwhile. Like auditioning for Light The Way." I take a deep breath. "You have to get in and beat him."

"There's no way," Sky says, shaking his head. "We're not ready. That's happening at the end of the summer. I don't have enough time to write new songs by then, and the boys would still have to learn them even if I did, and there's no way—"

"Sky, shut *up*," I say, and he miraculously listens. I hesitate for a second before blowing a harsh breath. Fuck it. "I *never* said this if anyone asks, but Jhilmil Sarkar will be attending. He's one of the judges. And so is Oliver Andrews. So you have to enter, okay?"

Sky scrambles to sit up, staring at me with wide brown eyes. "What? Oliver Andrews? As in the CEO of Ripple Records? Are you joking?"

"No, I'm not joking," I say. "Which is why I need you to get your shit together and prep for the audition."

He shakes his head, fish-mouthing. "But I don't—I don't—"

"I know," I say, firming my lips. "Which is why you need to let me help you. I'm at the record label every week. I know what people like them are thinking and what they're looking for. If we all work together, I know this can work."

"Why would you want to help us?" Sky asks, suddenly defensive. I can see his hackles rising and I want to physically shake him.

"Because I fucking *hate* Thomas, dude," I say, exasperated. "I don't want him to win this stupid competition and get a record deal out of it. He's doesn't have material of his own, so there's no way this will work out for him long-term, but if you and I team up, we can end this before it even gets anywhere. He's digging his own grave. We just need to put the final nail in the coffin."

Sky frowns, considering me with narrowed eyes, and I groan. "Come on, Sky. Are you really going to let Thomas get away with this? You *know* we can do this if we work together."

After a long painful silence, Sky nods shortly. Before I can thank God and Christ and whoever else, he squints at me. "I'm *only* agreeing because I don't want all of Third Eye to go down for this shit."

"Yeah, yeah, real martyr you are," I say, waving him off. "Now here's what we're going to do…"

26

NEW ANGEL—NIALL HORAN

"Why are you just staring at us?" Mohammed asks after ten minutes. "Aren't you supposed to be like, cleaning up?"

I raise an eyebrow and make a note on my clipboard. *Mohammed has no filter.*

"What are you writing down?" Mohammed asks, suddenly alarmed. "Are you writing that down? Why are you writing that down?"

I hum and jot down another note. *Mohammed is prone to panicking under pressure.*

"Sky, what is going *on*?" Mohammed asks in a high-pitched voice. "Why is she sitting there and taking notes about—about us?"

I make an amendment. *Really* panicking.*

"Sky!"

Ethan is laughing under his breath, which is true to what I know about him. He's definitely going to get the boy-next-door moniker.

Skyler sighs, scrubbing a hand over his face. "Don't worry about it, Mohammed. I'll explain later."

"Or you could explain now," Mohammed says, pouting at Sky and making some failed attempt at puppy-dog eyes. I roll my own eyes. As if Sky is going to buy into that.

"Oh," Sky says, his face falling. "Okay, yeah, let's have a band meeting."

I give him an incredulous look. Jesus.

Sky is absolutely incapable of saying no to his band members, I write down and scoot over when Ethan comes to sit beside me on the couch.

"So Liana and I got to talking the other night," Sky says.

"Oooh," Ethan says under his breath and I elbow him. Vincent glares at me from across the table, and I pretend not to notice.

Vincent is insanely protective of Ethan.

"And, what? Is she the band's secretary now? Why is she taking minutes?" Mohammed asks.

"I mean, no, but kind of?" Sky says and I immediately launch my pen at his head, which he dodges easily.

"I'm not anyone's secretary," I say darkly. "Don't ask me for shit. I'm not getting anything for anyone."

"She's scary," Mohammed stage-whispers, and I contemplate grabbing another pen to lob at his head.

"She's our pseudo-publicist," Sky says, trying to come up with a smile, but it falls short. "She's going to help us craft our image so we can win Light The Way." A pause. "If you guys are okay with auditioning?"

"Light The Way?" Ethan says, visibly vibrating with excitement.

"Publicist?" Vincent says, clearly having the opposite reaction.

"The music competition *Thomas* is going to?" Mohammed asks, disgust written all over his face.

Sky stops trying to smile, opting for a grimace. "I know we've never done anything on this level before but…" He chances a look at me, and I nod. "Jhilmil Sarkar and the CEO of Ripple Records are going to be there as judges. This is our chance to clear our name and take back our sound."

Vincent's brows furrow. "How do you know that?"

I raise my hand. "I told him. But it's top secret, so it *cannot* leave this room, do you understand? The judges are supposed to be anonymous until a month before."

"But *you* know," Mohammed says slowly, and there's an implicit question there.

"Yes, I found out at my internship," I say, trying to sound casual. "And it's obvious Thomas knows, too. I have no idea if Mr. Sarkar told him, or what the case is, but there's no other reason for him to be so determined to win." I look around, meeting their individual gazes. "Which is why we can't let him."

"I'm sorry, I'm not understanding why she's a part of this," Vincent says, looking back at Sky. "Why do we need to craft our image?"

Sky sighs, rubbing his eyes. "Well, for one, we only know any of this because of Liana's internship at Ripple Records. She has hands-on experience from there, and she's majoring in music management and marketing at UCLA in the fall. She knows more about that side of the industry than any of us. Thomas already has a leg up with his connection to Mr. Sarkar. This is our way to even the scale."

"We have Google, we could figure it out on our own," Vincent says, and I make a note. *Vincent is resistant to accepting help from others.* "Why is she writing that down? Stop writing that down."

I raise my clipboard in a white-flag gesture. "Hey, I'm just trying to help."

"Vinny, let's give her a chance," Ethan says, offering Vincent a hesitant smile. "I'm sure she's as mad at Thomas as the rest of us."

"You are quite seriously my favorite member of this band," I tell Ethan earnestly.

Mohammed frowns at the pair of us. "Ethan, she's basically a stranger."

Ethan shrugs. "We were all strangers at one point. Now we're a family, aren't we?"

If anyone had any other protests left, they seem to die right there and then. Sky, Vincent, and Mohammed all look at their youngest member with soft eyes and nod slowly.

Sky may be the leader of this band, but Ethan has everyone wrapped around his finger.

"I'm buying you a bottle of vodka for your birthday," I say to Ethan. "Bless your heart."

"Liana, do *not* buy him alcohol," Skyler says at the same time Vincent says, "Absolutely not."

"Haters," Ethan mutters.

"I'll still buy it," I whisper and ignore the glares the rest of the band shoot me. If Ethan wants alcohol, I'm buying him alcohol. Or Riya will, on my behalf.

"*Anyway*, the point is that Liana is going to be here more often, giving us pointers when we need them and trying to help us where she can," Sky says, looking around at all his band members. It's so obvious their opinions mean the world to him. If they said no to my presence, I think he would kick me out in a split second. I'm no one, but as Ethan said, this is his *family*.

"Just ignore me," I say, offering them a smile that only Ethan returns. "Pretend I'm not even here."

"Easier said than done," Mohammed complains, but stands up and returns to the piano. "We'd better practice hard if we want to make it into the competition, huh?"

Sky's answering expression makes my heart do a strange tumble. He looks at Mohammed like he put the stars in the sky. "Yeah. Yeah. Let's do it."

Ethan whoops and hops back over to his drum set and Vincent gets to his feet, grabbing his bass guitar.

I settle back in my seat and close my eyes. This is going to be a long summer. I've never had to undertake a project like this before.

But it's going to be worth it.

27

THE ARCHER—TAYLOR SWIFT

Evie shakes her head at me over FaceTime. "No, I need pictures, Liana. My imagination isn't doing it for me."

"I'd say search up their band's Instagram, but it doesn't have a single photograph with their faces in it," I mutter, looking through it myself. "Hold on, let me go to their individual pages. I'll send you screenshots."

It takes me much longer than it should to find all of their handles, and I end up having to resort to checking Thomas' profile to find them. *skylermoons, vinny.alvarez13, e.mitch.ll,* and *momo.anwar.* "This is so unmarketable," I say to Evie in despair, but screenshot their profiles anyway. "I need all of them to change their usernames *immediately.*"

I follow all of them shortly after, Ethan being the first to follow me back, followed by Sky, and then eventually Mohammed and Vincent.

"What is this *filter?*" I ask, dragging my fingers down my face at Vincent's profile. "Oh my God."

"At least they're all hot," Evie says, but it does little to reassure me. "And I'm saying that as someone who would rather rip off my arm than date a man."

"It's not good enough!" I say, before swinging my phone around to face my laptop so she can see the awful selfie Vincent has on his profile taken from the worst angle in human history. "What am I supposed to do about *this*?"

Evie grimaces. "It's not…great. But you can fix this. I know you can."

I groan and shove my face into an avocado plushie. "This is a nightmare."

"Listen, they're conventionally attractive and they make good music," Evie says, her voice soothing. "That's all you need at the end of the day. You can fix everything else. Think of it as practice for the future."

"I should be able to put this in my résumé," I complain, but look up from the stuffed avocado. "Tell me something good about your life before I start screaming."

Evie scratches her head, clearly at a loss, before she snaps her fingers. "Okay! Okay. The girl across the hall—Sam— she asked for my number the other day. It was because of an assignment but *still*."

"That's great!" I say, a genuine smiling pulling at my mouth. "Have you been texting her?"

"…No."

I groan. *"Evie."*

"I know, I know! But…what am I even supposed to say?" Evie asks, tugging at one of her dreadlocks anxiously.

"Start by asking her about school and take it from there,"

I say, shaking my head fondly. "You know this. You don't
need me to tell you this."

Evie grumbles something under her breath that I don't
even try to decipher.

"Get it together, Eve," I say. "Come on, shoot her a text.
It'll take two seconds."

"You are a menace to society," Evie says, scowling at me.
"I told you that to cheer you up, and now you're using it
against me!"

"Oh, come on," I say, rolling my eyes. "Text her, come on."

"But I don't want to," Evie says petulantly, and I huff in
amusement. I pull out my own phone, drafting up a text,
and shooting it to Evie who jolts at the sound of her phone.
"What's that?"

"A draft," I say, waving my phone pointedly. "See, I even
made it easier for you. All you have to do is copy and paste
it into Sam's text thread and press send on it."

"Menace," Evie repeats. "I'll think about it."

"Or you could just do it," I say, demonstrating myself by
sending her the same text again. "See that? Only two seconds."

"I'll think about it," Evie says steadfastly.

"What does that even *mean*? What is there to think about?
All you have to do is press Send."

"I said I'll think about it!" she says, a whine in her voice.

"Oh my *God*," I say. "Whatever. Send it, don't send it.
What do I care."

Evie sticks her tongue out at me. "I'll think about it."

"I'm going to fly to New York and commit crimes against

your person," I say darkly, and Evie just smiles. "I'm being serious."

"Do it," Evie says with a shrug. "And then take me back home with you."

I make a face at her, which she returns back tenfold, until we're both making awful faces that are more silly than anything else and break into laughter.

But a part of me knows she means it. She misses her family. She misses LA. There are certain growing pains that come with upending your life and moving across the country. I'm more than familiar with missing a place while knowing it's best for you to stay exactly where you are. But knowing that doesn't make it any easier.

"You should come visit for the Fourth of July," I say lightly. I think she needs a gentle nudge, to believe she's visiting LA for someone other than herself. "I miss you a lot. I don't know if I can wait until Light The Way to see you."

Evie cocks her head. "Fourth of July, huh?"

I brighten, sensing the possibility of agreement. "Yes. Evie, please? It would be so much fun."

"I don't know," Evie muses. "I'd have to be in the same city as Thomas. I can't promise I won't end up in jail."

"I already have the bail money ready," I say seriously, and Evie bursts into laughter.

"Well, how can I say no to that?" Evie asks, smiling so wide her eyes crinkle in the corners. "I'll talk to my mom and keep you updated, okay?"

"Okay," I say, and hold my pinky up to the camera.

Evie pretends to link hers with mine, completing the promise from all the way across the ocean. "If nothing, else, I'll see you at Light The Way, yeah?"

"Yeah," I say, smiling softly.

Well. If this all goes terribly, at least my best friend will be there to put the pieces back together, the same way I'm happy to do for her, even when we're three thousand miles apart. Maybe especially when we're three thousand miles apart.

After Evie and I hang up, I spend a little too much time scrolling through the Third Eye members' Instagrams. The more I scroll, the heavier my heart feels.

There are so many photographs of them with Thomas. Especially on Sky's profile. From just a few months ago to when they were just tiny preteens who bonded over their shared love for music.

In contrast, Thomas has few to no pictures of Third Eye. It's almost entirely pictures of himself, most of them thirst traps. I gag a little when I remember I wanted to *date* him.

I force myself to turn back to Ethan's Instagram. It's clear that they have something here—something beyond being young attractive kids who make fun, meaningful music. It's love. In every picture, it's obvious how much all of Third Eye adore each other, and how it takes precedence over their music.

Their friendship is the key to their marketability. I feel icky even thinking it—to monetize something so wholesome, so genuine feels *wrong*. But it's what sets them apart from people like Thomas, who think only of themselves. And I'm going to have to use it if I want them to rise to their full potential. It'll help them in the long run.

"Am I an awful person?" I ask Willow. She doesn't respond, but her tail thumps me in the thigh, which really could go either way.

I sit up, reaching over to pull her into my arms. She comes easily enough, but I know in approximately thirty seconds she's going to try to hit me with her paw.

For now, I bury my face into her fur, pressing kisses against her back. "At least you'll love me no matter what."

I imagine if Willow could speak, she would say that's debatable, but she can't, so I allow myself to live in delusion. Predictably, after half a minute, she begins to squirm around in my arms, trying to get free, and I set her down with a sigh.

There's a lot of work to be done yet, and I've already committed to the bit. Now I just have to see it through.

28

RIPTIDE—VANCE JOY

I set down four near-identical agendas in front of the Third Eye members. "Today's my day," I say, and ignore the panicked looks from Vincent, Mohammed, and Ethan. "Sky said I get at least one day a week, so we're making use of it."

"I don't like this," Mohammed says, tugging at the neckline of his T-shirt.

"No one cares," I say cheerfully, before tapping my pen against my clipboard. "First thing on the agenda. Username changes. Everyone pull up Instagram, we're going full rebrand."

"I *really* don't like this," Mohammed says, but when the others reluctantly take out their phones, he has no choice but to follow suit.

"Alright, your new usernames should be on your agendas. No, don't make that face, go and change it." I meet Sky's grimace with a raised brow. "Now."

It takes too long—Vincent doesn't even know *where* the

setting to change your username is—but it gets done. Now they're *thirdsky, thirdvinny, thirdmo,* and *thirdethan.* Perfect.

"And the main Instagram needs to be *thirdeyeband*," I say to Vincent, raising my brows. "I hear you're in charge of socials, for *God* knows what reason."

Vincent gives me a flat look. "And what is that supposed to mean?"

"That you have no idea how to properly use social media," I say. "So if it's possible, I want the passwords to all the official band socials. I'll handle it for now and eventually train *Ethan* in how to use them. Got it?"

"I don't like her," Vincent says, louder than necessary.

"You don't need to like me," I say with a shrug. "You just have to listen to me."

"Why did you do this to us?" Mohammed asks Sky. "We were doing fine without her."

"Mhhm," I say, before pointing at the agenda again. "What other socials are we working with? I found your YouTube channel, but what about everything else? Do you have Twitter, TikTok, Facebook, Pinterest?"

Ethan glances at the other members before nodding. "We have a Twitter account. Maybe a TikTok? I can't remember."

"Alright, we're going to change those usernames to *thirdeyeband*, too. I want consistency across the board. Do you have a website? When I looked up Third Eye on Google, I couldn't find one."

"A WordPress one?" Sky says, but his voice goes up at the end making it a question instead of an answer.

My eye twitches, but I nod. This is going to be more work

than I expected. "Okay. We can work with that. What kind of stuff are you uploading?"

Vincent shrugs. "I post when we have shows."

I wait, expecting him to say more, but nothing comes. My eye starts twitching a little more.

It's fine. My plan is to get them to ten thousand followers on Instagram by the end of summer, and at least four thousand on Twitter. I'll also fix up their website, change the URL to something easy to search, and take new headshots. Their YouTube account will be a little bit more of a challenge, but if I really put myself to work, they might be able to break five thousand subscribers. We'll have to set up a schedule to upload weekly videos with a range of content, but I have faith we can do it.

Tangible goals are the key to success, and I have no intention of failing at this.

"Okay," I say and take a deep breath. "I need to see you one by one. Mohammed, you're up."

"Why me?" Mohammed asks, turning to the others for help. "Can't I be last?"

"Mohammed," I say, tapping my foot pointedly. "Come on."

"If she kills me, I hope it weighs on your conscience," he says to Sky, but jumps to his feet with a grumble. "Let's get this over with."

"Great attitude," I say dryly and lead him out of the practice room, up the stairs to where our back room is. There's a table near the front and I sit down, gesturing for Mohammed to take the other seat.

"First things first, you need to take your account off private," I say, pointing at his phone.

Mohammed looks at me in disbelief. "I can't do that."

"Yes, you can," I say easily. "I'll show you how."

"No, I know how, but I *can't*," Mohammed says, shaking his head. "Come on, you get it, you're brown, too."

"What does that have anything to—oh." I frown, not having considered that. My Instagram is private, too, for the exact same reason. My dad doesn't give much of a shit what I do, but it's better to be safe than sorry in case the day comes when he *does*. The last thing I need is for my dad to lose his mind after finding out I spend a vast majority of my free time with four teenage boys.

"I thought you and your parents have a good relationship," I say slowly.

"We do," Mohammed says immediately. "But they're still brown parents, and I'm too young to die."

I lean back in my chair, tapping my pen against my bottom lip. "Okay, new plan. Change your username back."

"So I'm free?" Mohammed says hopefully.

"Absolutely not," I say and motion for him to get on with it. Once he's done, I hold my hand out for his phone.

"I'm not giving this to you," Mohammed says, and I sigh.

"All of you need to be more trusting," I say, but concede, instead pointing out what I want him to do.

Mohammed blinks. "You want me to make a new Instagram?"

"One personal, one professional," I say easily. "Don't post any stupid shit on the professional one, and your parents won't want to kill you. It's that simple."

"I don't quite believe you," Mohammed says, but he listens

to me and makes a new account. I direct him to follow the other boys, and the official band account, which he does but not without some muttered complaints about how this is all dumb.

"Alright, pull up five of your best selfies. Let me see them," I say, tapping his phone with my pen.

"My *selfies*?"

"You need a profile picture, dude."

Mohammed groans, burying his face in his arms. I poke him incessantly until he sits back up, glowering at me.

"When you're done with that, change your bio to this," I say, underlining the sentence in his agenda.

1/4 of @thirdeyeband. pianist.

"And link your website, too," I say, before pausing. "Who runs the website?"

"Sky, I think," Mohammed says, scratching his head. "Do we really have to do all this to win Light The Way? What's wrong with what we were doing before?"

"There was nothing *wrong* with it," I say, patting his head. "But it's about building a brand. We want Third Eye to be as accessible as possible, so that you can gain a following easier. With limited funds, word of mouth is by far the biggest marketing tool in the game."

"I'm going to pretend I know what you're talking about so I can leave this room sooner," Mohammed says, flashing me a thumbs-up.

I click my tongue. "Just show me the selfies, Mo."

Once I've picked out a profile picture for Mohammed, I send him on his way with a promise to text me before he even thinks about posting anything to his main feed.

"Call in Vincent next!" I yell after him.

★ ★ ★

After forcing Vincent to archive over half of his posts, showing Ethan how to create reels and highlights, and telling Sky to unfollow Thomas on all platforms, I finish up with revamping Third Eye's website.

It takes a few hours and FaceTiming with Evie before I'm happy with a site design.

Then I realize Third Eye still needs a logo.

3E + Liana

Me: who can draw

Ethan Mitchell: not me

Mohammed Anwar: definitely not

Mohammed Anwar: oh wait actually

Vincent Alvarez: I don't think crude drawings of dicks count

Mohammed Anwar: ...nevermind

Vincent Alvarez: yeah me either

Me: ok what about photoshop

Me: any takers

Vincent Alvarez: why

Me: y'all need a logo

Skyler Moon: what about this one??

Sky sends an image and I stare at the minimalist eye design for a few moments, thrown back to when I saw it on the cover of their demo in my dad's car.

That feels like a lifetime ago, but it's only been a month and a half.

Me: it'll do for now but I want something more commercial

Me: so get to brainstorming

I close out of the group chat and turn my attention back to their website. After linking all their social media accounts and putting together a short bio, I create an events page, listing all their upcoming gigs as well as the Light The Way music competition, even though it's not confirmed yet. Might as well speak it into existence. I hope Thomas checks their website and knows exactly who he's going to be up against.

Every time I think about his smug face, *taunting* the Third Eye members, I understand Mohammed's desire to hit something. It's not fair that he did this—and it's not fair that I helped him.

But I'm going to make up for it. Hopefully I already am.

29

WHAT ABOUT TODAY?—LEWIS WATSON

I take a peek at my dad's schedule on the car ride to Ripple Records to get an idea for when he might take his lunch break. I play it off as using his phone to choose an alternate Pink Floyd song, switching from "Time" to "Money" while at the same I glance at his Google Calendar.

"How is Riya Apu?" Baba asks when I set his phone back down. It's a normal conversation for once, but I don't like the direction it's heading in. "Has she started looking for a real job yet?"

I keep my gaze trained on the horizon to keep from glowering at my father. "No, I think she likes being the manager at the record shop."

Baba frowns. "She studied business, no? She could do something more."

"She likes it, Baba," I say, maybe a little too sharply. I force myself to soften my tone. "Let's leave it at that, okay?"

My dad hums in disapproval, but he doesn't say anything

else. I try not to be too upset that he hasn't asked how *I* am or what I've been doing for the entirety of the summer. It's not like I could tell him if he asked, but it would be nice to be asked.

I hoped that maybe the change in our dynamic at work might carry through into our relationship at home, but it seems more and more unlikely as the days go by.

Baba clocks around an eighty-hour workweek, if not more. He's always at the office, always in meetings, always out at different events, scouting talent.

And when he's not, he's sleeping.

It doesn't really leave much room for anything in his life, which I'm all too aware of.

"Riya Apu's birthday is coming up soon," I say, changing the subject. "Did you get those concert tickets I told you about?"

"For that K-pop group? Yes," he says, though he's making a face. I roll my eyes. Even though he says he's not, he can be a music snob at times. I'll listen to everything once, but I'm unabashedly a fan of all kinds of pop music. Riya is the same, which is why I figured tickets for the upcoming SEVENTEEN concert would be a perfect gift.

If I weren't also a fan of music from the '70s and '80s and '90s—things Baba knows and understands—I'm pretty sure my dad would judge my taste as well. As it is, I tend to listen to my pop music away from him.

It's kind of ridiculous given it's Baba's *job* to find people who can break into the top 100. I guess he doesn't need to like it to be able to objectively see its worth, but it still doesn't make any sense to me.

Sometimes, I wonder if Baba even likes his job.

He has to—otherwise how could he let it define his entire

life like this? He lives and breathes his career. It's inconceivable to think that he might actually be miserable.

But if he was, at least we'd have something in common.

When Baba leaves for lunch with a client, I sneak into his office, prepared to snoop as much as I can within a half hour.

I go through his cabinets, looking for files dated from this summer. I need to know which artists he's been looking at recently, and what factors have gone into choosing them—and if there's any commonality between them and Third Eye that I can leverage.

When I come across Thomas' file, I sneer. If it wouldn't set off the smoke alarm and raise too many questions I can't afford to answer, I'd light a match and set it on fire.

I skim through Baba's notes on him before my eyes flick back up to Thomas' headshot. I stare at his stupid smug face for half a second before pointedly closing the file and putting it away. There was nothing in his file that I didn't already know, which is simultaneously relieving and frustrating.

Ugh. This is useless. I move on from his cabinets, going to my dad's desk and sitting down in his chair, rolling it closer so I can open up his drawers.

When I see a folder marked *Light The Way*, I immediately grab it. I flip it open and read through the materials inside.

Five judges, twenty contestants, last week of August… I turn to the next page, noting all of that in the back of my head. The rest details past winners, which I briefly skim through, but I've already seen most of it online and none of it catches my eye.

Either way, it's more information than I had before.

I close the folder, putting it back in the drawer, when something glints in the corner of my vision.

I lift up all the folders in Baba's drawer, sliding my hand down to the bottom until I gain hold of whatever it is. Carefully, I pull it out and confirm my suspicions.

It's a photo of Ma.

Well, to be more specific, it's a photo of Ma and Baba on their wedding day.

Ma looks absolutely beautiful and resplendent in a glittering red sari, mehndi covering her hands and arms. She's wearing so much jewelry I'm not sure where to look first—her bangles, her necklaces, her tikka headpiece. Her eyes are bright as she grins at the camera, and I absently touch my own face, wondering at the resemblance between us.

Beside her, Baba looks like the happiest man alive. I'm not sure I've ever seen him smile like that in my *lifetime*. If I have, it's a long forgotten memory.

I brush my thumb against their faces and wish my heart weren't lodged in my throat.

I know Baba misses her. I'd be stupid to not know that. But why doesn't he ever talk about it? Why doesn't he ever tell me about her?

What would Ma think if she knew we can't hold a conversation about her for more than a minute?

The question aches inside of me, and I shake my head, trying to clear all thoughts of Ma. I can't afford to do this right now. I put the photo away and close Baba's drawer.

I force myself to leave Baba's office, making sure to grab all my stuff before I go.

It shouldn't hurt this much to exist in the same space as Ma's memories, but it does. And it probably always will.

30

KEEP DRIVING—HARRY STYLES

I knock on the door to the practice room before pushing it open. As usual, Sky is sitting on the floor, messing around with his guitar.

"Don't you have a home to get to?" I ask, raising a brow.

Sky makes a face that makes me physically nauseous. That's the face *I* make when I realize there's nothing left for me to do but go back to my house, where no one and nothing awaits me.

Why would he make that face? What's wrong with going home? How can he possibly dread it as much as I do?

"Sorry, I just meant…you stay late after practice a lot," I say, fidgeting with my hair.

Sky releases a deep breath, one that's so heavy I can feel the weight of it from across the room. "It's just…easier to work here."

I hesitantly venture inside, coming to a stop a few feet

away from him. "Well, what did you do before you guys practiced here?"

Sky smiles humorlessly. "I spent a lot of nights at Thomas' place."

"Oh," I say, my shoulders drooping. "I'm sorry."

"No, it's not—I didn't say that to make you feel bad for me," Sky says, getting to his feet. "It's just—I don't know. It's weird not being able to go there when I need to get out of my head. I came up with so much of my music there. And now I don't even have that option anymore."

I suck my bottom lip into my mouth, staring at him uselessly. I don't know what to say to him. I've never lost a best friend so suddenly before. I'm no longer in touch with most of my friends in New York, but that was because I moved away and we slowly drifted apart—not because they turned around and stabbed me in the back.

"Sorry, I know my writer's block isn't your problem," Sky says, looking away from me. He puts his guitar in his case, zipping it up, and then goes to gather his sheet music and journal.

The entire time, I stand there, wanting to say *something*, but unable to put it into words.

Right as he starts for the door, I move, putting myself in front of him. "Hey, I didn't mean anything by it. As long as the store is open, you're always free to be here."

Sky offers me a dismal smile. "Thanks, Liana."

"No, I mean it," I say, maybe a little too vigorously. Sky looks at me quizzically, and I force myself to *think*. Surely, I can give better advice than this. "Uh, when I'm stuck on something or really anxious, I've found walks to very helpful? Or long drives."

Sky's brows furrow. "And that works?"

I nod eagerly, glad to finally say something of use. Walks are something I started doing when Ma passed away, unable to stomach being in our New York apartment anymore, Baba's grief thick and heavy in the air. It's part of why we moved across the country, to somewhere new and fresh and devoid of any memory of my mother.

It's helped in a lot of ways, but it also somehow feels worse. Our house in Los Angeles isn't heavy with grief, but it's empty and quiet and nothing like a home. Baba has taken his sadness and anger and hurt and buried it within his work. If he works all the time, he doesn't have to think about Ma. He doesn't have to think about me.

I wish it were that easy for me. Instead, I end up leaving our current house frequently for entirely different reasons than our old one. Back in New York, I would leave our apartment and just ride the first subway train that came to wherever it would take me.

Here, on the days that are particularly bad, when I really think my head is going to explode and I'm going to vibrate right out of my skin, I call an Uber and put in a random destination across the city.

It doesn't fix things, but it makes them a little better.

And Sky drives, if I'm correct.

"You have a car, right?" I ask, nodding at the door. "Come on, I have the perfect playlist for this."

Without waiting for an answer, I hop the stairs two at a time and make my way to the front door. Sky follows at a slower pace, looking at me skeptically.

Tiana is on the closing shift with me, and she's watching the two of us with wide eyes.

"You're good to lock up, right?" I ask her and she nods. I pretend not to notice when she discreetly lifts her phone to take a picture of me and Sky. I already know it's going to make its way into our work group chat and Riya will be making fun of me by the morning, but that's not my concern right now.

I hold the door open for Sky. He shakes his head but slips past me, heading for his car, and I follow him.

"It'll be fun," I say, and pray he doesn't hear the slight hysteria in my voice. "It's nice to just shut your brain off and relax."

"I don't think my brain ever turns off," Sky says but unlocks his car anyway.

"I used to think that, too," I say, climbing into the passenger seat without pause. "But you'll see. Hurry up!"

Once he's in the car, I grab the aux cord and pull up Spotify.

songs to scream at the top of my lungs while driving down the highway:

Haunted—Taylor Swift

august—Taylor Swift

Style—Taylor Swift

Maroon—Taylor Swift

Last Kiss—Taylor Swift

All Too Well (10 Minute Version)—Taylor Swift

You're On Your Own, Kid—Taylor Swift

I Can See You—Taylor Swift

Wildest Dreams—Taylor Swift

cardigan—Taylor Swift

Better Than Revenge—Taylor Swift

You're Not Sorry—Taylor Swift
You Belong With Me—Taylor Swift
Cruel Summer—Taylor Swift
Getaway Car—Taylor Swift
Stay Stay Stay—Taylor Swift
Would've, Could've, Should've—Taylor Swift
Should've Said No—Taylor Swift
Speak Now—Taylor Swift

Sky looks at the playlist on my phone and then back at me. "This is all Taylor Swift."

"Yes," I say easily. "Is there anyone better to scream at the top of your lungs?"

"...You make a point," Sky says, and nods. "Add 'My Tears Ricochet' to the playlist."

I shake my head. "That song is too fucked up to be on this playlist. We're trying to have fun, not jump out of the car while it's going at full speed."

"You have 'Haunted' as the first song," Sky says, staring at me incredulously. "How does that song not make you want to walk into traffic?"

"It *does*, but it's a fucked up bop, not a fucked up I'm-going-to-lie-on-my-couch-and-spiral."

"Half of these songs are spiral-worthy," Sky argues. "'August'? 'Cardigan'?"

"I can't help that *Folklore* was an absolutely unhinged album," I say, but with a drawn out sigh, I add "My Tears Ricochet" to the playlist.

31

TUM SE HI—MOHIT CHAUHAN

Sky turns on the engine, and before I know it, we're cruising down the road to the sound of "Getaway Car."

I roll down the window and laugh when the breeze blows my hair out of my face. "See? Isn't this nice?"

Sky harrumphs, but I can see the ghost of a smile in the curve of his lips.

"Come on, roll down your window. In fact, open the sun roof," I say, thumping the top of the car. "Let loose a little."

"You're way more uptight than I am," Sky says, though that doesn't stop him from following my instructions. "There, happy now?"

"Elated," I say and pull out my phone. I should've done this sooner. "I'm gonna take a video for Instagram. Your fans will love this content."

"We don't have fans yet," Sky says, but his dimples are showing now. "What are you trying to say, anyway? Do I look good right now?"

"Um, if I recall correctly, I've *already* doubled your follower count across socials, so you definitely have fans," I say, raising an eyebrow. "And don't try to scam a compliment out of me."

He does look good, though. The breeze plays with his hair, and his smile is wide and easy, his dark eyes bright like the stars. He looks at home on the open road. I try not to think about it too much.

"Smile!" I say and record him rolling his eyes at me, a crooked grin betraying his amusement.

"What's your favorite song?" I ask, still recording. It'll be good content for Third Eye's page, but I'm also kind of curious.

He glances at me, noting my phone mere inches away from his face. He purses his lips, clearly thinking about it, before his face lights up. "'Chasing Cars' by Snow Patrol."

I blink, lowering my phone. "I love that song."

"It's a good song," Sky says, but it's obvious he's pleased by my response. "What's yours?"

"'Sweet Disposition' by The Temper Trap," I say, finally putting my phone away.

Sky cocks his head. "Don't think I know it."

"It was in *500 Days of Summer* briefly," I say, brushing my bangs out of my face. "That's not why I like it, but you might've heard it there."

"That's the movie with Jess from *New Girl*?" Sky asks, scratching the back of his neck.

"Yeah," I say with a grin. "She's way better in *New Girl*, though."

"Well, *New Girl* is a classic," Sky says easily. He switches from the highway to local roads, clearly driving without any aim. "Play me the song. I wanna hear it."

My eyebrows lift slightly. "Right now?"

"Yeah, put it on," he says, gesturing toward my phone. We stop at a red light. "Taylor Swift can wait. We'll come back to her."

"Okay, but I'm telling her you said that," I say and ignore how comforting the sound of Sky's laugh is. "Here we go."

The first few notes of "Sweet Disposition" filter into the car, and I lean back in my seat, letting the music wash over me.

I turn to the side to watch Sky's reaction to the song, and he's listening with his head tilted toward the speakers, his eyes narrowed with focus. After a few seconds, his fingers start tapping along on the steering wheel, matching the song beat for beat.

It reminds me of my dad, who also automatically matches the tempo of any song he hears. I push that thought out of my head.

Sky starts making this face that I can't even fully describe. I'd almost say angry, with the way his features are screwed up, but his *eyes* look so bright and his head is without a doubt bopping along to the song. Maybe *concentrated* is the right word.

The song slowly comes to an end, the drummer hitting the last few beats, before Spotify launches back into my playlist and "I Can See You" by Taylor Swift comes on.

"Well?" I ask, suddenly nervous. I don't know when I started to give a shit what Sky thinks, but it clearly happened at some point or another.

My nerves only heighten when Sky pulls over, idling in

front of a McDonald's. It looked like he liked it well enough, but maybe I read his body language wrong.

Sky turns to look at me, and I count backward from ten, willing him to hurry up and say his thoughts already.

"I thought it was really good," Sky says after a moment. His eyes are closed now. "I love the chorus."

Relief sweeps over me. "Yeah, me, too. I want to get a tattoo from it."

"What would you get?" he asks, blinking his eyes open. It feels so strange to be the center of his undivided attention.

"The last line," I say, willing myself to keep it cool. There's no reason to react to him *looking* at me.

Sky hums. "Any reason why? Or just because it's your favorite song?"

It would be easy to take the out. I don't have to explain myself to Skyler Moon.

But no one's ever asked before, and I find that I want to tell him.

"There's two reasons," I say, holding up my fingers like he doesn't know how to count. *Get it together, Liana.* "I like the idea of not wanting to surrender, no matter what happens. To keep fighting, even when it seems like everything is going wrong. To stay as strong as you can. I don't know if I'm there yet, but I think the tattoo would be a good reminder to myself to keep pushing."

Sky's gaze is warm. Almost fond. "That's a lovely reason, Liana. Do you want to talk about the other one? You don't have to."

"No, I don't mind. Actually, maybe you'll get it better than most." I tuck my bangs behind my ears, though they slip forward again in a moment's notice. "The song is about being young. And I—I don't know, I feel like a lot of people of color don't get to have the same youth we see portrayed in media."

Sky nods, lifting a knee to his chest so he can rest his chin against it. "Yeah, definitely. Having immigrant parents will do that to you."

"Right, yeah! It's like…we have to grow up too fast, but we also don't get to grow up at all. When do we get to have a *normal* childhood?" I shake my head. "I don't know. I like the idea that I can still have my youth, even when I'm no longer a kid. And that my tattoo can be a reminder to live for the younger version of myself who didn't always have the same opportunities. It's part of why I want to go into the music industry—to help people like me, with dreams bigger than they know what to do with."

I feel out of breath when I finish talking, even though I really didn't say all that much.

Skyler is still watching me, his eyes soft with understanding. "Where would you get it? The tattoo?"

I point at the inside of my wrist. "Right here."

My heart climbs into my throat when Sky grabs my arm, his fingers gently wrapping around my wrist. "It'll be sensitive here. It's right on the vein. If you're not set on the positioning, I'd get it a little lower." He draws a line across my forearm with his finger.

I laugh nervously. "Right, well. It'll probably be a while until I get it, so I have time to figure it out."

"Are you not eighteen yet?" Sky asks, peering up at me.

"No, not yet," I say and control the urge to pull away, my arm buzzing where his skin meets mine. "My birthday is in August. Maybe I'll get it then. I'm just…a little anxious about it."

"Ah," he says, nodding his head. "Don't worry. It seems worse than it is."

My eyes go to his tattoos, littered up and down his arms, and more noticeably twined around his neck. "You've got quite a few."

Sky finally lets go of me to touch one of his own tattoos. It's a bird, the body mostly on the side of his forearm, the wings stretching onto the back of his hand, right below his knuckles. "I think I've got about…six now? I turned eighteen in February, and I think I've gotten one every few weeks since then."

I look him over. Flowers and vines on the side of his neck, the bird on the back of his hand, some words scribbled on the inside of his elbow, a constellation on his forearm, and… I don't see another one.

"Where's the last one?" I ask.

Skyler smirks, and I realize I don't want to know the answer after all. When he reaches for the edge of his shirt, I scramble to stop him. "No, I'm good!"

He laughs loudly, throwing his head back. "If you say so. It's something my mom drew, on the side of my ribs."

I clear my throat. I've been feeling more sensitive about Ma lately, but that's not Sky's fault. The last thing I want is for him to pity me. "Oh. Are you and your mom close?"

Skyler falters, and there's a sudden tension in the car that wasn't there before. I can sense my misstep, but I'm not sure what it was. It felt like a natural conclusion to draw—he has his mother's drawing *permanently* inked on his body.

But then I recognize the look in his face, the hesitation

spreading across his features, the *reluctance* and everything clicks into place. He must have gotten it in her memory.

"She's dead," he says, confirming my thoughts. "Please don't do the pity thing where—"

"My mom's dead, too," I blurt, and his face falls slack in surprise.

"Oh." Both of us stare at each other, clearly unsure what to say, before I giggle almost nervously. Sky's expression eases and he chuckles in response.

The next silence is more welcome, full of understanding. He's the one who breaks it now with a simple, quiet, "I'm sorry."

"I'm sorry, too," I say, sharing a sad smile with him. It's been a long time since I've been able to look at someone and know they *get* it, but it's undeniable that Sky does. "It looks like we have more in common than I thought."

"Yeah," he says, his voice gentle, "I guess so."

32

GOLD DUST—SYKES

There's no reason it should take four teenage boys an hour to record a fifteen-second video, but here we are.

"All you have to do is lip-synch along," I say, rubbing at my temples. "A *toddler* could do this."

"I need to go to work soon," Mohammed says with a pout. "Can't we just call it a day?"

"Not until you finish making this video," I say, turning a death glare on him. "I know for a fact your shift doesn't start until four p.m."

Mohammed gapes at me. "How do you know that?"

"Don't worry about it," I say with a bright smile before pointing at the tripod again. "Line up. Come on."

"I don't see why we have to use every godforsaken app on the internet," Vincent says grumpily.

"And that's exactly why you are no longer in charge of social media," I say. "If you're going to make a reel, you might as well crosspost it as a YouTube short and a TikTok. It's just common sense. It's how to maximize views."

"It's not that bad guys. We almost had it the last time," Ethan says, squeezing Vincent's shoulders.

Vincent looks at Ethan, a frown on his lips, but it slowly disappears the longer they hold eye contact. "Yeah, okay, fine. Another try."

I narrow my eyes and reach for my clipboard. *Vincent… might have a crush on Ethan?*

"Sky, she's taking notes on us again," Mohammed whines, draping himself across Sky's back.

Sky laughs, sliding his hands down and around the back of Mohammed's thighs so he can give him an impromptu piggyback ride. "You'll live, Mo."

I squint. *…or they're all just really close. Maybe both.*

"Right, well, I need you in front of this phone, stat," I say, gesturing to the empty space in front of the tripod. "Come on."

It takes another fifteen minutes, but we finally get a good take, complete with Ethan bursting into laughter, Vincent half-carrying him to keep him from tumbling over, Sky's heart-wrenching smile, and Mohammed jumping on Sky's back again.

"Okay, great!" I flash them a thumbs-up. "Feel free to run off to work, Mo."

"Thank God," Mohammed says, before grinning at his bandmates. "I don't envy you."

"Get lost," Vincent says, tossing a guitar pick at him.

Mohammed sticks his tongue out and grabs his leather jacket before disappearing up the stairs.

Sky slumps on the couch, massaging the bridge of his nose. "I wish we didn't have to do any of this stuff."

I whirl around to give him the evil eye. "You know how important all of this is."

"No, I know, I know," Sky says, running his hands through his hair before pulling on a beanie like it's not the middle of summer. "But I just—I want it to be about the music. All of this feels so extra and unnecessary."

"Well, it's not. It's already July and we only have a month or so to prepare for Light The Way," I say, and I can't help the small part of me that feels slighted. He thinks my future career is *unnecessary*?

Even though I know I shouldn't, I open up Instagram and pull up Thomas' profile. "See this? He clearly knows how important marketing is. He has nearly eight thousand followers and so far, we're only at five thousand."

Vincent and Ethan lean over to see my phone screen as hurt flashes across Sky's face. I immediately feel bad, but it's too late to take it back. Instead, I push forward.

"This is why you can't afford to sit back and do nothing," I say. "He's trying to stay one step ahead of us, but we can't let him."

Sky nods shortly, looking away from me. "Right. Yeah. Okay. We'll do whatever we need to do."

Ethan looks over at him, his expression heavy. My skin itches. "Sky…"

"No, she's right," Sky says, straightening his back. His expression is devoid of any emotion except for determination. "What else do you need us to do, Lia?"

The nickname takes me aback, and a protest rises to my lips, but I swallow it down. I refer to him as Sky all the time—I've never thought twice of it. He's never called me out on it, either.

"Can we pick out what outfits you're going to wear for your next gig?" I ask, tapping my pen against my clipboard. "I just want to make sure you all coordinate. Do you have photos from previous gigs I can use as a reference? And do you have any official band colors?"

Vincent sighs, and despite his obvious attempt to be discreet, I can see where his hand slips between his and Sky's thighs, grabbing his hand and squeezing it.

Something inside my chest feels wet and loose, and I force myself to ignore it.

"Yeah, of course," Sky says, squeezing Vincent's hand back before coming to stand beside me, bringing his iPad with him. "No official band colors, but these are pictures from our last few shows…"

I nod, looking over them with him, but I'm painfully aware of Ethan and Vincent whispering among themselves, casting us looks every now and then.

That night, I sit in my room with Willow in my lap, musing on if I'm going about this the wrong way with Third Eye.

To some degree, I understand. I hate being in front of the camera, much less widely perceived. My anxiety is skyrocketing just at the thought of it.

But I don't know any other way *to* do this. I've watched Baba do his job for years. This is how it works. Everything is about numbers, statistics, how to garner the most interest. If it's not quantifiable, there's no proof of progress.

I have to help them become the best version of themselves.

And maybe they won't enjoy it, but at the end of the day, they're a product, no matter how awful it sounds. They're trying to sell their music, which means they're trying to sell themselves.

It's that simple. It has to be.

But it still leaves such an awful taste in my mouth.

33

MESS IT UP—GRACIE ABRAMS

"I still don't know why you're here," Mohammed says, and his mouth is filled with popcorn. He must have worked out or something before he came to Ethan's house, because there's no other explanation for the way he's inhaling his food like it's air.

"You're the one who came up with idea," I say, raising a pointed eyebrow.

"I don't even know my own name half the time," Mohammed says, and I flip him off. The two of us are alone in Ethan's living room, while Ethan and Vincent are at the convenience store around the corner discreetly getting chasers, so we can properly celebrate the Fourth of July.

Ethan's parents are in the backyard, hosting a party that we've been repeatedly invited to. We opted out for the time being, but I'm sure we'll finish the night out there.

Evie is supposed to arrive soon, too, which fills me with an inexplicable delight. I'm going to squeeze her until we meld into the same person.

In the meantime, the basement downstairs is absolutely decked out with a pool table, various gaming sets, a Pac-Man arcade, and two large flat-screen televisions. It reeks of teen-age boy, and Ethan being an only child explains it.

"You're literally obsessed with yourself," I snap and tug use-lessly at a box that won't move. I'm halfway inside a closet, and covered in sweat. Mohammed is getting on my last nerve, considering it was *his* idea for us to join in on the Mitchell family festivities. "Also, why the fuck am I doing this while you're eating popcorn? You're, like, *super buff.*"

Mohammed makes a muffled noise of disagreement but he does eventually set down the bowl of popcorn and join me inside the closet. He uses only one hand and pulls the box out like it's a sack of fluff. I honest to God consider smack-ing him, but he would just laugh in response.

Using his foot, he nudges a different box toward me. I glance inside to see paper plates and cups.

Mohammed doesn't wait for me to pick it up before he leaves for the basement. "Hurry up, Lia!"

"I'll hurry up and poison your popcorn while I'm at it," I say under my breath and, of course, Mohammed hears it because he starts cackling halfway down the stairs. "And no one said you could call me Lia!"

"Sky does it!" Mohammed shouts back.

I huff to myself and pick up the box that Mohammed pointed to. It's not nearly as heavy, thank God, because I re-ally would've gone downstairs and dragged Mohammed back upstairs by the ear to carry it.

Earlier today, we were all sitting around, me half-heart-edly organizing albums and three of them working on a song, when Mohammed burst in, having finished his shift at Dear Paneer, and declared we all need to take some time off to actually celebrate the Fourth of July.

Ethan threw one of the couch pillows at him, but it worked against him when Mohammed's eyes lit up. "Didn't you say your parents were hosting a barbeque today?!"

Riya is going to kick them out of the basement at this rate.

At first, I made a face and went back to organizing, already busy with plans to see Evie later, but as the boys got more hyped, an idea formed in the back of my head. This would be a perfect time to get some genuine content of their friendship.

Sky gave me a frown when I said I was coming along to film stuff for social media, and it didn't go away, even when I promised I would leave within a few hours.

Later, I asked Ethan if it was okay to invite Evie, and he looked at me like I was being ridiculous before saying, "You don't even have to ask! Of course!" I don't know why I expected anything else.

"Mohammed!" I call when I make my way to the basement. At first, I can't figure out where he went, but then he shouts back from—the kitchen? How is there a *kitchen* down here?

I set the box down and walk over to where his voice is coming from to see him sifting through bottles of alcohol.

"Can you find the shot glasses?" he asks without looking up, busy scanning the labels. I don't think I've ever seen him so focused on something. "They're in one of the cabinets upstairs."

I scoff in disbelief. "I'm not going through Ethan's cabinets."

Mohammed snorts. "Fine. Make Sky do it when he gets back from his family stuff. You've got him whipped, anyway."

I splutter. "That's not—what?"

"Oh, are we not talking about it?" Mohammed asks, looking up at me with raised brows. "My bad. Pretend I said nothing."

"Mohammed Abdullah Anwar," I say, eyes narrowed. "I will kill you where you stand."

He holds his arms out in surrender, a bottle of vodka in one hand and a bottle of rum in the other. "I said to pretend I said nothing."

"I feel like you *want* to die," I say, snatching the bottle of vodka out of his hand. "Sky is not *whipped* for me."

"No, he's just letting you commandeer the band for no reason whatsoever," Mohammed says, rolling his eyes.

I gape at him. "He's doing it for the good of the band!"

"The good of the band, my ass," Mohammed says, snagging the vodka back from me. He bends down to pull out a handful of plastic cups from the other box as he adds, "You think he let you come to this barbeque for the good of the band? Be fucking for real."

"That's not true," I say, frowning. "He wants Third Eye to have the best chance possible."

"He absolutely hates doing all of this shit," Mohammed says, pouring vodka into two cups and following it up with Coke. "He's just not complaining about it to you."

"You're lying," I say, squinting at him. I know Sky doesn't *love* doing this—it's clear none of them do—but hating it is a far jump from that.

Mohammed only smiles at me before offering me one of the red solo cups. "Drink up, it's going to be a long day."

34

HEAL—TOM ODELL

After I'm done coughing and gagging at the drink Mohammed made, with way too much vodka and not enough Coke, I wander back into the common space.

Mohammed appears in the doorway, eyes glassy but bright. "Ethan and Vincent are back. We can actually get shit done now."

"How do you even know that?" I ask, but it's pointless because Ethan and Vincent appear at the base of the steps, holding multiple plastic bags.

"Sorry, it was really busy," Ethan says in apology before turning to Mohammed in suspicion. "You didn't touch any of my stuff, did you?"

Mohammed gives him a dry look. "Because I touch your stuff all the time."

"Yes, you do, frankly," Ethan says and snatches the cup out of Mohammed's hand. "Thanks for the drink."

"You're not welcome!" Mohammed says, but like always,

he folds. Ethan really does have everyone wrapped around his finger.

I take out my phone now that more of them are here, and Mohammed pulls up short to stare at me incredulously. "Are you really just gonna sit around and film us? That's so boring."

The look I shoot him is nothing short of scathing. "Yes. That's the entire reason I'm here, in case you forgot."

"I know you secretly love spending time with us," Ethan says, coming to stand by my side and butt his head against mine. "You adore us."

"I'm not even going to comment on that," Vincent says, waving a hand at the pair of us. "Now excuse me while I go set up the PlayStation. Mohammed isn't allowed to touch electronics."

Mohammed protests half-heartedly, but then gets distracted by the box of alcohol again. Ethan's eyebrows lift so high they nearly touch his hairline and he immediately follows Mohammed into the kitchen.

I'm left alone with an empty cup and the feeling that this is the beginning of the end. Why did Sky leave me alone with these people? He didn't even explain what his family thing was before he disappeared in a rush. And now I'm going to end up dying tonight because of these three hooligans, and I have no choice but to live with it.

Two hours later, the boys have eaten through almost an entire table full of popcorn, nachos, pizza, and drinks. Vinny also promised Ethan's parents we'd come upstairs once they fired up the grill, so there's even more food on the way. I know they're growing teenage boys, but *Jesus Christ*. I have no idea how they manage to eat as much as they do, but I'm not going to start questioning their stomachs.

Mohammed has a stack of DVDs set up and Ethan is writing what may or may not be a song—but he flips his notepad over every time Vincent wanders over, making the other boy scowl at him.

Ethan is probably writing a song about Vincent. Then a pause. *Ethan wants to write songs?*

Slowly, I wander over to where Ethan is sitting. He eyes me suspiciously, but doesn't turn over his notepad, which I take as a good sign.

"Hey," I say, offering him some tortilla chips. "Are you working on a song?"

The apples of Ethan's cheeks flush red. "N-no."

"You need media training because that was possibly one of the worst cases of lying I've ever seen," I say, popping a chip into my mouth.

"Was it that obvious?" Ethan asks, groaning and hiding his face behind his notepad.

I snort, bumping shoulders with him. "A little bit, yeah. I didn't know you wrote songs?"

Ethan shakes his head. The flush has started to climb up his neck. "I don't. I mean. I haven't, before. It's just that—Thomas thought writing our own songs was stupid, and he was so mean to Sky about it, and—yeah."

My blood feels like it's boiling under my skin with the sudden rage I feel. "The same songs he took credit for?"

Ethan gives me a bittersweet smile. "The one and the same."

I close my eyes, shaking my head. I can't think about how

much I want to wring Thomas' neck right now, three mixed drinks in, or I'll sink into a pit of self-loathing.

I open my eyes again. "Okay. Well, fuck him. Have you told Sky you want to write songs?"

Ethan grimaces. "Well, not exactly." Before I can interrupt with a demand for him to explain, he squeezes my arm. "I just—I know how hard he's been working to write these new songs for the band, and I don't want to throw something into the mix and complicate everything."

"Ethan Mitchell, don't you dare self-sabotage and say it's for the benefit of the band," I say, smacking his hand off my arm. "You know Sky would be overjoyed to look at anything you worked on."

Ethan bites his lip, looking down at his notepad. "What if it's bad? What if I'm not good enough?"

"Then Sky will help you get better," I say, poking his cheek. "You're the one who always says you guys are more than a team. Do you really think Sky would hang you out to dry?"

"I mean, no," Ethan says, clicking and unclicking his pen. "He would never do something like that."

"Then why would this be any different?" I ask.

He sighs. "Stop being so reasonable, Lia."

"No," I say, but scratch his head affectionately. "Let's talk about this again when we're both sober, okay? I really think you should tell Sky, but maybe now's not the best time for any decision-making."

Ethan whines, but he leans into my touch. "I guess."

"But since we are both tipsy..." I glance over my shoulder, but Vincent and Mohammed are both distracted by some video game. "What's going on with you and Vinny?"

Ethan's eyes bulge. "I—I don't… What do you mean?"

"Didn't we just talk about the fact you're a bad liar?" I ask, giving him an exasperated look. "You don't have to tell me anything, I've just been a little curious. I've seen the bi sticker on the back of Vincent's car, and when I screened your Instagram, I saw your post for National Coming Out day last year, so…"

"It's not…" Ethan sighs again. "Vinny and I aren't hiding the fact we're both bisexual. Mo and Sky have always been supportive of us, and we're proud of our sexualities. But we both also know the reality of the industry. We know it's better for marketing if the four of us appear single and attainable. So that's that."

My heart feels like lead. "Ethan, that's not—"

Ethan cuts me a look, and I trip over my tongue.

Once I get my bearings again, I shake my head. *This* is exactly why I want to work in the music industry. To champion the people with the odds stacked against them. To be in their corner no matter what and do what I can to make sure they come out on top.

"No. Don't do that to yourself," I say firmly. "Don't sit here and deny yourself what you want because of people you don't even know. Any record label or management company that asks you to hide your relationships is *shitty* and not worth it. Does—Sky doesn't know about this, either, does he?"

Ethan makes a face. "He already has enough to worry about."

"You're so *silly*," I say, shaking him by the shoulder. "That boy would sacrifice anything for you. He would never ask this of you—or of Vincent."

"And that's the problem," Ethan says, crossing his arms, a grumpy tilt to his mouth. "He wouldn't ask, even though it would be better for the band and for our careers. He loves us too much. So Vincent and I decided it's better for him to not know. He deserves to have his dreams come true."

I stare at him in disbelief. "Do you hear yourself? You think you're doing this *for* Sky? Ethan, shut up. If you want to be in a relationship with Vincent, do it. Fuck the marketing, fuck the PR." I raise both my hands to my temples, rubbing circles into them. "Fame is *not* worth losing what matters to you. Anyone who recognizes your talent should also be able to recognize it's doesn't require compromising yourself and your morals."

"Liana, you don't know what you're talking—"

"But I do! That's literally why I'm here!" I say, throwing my arms up. "You—we're having *so* many conversations when we're sober." I point a threatening finger at him. "I'm circling back to this."

Ethan shrugs. "It's not going to change anything."

I resist the urge to pull out my hair. "I need more alcohol," I say, pat his head once, and leave the couch.

35

SOMEONE TO YOU—BANNERS

When Evie shows up, I shriek so loudly that everyone else in the vicinity winces. "Evie!"

She immediately launches herself into my arms and I squeeze until I lose feeling in my limbs. We've migrated to the backyard now, sequestered in our own little corner of the patio. I've sobered up somewhat, but I'm still pleasantly buzzed.

"So this is the infamous Evelyn?" Mohammed asks once we finally separate.

Evie gives me an amused look. "Have you been telling people my name is Evelyn?"

I shrug, grinning. "Maybe."

"Is that not your name?" Mohammed asks, thick brows furrowed.

Evie shrugs. "Who can say? I'm guessing you're Mohammed, though."

Mohammed narrows his eyes. "How did you know that?"

"I've read Liana's notes on all of you," Evie says easily, sitting down on one of the hammocks. I take the seat beside her, leaning my head on her shoulder. There's an overhead awning shielding us from the sun, but I made Ethan put on sunscreen before we came outside. I told the others, too, but I'm not as concerned about them turning tomato red.

"You were *actually* taking notes?" Mohammed asks, his voice rising several decibels as he frantically looks between me and Evie.

I snort. "You're screaming, Mo. You're gonna give the old white men behind you a heart attack."

Mohammed glances at the rest of the backyard, filled with the Mitchells' guests, and turns back, looking properly chastised. "I can't believe you were actually taking notes on us," he whisper-yells.

"I can," Vincent says, sitting down on one of the lawn cheers. Earlier, Ethan's dad offered him a beer and Vincent stammered for a good half a minute before Ethan accepted it on his behalf, giggling the entire time. "Liana has narc energy."

I gasp. "Take that back."

Vincent offers me a catlike smile. "No."

Ethan rolls his eyes and sits down on the patio floor, tucking himself in between Vincent's legs. Evie takes stock of it with interest, her eyes bright. "Vincent and Ethan, I assume," she says, pointing at them respectively.

Ethan grins, tipping an imaginary hat. "At your service, m'lady."

Vincent lightly smacks the back of his head and when Ethan

pouts at him, he cards his fingers through Ethan's hair in apology.

"You two are cute," Evie says, a small smile on her face.

Ethan turns to me slowly, his eyes questioning, and I shake my head minutely. I didn't tell Evie anything specific about Ethan and Vinny, but I'm not surprised she figured it out.

"So how are things going with you and that girl back at Columbia?" I say loudly.

Evie cuts me a look, clearly catching on to my attempt to change the subject, but she rolls with it anyway. "It's fine. I'm just in my yearning era, that's all. Nothing new to update."

"Wait, I want to hear about this," Ethan says, scooting slightly forward. "What girl?"

I hide my smile by tucking it into Evie's shoulder. She sighs forlornly but starts recounting every single interaction between her and Sam in vivid detail, down to the time stamp.

By the time she's finished, both Vincent and Ethan are deeply invested, scrolling Evie's text thread with Sam with wide eyes, muttering theories to each other.

"It's obvious Sam likes her, I don't understand what you guys are investigating," Mohammed says through a mouthful of corn on the cob.

"There are levels to this, you wouldn't get it," Vincent says, waving him off with a hot dog in hand, and I snort.

Mohammed scowls, wiping barbecue sauce off his mouth. "I'll remember that, Vinny."

"When is Mr. Skyler Moon showing up?" Evie asks me, nudging my foot with hers. "Mom said she was going to pick me up in like…two-ish hours? We're going to watch fireworks on the beach."

I pout. "That soon? You haven't even been here that long."

"I know," Evie says, giving my hand a squeeze. "I wish I could stay longer."

"You can," I insist, and reach over to snatch her phone out of Ethan's hands.

"Hey!" Ethan and Vincent say as one.

I ignore them, holding the phone out to Evie. "Call your mom. I'll talk to her. She loves me!"

"It's not gonna work, Li," Evie says, leaning back in the hammock. "It's Khodabux family tradition. I can't miss it."

"You don't have to miss it," I say, shaking my head. "You can just be fashionably late."

"Li," Evie says gently. "I can't."

"Can you pass the ketchup?" Mo whispers loudly, and Ethan smacks his arm.

I don't register it, too busy staring at Evie's expression, trying to dissect it. It hits me all at once—the mentions of her homesickness through the past few weeks, how much Evie has missed her mother. She's saying *I can't*, but what she means is *I don't want to*.

I swallow the protest in my throat. Even if a small selfish part of me wants her to stay, I can't keep asking her to. She deserves to spend some quality family time before she has to go back to school. At the end of the day, I want her to be happy.

"If you want to stay longer, we can give you a ride to wherever you need to go," Vincent says quietly, startling me despite the low volume of his voice. "We don't mind."

"Thanks," Evie says, smiling slightly. "But it's okay. I'll be good. And so will Liana, since she has all of you to keep her company." She shoves at my shoulder. "Cheer up, buttercup."

I sigh and wrap my arms around her in quiet acceptance, before turning to the boys. "Where is Sky, anyway? How am I supposed to film content if he's not here?"

"You're not," Mohammed says with a self-satisfied grin.

"You're annoying," I say, flipping him off. "But really, has Sky talked to any of you? He's been out with his family for a while, hasn't he? Do they have specific plans for the fourth?"

"I think they went to visit his mom's grave," Vincent says, and I instantly fall silent.

I haven't visited my mom's grave since I left New York. I still remember exactly what it looks like despite the time that's passed. The words written on it are inscribed into my brain.

In loving memory of Zaynab Ahmed, beloved wife, wonderful mother, and inspiring woman. Always in our hearts.

"Oh," I say. Evie interlaces our fingers, rubbing her thumb over my knuckles. I offer her a small grateful smile. "Is it the anniversary of her death?" I ask the boys.

"No," Mo says. "It was a last-minute decision. I think Sky and Kate visit every few weeks, just to talk to their mom."

"Just to talk to their mom," I repeat, slightly at a loss. I can't fathom visiting my mother's grave that often and opening myself up to that grief. Even thinking about her for too long *aches* like a tender bruise.

But maybe that's a problem in and of itself. I constantly complain that my dad never talks about my mom, but it's not like I really do, either. It hurts too much.

"Yeah, and they said something about getting donuts after," Mo says with a shrug. "Kate loves them."

"You know an awful lot about what Kate likes," Ethan teases.

Mohammed's cheeks warm and he waves Ethan off. "I just actually listen when Sky tells us things."

"Yeah, when it involves Kate," Ethan sing-songs and leans away when Mohammed threatens to swat him.

Evie nudges me as Mo and Ethan continue to bicker. "You okay, bubs?"

I blink away the strange dust caught in my lashes. "Yeah, I'm good. I don't think you'll get to meet Sky, though."

"Who cares?" she says, tossing one of her legs over mine. "As long as you're here, I'm good."

"I love you," I say, leaning into her side. "I wish you didn't have to go."

Evie squeezes me. "I love you. I'll see if I can convince Mom to include you in our plans tomorrow."

"Please do," I say. "And if she says no, send me the address anyway and I'll hitchhike there."

Evie laughs, and it's a warm and familiar sound.

When Evie leaves, promising to call me later tonight, I pointedly do *not* cry, but Ethan initiates a cuddle pile on one of the massive swings in his backyard anyway.

At first, Mohammed and Vincent give him an incredulous look. But then all Ethan has to say is, "Oh, come on. We cuddle all the time. Who cares if Liana knows?" before they all climb in.

I'm the last one left, staring at the three of them in bewilderment until Ethan glares at me.

"What?" I ask defensively, wrapping my arms around myself.

"You're a part of this now," Ethan says, patting the spot next to him. "Accept it."

I let out some mix between a scoff and a laugh. "You're not being serious."

"Come on, Lia, don't be so stubborn," Mohammed says, using his feet to give the swing some momentum. "Everyone does what Ethan wants. Including you."

"That's not true." But isn't it?

I blink a few times, my eyes suspiciously itchy, but make my way to the swing, sitting next to Ethan. It's nice of them to pretend they're not doing this because I look sad and pathetic in the aftermath of my best friend leaving. Nicer than I deserve, probably, but I won't complain about receiving free cuddles.

"There you go," Ethan says, tossing a throw over the four of us. He looks far too proud of himself. "Now we wait for Sky. I'm sure he'll be here before the fireworks."

Right as the sky begins to darken, Skyler shows up, looking out of breath. He spots the four of us, a mess of limbs, on the swing and decides not to ask any questions. Instead, he climbs in beside me and offers us a box of donuts.

"Kate's obsession is getting out of hand," he mutters to Ethan who laughs, taking a chocolate donut and passing the box along to Vincent.

When the fireworks eventually start, it's like a scene out of a movie. They light up the sky with rainbows of color, starting off as small dots before expanding into showers of light. I jump at the first *boom!* and Sky puts a hand on my shoulder, steadying me.

"Are you alright?" he asks, so close that his lips almost brush against the shell of my ear.

"Yeah, sorry, I was just startled," I say, slightly embarrassed.

Sky leans back to look at me, tracing the features of my face with his gaze. "Don't apologize. Are you alright?"

You already asked that, I want to say, but it's obvious he's asking a different question now.

I take a moment to think about it. "Yeah," I say eventually. "I'm alright, Sky. Are you alright?"

He smiles, squeezing my arm. "Yeah, Lia. I'm alright."

We both turn back to the fireworks, watching as they explode in the sky, beautiful and mesmerizing.

It's only later, after the boys drop me off at my house, that I realize I didn't take a single video the entire time I was there. And I have no idea how to feel about that.

36

THE CHAIN—FLEETWOOD MAC

It takes me by surprise when the end of my shift at the record shop rolls around a few days later, and Sky has actually come upstairs without me having to go get him.

I falter where I'm wiping down the counter to stare at him. "Oh. Are you…leaving?"

Skyler nods, but he's looking at me in a strange way. It sets me on edge, and my knee starts jiggling up and down. "Yeah."

"Right," I say, the syllables stretching out to a point that's uncomfortable. "I'll see you tomorrow, then."

I expect Sky to leave, but he keeps standing there, like his feet are planted to the ground. "Uh, well—I was wondering if…"

"If…?" I ask, brushing my hair out of my eyes.

"Well," Skyler says, rubbing the back of his neck. "Did you want to go on a drive? Like the other night?"

Like a date? I want to ask even though I know it's not.

"Yes, she does!" Riya says, coming up behind me, startling both of us. "I'll close up, you go on."

I shake my head, eyes wide at her arrival. "I don't—"

Riya grabs the cloth rag out of my grasp and hands me my purse in the same motion. "Go, go. Before I change my mind."

"What are you *doing*?" I hiss under my breath.

"Ē'i chēlē tōmākē pachanda karē," Riya says, a scary smile on her face. "Chup koro, ēkhon *jā'ō*."

Sky raises his brows, clearly not understanding what my cousin is saying. I thank *God* for that because the last thing any of us need is for Sky to know Riya is accusing him of having a crush on me. In fact, my plan is to make sure he never finds that out.

"You are an *insane* person," I say, taking my purse from her. She nudges me toward the door without responding. "Okay, I'm going, I'm going!"

"Use protection!" Riya shouts out the door. Well, there goes that plan. I contemplate sinking into the ground. Sky lets out a noise that's a mix between a laugh and a cough.

"Shut the fuck up!" I yell back and refuse to look Sky in the eye. "Sorry, I don't know what's wrong with her."

"No, it's fine, my sister is like that, too," Sky says, and I chance a glance at him. The tips of his ears are red, but he's smiling like he thinks this is funny and not weird as hell.

"Kate, right?" I ask, looking down the block for Sky's car.

He peers at me curiously just as I spot his shiny black Toyota Corolla across the street. "Yeah, how'd you know that?" A pause before his eyes narrow. "Was it Mohammed? It was Mohammed, wasn't it?"

"I just know things!" I say and run away from him before he can press more, shrieking when he tries to grab for me. "Stop that!"

"You're so annoying," he says, out of breath by the time he catches up to me. "Get in the car, Ahmed."

I inhale sharply at him using the wrong last name but manage to cover it up by clearing my throat. "Yeah, okay."

The more time that goes by—and the closer we get to Light The Way—the more I realize how precarious my situation is.

Third Eye is going to find out who I am eventually. And even if they don't find out what I did, how I helped Thomas and got them into this mess, they'll still find out that Jhilmil Sarkar is my *father* and I could have gone to him at any point and told him what Thomas did.

But I can't—I can't look my dad in the eye and tell him I fucked up. Not when he's finally starting to take me seriously in the workplace and look at me as something other than a nuisance. I can't stand to bear the brunt of his disappointment.

The problem is that it's looking like I'm going to face Third Eye's disappointment instead.

I bite the inside of my cheek until I taste the tang of blood in my mouth. I can't think about this right now. There's too much at stake for me to lose focus.

"Penny for your thoughts?" Sky asks, drawing my attention back to him.

I blink back to reality. "My thoughts are more expensive than a penny."

Sky makes an amused noise. "Okay. A dollar for your thoughts?"

I put my seat belt on before holding out my hand.

Sky stares at it beseechingly for a moment before he slowly places his hand in mine.

My entire face warms. "That's not—where's the dollar?"

"Oh! Oh," Sky says, pulling his hand back. Great. Now we're *both* blushing. "Right. Here." He pulls out his wallet and hands me a dollar. "There you go."

"Thanks," I say, wrapping my fingers around it. "Uh, I was thinking about how I don't really know much about your family. I know Mohammed has three older sisters, Vinny has a younger brother, and Ethan is an only child. You have... one younger sister. Is Kate younger?"

"Yeah, Kate is younger," Sky says, but his nose is wrinkled. "I think I probably fall into the overprotective brother stereotype. In my defense, she's going through a rough breakup right now."

"Is that why you've been seeing her so often?" I ask, tilting my head curiously.

Sky sighs. "Yeah, I just hate seeing her so sad. She keeps taking me to this donut place in Hollywood and stuffing her face, and I can't bring myself to say no. Her ex-boyfriend's lucky I'm busy with this competition."

I hide a smile as I imagine him standing up for his sister in the most dramatic way possible, valiantly fighting for her honor. Instead of telling him where my imagination is taking me, I ask, "Why'd they break up?"

"I can't get into it right now or *I'm* going to need donuts," he says, grimacing so hard one of his dimples appears. "What's tonight's playlist?"

Sky is terrible at changing the subject.

"I just picked a random one," I say, pulling it up. "I can find something else, though, if it's not the vibe."

vibes 24/7:
Go Your Own Way—Fleetwood Mac
That's All—Genesis
Sirius—The Alan Parsons Project
Leave It—Yes
Sultans of Swing—Dire Straits
Mother—Pink Floyd
Still Loving You—Scorpions
Broadsword—Jethro Tull
Dreamer—Super Tramp
Solar Fire—Manfred Mann's Earth Band

Skyler shifts the car into Drive. "Sounds good to me. Shall we?"

I nod, lowering the windows. "Go for it."

37

DOMINO—ITZY

Over an hour later, Sky glances at me from the corner of his eye. "You know, you don't really talk about yourself much, either."

I stiffen, wondering how to talk around my father's existence. The last time I did this was with Thomas, and that could not have turned out worse.

What can I talk about that won't make all of this implode?

"My best friend's name is Evie," I say eventually. "You just barely missed her the other day. She's back in New York right now. She's attending Columbia in the fall, but they wanted her to come early for a pre-college summer program, so that's where she's been the last two months. But she'll be back in time for the Light The Way music competition! She promised to come."

"That's cool," Sky says, a small smile playing at his lips. "I'm excited to finally meet her."

"She's a lesbian, so your usual charms aren't going to work," I say and try not to sound too gleeful. "How will you live?"

"You know, I think you've got it in your head that I'm some kind of sleazy fuckboy and I have no idea why," Sky says with an amused shake of his head. "Is this because of the party we first met at?"

"Uh, yeah," I say, giving him a skeptical look. "You were *literally* offering to take anyone who named three of your songs on a date. Do you know what a douchebag move that is?"

"Okay, well, the part you *don't* know is that Mohammed dared me to do that," he says, and my mouth falls shut with a loud clack, my teeth grinding against each other.

"You're lying," I say, because there's no way—

Realization hits me like a truck. Fucking Thomas. He led me to believe that's what Sky was always like, made him out to be an obnoxious asshole when he probably *knew* Mohammed dared him to act like that. "Oh my God."

"I'm not gonna lie, though, I was genuinely impressed you knew our songs," Sky says, blowing past it like I'm not having an entire crisis over misjudging my first impression of him. "I would've actually taken you on the date if you let me."

I cough abruptly. *"Huh?"*

"I mean, you knew our music and you were beautiful," Sky continues. I'm gonna go into cardiac arrest at the tender age of seventeen at this rate. "And I could tell you were pissed near the end, but it was kind of hot."

"What?" I ask.

Skyler smirks at me. "Cat got your tongue?"

"Are you—are you fucking with me right now?" I ask, smacking his arm. Oh my God, I cannot *stand* this boy.

"Maybe," Sky says, his expression entirely too mischievous. "But what if I wasn't?"

"I will take the wheel and crash this car," I threaten him.

Sky pulls over without a moment's notice and I jolt in my seat. We're on a local road, but that still doesn't explain why he's parking. He unbuckles his seat belt, all while I stare at him in bewilderment. "Okay, let's switch, then. Take the wheel. We can pretend you have a driver's license."

"You—I'm gonna end your life," I say, unbuckling my own seat belt just so I can lean across the car and shove his head.

Sky bursts into laughter, pushing me away half-heartedly. I shift forward, sitting half on the console to wrap my hands around his neck.

"I'll squeeze, I swear to God!"

"Go ahead," Sky says, but the words are barely coherent through his laughter.

"You are so unbelievably obnoxious," I say and, all of a sudden, realize how close I am to his face.

There's a beauty mark on his nose. I've never noticed it before.

Sky slowly stops laughing, and eventually gives me a small smile, his eyes impossibly warm. "What's wrong, Lia?"

"Uh," I shake my head, scooting backward. "Nothing."

My elbow bumps into the wheel and the horn honks loudly, making me startle and fall back into my seat haphazardly.

Sky laughs again, steadying me with a hand on my arm. "Be careful."

"Right. I'll try," I say, ignoring the urge to press my hands against my cheeks to see if they're really as hot as they feel. I need him to start driving again and I need to find something to do with myself before I start astral projecting. "So, uh, back to Evie, we've been best friends for three years now."

"About the same as me and Mohammed," Sky says with a nod and thankfully turns the engine back on. "How'd you meet?"

"It was at a concert, actually," I say, blinking in realization. "Like you and Ethan?"

"Yeah! Yeah. What concert?"

"SZA," I say, smiling at the memory. Both Evie and I had queued up for the pit several hours early, determined to be as close to the stage as possible. I was alone since I didn't really have any friends in LA yet and my dad had no interest in accompanying me. Evie was alone because her friends didn't want to wait around all day for the pit and bought seats in the stands instead. It was only natural the two of us became fast friends, especially when we realized we go to the same school.

I relay it all to Sky who looks a little too surprised at how unhinged the SZA pit ended up being.

"Hey, you know it's going to happen with you guys at some point, right?" I ask, eyebrows raised. "Like…people are going to queue for your concerts. You'll have girls throwing bras at you in no time."

Sky snorts. "I mean, I guess we can hope."

"No, but seriously," I say, turning in my seat to face him better. "Especially since most shows are general admission when you're first starting out in the industry."

"No, I know, but—it's insane to think we could play at the Troubadour or something." Sky's face is so full of yearning that it makes my heart skip a beat. His dream, his future feels so real and palpable around us.

"We should go see a show there sometime," I say, poking his shoulder gently. The last person I asked to come with me to a concert was Thomas, only for him to ignore me, but this is different.

Sky glances at me, his features bright with mirth. "Are you asking me on a date?"

"You wish," I say, pulling my hand back with a shake of my head. "I meant as friends, dumbass."

"So we're friends?" Sky asks, and the question takes me by surprise even though it shouldn't.

Me and Sky as friends. It's not something I ever saw happening. But it's undeniable that I'm sitting in his car at midnight for no reason aside from wanting to listen to music with him. That's not something you do with your casual acquaintances.

"I guess we are," I say and ignore the flutter in my stomach at the sight of his responding grin. "Now drive me home, I need to feed my cat."

Sky laughs and it sounds like music. "Your wish is my command."

38

COOL (YOUR RAINBOW)—NMIXX

Evie is smiling at me with a devious look in her eye. It's our weekly sleepover, and I called her as soon as I finished my shower, deciding to let my hair air-dry tonight.

"I don't like the way you're looking at me right now," I say, wrinkling my nose as I rub my towel through the wet strands of my hair. "What's wrong with you?"

"You have a crush," Evie says in a singsong tone that makes me want to slam my laptop shut and never open it again.

"I *just* told you that we're officially friends," I say, throwing my hands up. "How does that translate to having a crush?"

"Because I know what you look like when you have a crush," Evie says, way too smug for this entire conversation. "I had an inkling when I saw you last week, but now it's obvious."

"You literally have no idea what you're talking about. It's not even like you actually saw me interact with Sky when you were here," I say, shaking my head and grabbing my hairbrush from my bedside table. "You're projecting because *you* have a crush."

"See, the thing is I don't do that," Evie says, flashing her teeth in a grin. "You're the one who does it."

"When have I done that?" I ask in disbelief, stopping halfway through brushing out a knot.

"You're doing it right now! You love to deflect," Evie says without missing a beat. "But if you really want to play it like that, we can. I'll run you through my life. The summer program is still going great, I'm having a good time and learning a lot, but I'm glad I got a little break when I came to visit. Sam and I had dinner last night with a few of the other girls here and it was a teeny-tiny bit gay. I already miss my mom but she said she would come and visit next week. I also miss my siblings, but that's way too many plane tickets to pay for, so I'll just have to wait. I also really miss *you* but I'm happy because you're actually having fun, which is all I wanted for you this summer! Oh, and the MTA scares the shit out of me. See? There. Now do you want me run through your life, too? Because I can."

"You are a terrifying person," I say, but there's something stuck in my throat, making the words fuzzier than they should be. "And I miss you already, too."

Evie groans. "I cannot wait for you to have a therapist."

"Yeah, yeah, we all want me to go to therapy," I say, squeezing the last bits of water out from the ends of my hair. "But it's still not a crush, Eve."

She stares at me blandly. "You know it's okay to have a crush, right? I know Thomas was an asshole, but Sky doesn't seem like that."

"He's just a friend," I say.

And I can't go through that again. I can't let my guard down only for someone to take advantage of me and hurt me again. It doesn't matter if Sky seems like a good guy. Trusting someone to treat me the way I want to be treated is too hard and too scary. I can't open my heart to someone and risk losing them in the process.

I don't have to say all of that aloud. Evie already knows it, which is why she's hounding me about this in the first place.

"As someone who *worships* 'You Are In Love' by Taylor Swift, you're really going to say that to me? Okay." Evie shrugs. "Whatever you say."

I gape at her. "Why would you invoke that song?"

"Because someone had to!"

"You're unhinged," I tell her very seriously. "So unwell I can't even stand to look at you right now."

"Drama queen," Evie says, and then gives me that awful smile again. "It's my turn to pick a movie, isn't it?"

"...Yes," I say, already sensing I'm about to regret it.

"We're watching *Love, Rosie*," Evie says brightly. "The friends-to-lovers blueprint."

I glare at her. "You're the devil. Know that."

Evie doesn't pay any attention to me, already in the process of queueing it up. I sigh and surrender to the fact Evie is going to die on this hill, and there's little for me to do about it.

Even though I refuse to have a crush on Sky, I spend that entire night tossing and turning instead of sleeping. What's going to happen when he catches me in my lie? What's going to happen when they all do?

I've been careful, but all it takes is Ethan looking me up in our school directory for them to find out that my last name isn't Ahmed. There's no reason for Ethan to do it, but the point is that he *could*.

There's also Thomas, who is a completely unknown factor in this game. At any moment, he could pop up and tell them what I did, expose me completely for the liar I am. I have to believe he wouldn't go anywhere near Third Eye willingly but if he does—

It's nauseating to think about.

There are so many things that can go wrong, and I'm at the mercy of most of them. I know it's going to come out at some point or another. There's no way to avoid it forever.

But I want to.

I briefly contemplate whether it would be better to just tell them now and get it over with, but…the competition. It would distract them too much, take away from too much.

Afterward. I'll tell them afterward and deal with whatever consequences I reap.

The thought of losing the tentative friendships I've built with all of Third Eye—with Sky, of all people—is an awful thought.

I wish the entire thing didn't feel so doomed.

39

EVERYTHING I WANTED—BILLIE EILISH

Riya's twenty-fifth birthday approaches at the end of July and everything predictably goes wrong. It wouldn't be a proper brown function without an impending disaster.

My outfit looks wrong on me. Probably because it belongs—belonged to Ma. I stare at the salwar kameez in the mirror, trying to figure out why it looked so beautiful on Ma, but it's so ill-fitting on me. It's too loose in the pants and too tight in the chest, and it scratches my skin, and I feel like I'm *losing* my shit.

I shouldn't have taken out the box of Ma's clothes. That was my first mistake. How did I think I could wear anything she owned? How did I think I could do it justice?

"Are you ready yet, Bibi?" my dad asks, coming into my room without knocking and pulling up short at the sight of me.

"Those are your mother's clothes," he says, and if the words are choked, we both pretend not to notice.

"I don't have any other Bangladeshi clothes to wear," I say, fidgeting with the dupatta. My anxiety is festering under my skin, insidious and awful. "None of my old ones fit me anymore."

Baba stares at me in painful silence before he nods shortly. "Be downstairs in ten."

"Okay," I say, my voice small, and turn away.

The entire car ride to Uncle Biptu's house is awkward and silent. Baba's knuckles are tight on his steering wheel and my gaze is firm on the horizon.

When "Call Me" by Blondie comes on my playlist, both of us flinch. Ma's favorite song.

By the time we arrive at Riya's birthday party, we're both prickly with tension. I greet Biptu Uncle and Shriya Auntie at the door with hugs and then quickly slip inside to find Riya and the rest of my cousins.

But even still, as I wish Riya happy birthday and give her the envelope with concert tickets, I'm acutely aware of the strain between me and my dad. I wonder if everyone else can see it.

Within the first hour of us being there, a few too many people stop me to tell me how much I look like my mother. It makes me want to hurl.

Baba can't even stand to spare me a glance.

It comes as no surprise when halfway through the party Baba pulls me aside to say, "Bibi, I'm going to duck out early. You'll be fine by yourself, won't you?"

"You're going to leave Riya Apu's birthday party?" I ask in disbelief. My skin feels itchy and I want to scratch at it until it bleeds. "They haven't even cut the cake."

"I don't care for desserts," Baba says, which is an absolute lie, and it's insane that he thinks I don't know that.

"Why are you leaving so early?" I ask tightly. "Won't Biptu Uncle and Shriya Auntie be upset?"

"They'll be fine," Baba says with a roll of his eyes. "I have a work thing to deal with."

My skin starts to crawl. "What work thing?"

"Don't worry about it," my dad says, waving me off. "You'll be good, yeah?"

"Stop," I say, shaking my head. "I don't want to stay if you're going to leave. Everyone's going to ask me where you went. Let me come with you, then."

"*No,*" Baba snaps a bit too loudly. Some of the aunties in the room look over at us in surprise, and my dad immediately lowers his voice. "No, you stay here. It's your cousin's birthday, you should be here."

"It's your *niece's* birthday!" I say in response and draw the attention of more of my relatives, but I don't really care at this point. "That's not—let me come with you."

"I already said no, Bibi," he says, typing something on his phone in a clear dismissal.

I grit my teeth. Maybe it's because I'm already oversensitive from being stared at all day and compared to Ma so many times, but I feel my impulse control giving away. "Why not? Is it because I'm wearing Ma's clothes?"

Baba stops short, staring at me in wide-eyed shock. "Bibi, what's wrong with you?" he asks, his voice a whisper.

"Why don't we ever talk about her?" I ask, my throat closing tight. "Do you think this is what she would want for us?"

"Please stop," he says weakly. "I have to go to work, okay?"

"You don't have to," I say, pulling on the sleeve of his kurta. I feel like a little kid all of a sudden, so small and scared and hurt. "You could stay. Please stay, Baba."

"You're causing a scene," my dad says, shaking me off. My arm falls to my side, heavy as a ton. "Don't do this on Riya's birthday."

"You're the one leaving on Riya Apu's birthday!" I say, my voice cracking. I thought things were different now. I thought things were getting better, even if slowly. "You can't keep doing this, Baba. It's not *fair*."

Baba finally looks at me, but his gaze is cold. "Bibi, stop this right now."

"No, I won't," I say, even though I want to rip my clothes off and set them on fire at this point. "You can't always avoid the topic of Ma. You can't value your job more than your family! I know you're grieving, but I'm grieving, too! I miss her, *too*. Can't you see that?"

"I'm not doing this with you," my dad says, pinching the bridge of his nose.

"I know Ma died, but you know I'm still alive, right? I'm still here!" I wave my hands in front of his face pointedly. "Does that even matter to you?"

"Bibi," he says, his disappointed tone leaving no room for argument. "Enough."

Fuck this.

"It's like you don't even care that I'm your daughter!" I shout finally. "It's like you think I don't exist!"

Baba flinches and turns around, walking away from me instead of fucking *admitting* to it.

Everyone in the room is staring at me with wide eyes, and

I bite the inside of my cheek to keep from bursting into tears. As much as I love Riya, I can't be here anymore.

Just as I move to leave the room, I realize someone is looking at me differently than everyone else. Near the entrance to the hallway, Mohammed is staring at me, his mouth dropped open.

Oh shit.

Oh shit.

40

ARCADE—DUNCAN LAURENCE

"Wait, I can explain!" I say, chasing after Mohammed as he disappears into the hallway. Shit, shit, shit. I knew he and Riya lived in the same community, but how the fuck do they *know* each other? He's not Bangladeshi, so it's not as if he's some random relative I forgot about. Surely, she didn't invite him and his whole family just because she knows him *tangentially* from the record shop? If that were the case, the rest of the band would be here, too.

"Mo, wait!" I shout and finally catch up to him on the steps leaving the house. "Just listen to me."

"Oh, I'd love to hear what you have to say," Mohammed sneers, and it cuts deeper than I expect it to. "That was your dad, wasn't it? Jhilmil Sarkar? A&R coordinator at Ripple Records?"

I feel lightheaded. "No! I mean, yes, but you don't—"

"What kind of sick game are you playing?" Mohammed asks in disgust. "You've been messing with our band this entire time!"

"That's not true!" I say, and then wince when I realize we're still standing in the open doorway. I've already caused a scene once today. Twice is a bit much, even for me.

I grab the sleeve of his kurta and pull him farther outside, toward the swing set in the side garden.

"Let go of me," Mohammed says, pulling his arm out of my grasp. At least he doesn't go running for the hills. "You have thirty seconds to explain or I'm leaving."

I shake my head desperately. "Mo, you don't understand, please—"

"Twenty seconds."

"Mo! I—" I suck in a deep breath. "Okay. Yes, my dad is Jhilmil Sarkar. I'm sorry, okay? I don't—" My head is *pounding*, but I can sense I'm losing Mo with each word. "It—it was Thomas!"

"Thomas?" Mohammed asks skeptically.

God, why is this *happening*?

"Yes, Thomas. I—Thomas lied to me. I told you Thomas lied to me. I just didn't… I didn't explain to what extent. He told me he wrote all the songs and that you guys were taking credit for it and that he wanted to leave the band but he was scared you'd be mad at him, and he said you and Sky and the others were all awful to him and that it would be even worse if he brought up going solo, and I just felt so *bad* and I really liked him and I didn't know better so I offered to give his demo to my dad, which was the biggest fucking mistake of my life but me and my dad have a really shitty relationship if you couldn't tell and—"

"Take a breath," Mohammed says, gripping my shoulder. "Hey, Lia, breathe."

I take a breath so fast I almost heave. "I'm sorry, I'm sorry, I—"

I swallow painfully. I can't have an anxiety attack right now. "My dad liked Thomas' demo and Thomas was so *happy* and I thought I was doing a good thing but then you guys showed up and it turned out it was all a lie and Thomas never even *liked* me, he was just using me because he knew who my father was, and I'm so fucking stupid that I didn't realize and I've been trying so—"

"Lia, *breathe*," Mohammed says again, and I feel like sobbing.

"I don't—" When the tears come, I don't even attempt to stop them. "I'm sorry. I've been trying so hard to make up for it, to help you guys however I can. I've devoted my entire summer to it. I've been giving Riya half my paycheck so you guys can rehearse in the basement and I've been trying to help build Third Eye's brand and I've been gathering intel from Ripple Records on what Thomas is doing and how we can stay ahead of him and I've—" I hiccup. "I never meant for this to happen, Mo. Please believe me."

Mohammed stares at me for a long moment. "You should've told us."

"I couldn't," I say helplessly. "You guys would've never let me help you if you knew."

"Why didn't you go to your dad and tell him the truth?" Mohammed asks, and I don't have an answer, not when my dad's disappointment is a visceral ache in my chest right now.

"I'm sorry," I say instead, scrubbing at the warm tears on my face. "I'm so sorry."

"You have to come clean to the others," Mohammed says, and I shake my head vehemently. "No, Liana, you have to."

"Mo, I *can't*. Sky will never let me help you. You know

how insanely protective he is of Third Eye and how hurt he is about Thomas. He barely let me help you in the first place!"

"You can't keep lying to them!" Mohammed says, his voice rising to meet mine. "They think you're their friend!"

"I *am*," I say, and the words feel so heavy. "I am their friend. Mohammed, please. Please keep my secret. I'll tell them after the Light The Way, okay? I swear. But I can't tell them now. Sky will flip out. You know I'm right."

Mohammed sets his jaw. "He would only flip out because he loves us. Because he can't *fathom* someone going back on their word. Because he values loyalty above all else."

I want to claw my eyeballs out so they'll stop fucking leaking. "I didn't know you! I would've never hurt any of you on purpose. It was an honest mistake."

"It doesn't matter if it was an honest mistake. What matters is that you've been lying to us day in and day out since then," Mohammed says coldly. "Thomas betraying us was bad enough."

The comparison to Thomas feels like a knife to the chest.

"Mohammed, please," I say, and if these weren't Ma's clothes, I would get down on my knees in the dirt and beg. "Just until Light The Way. I swear to you I'll tell them afterward. If I don't, you can. Just give me until then."

He grinds his teeth and looks away from me. It takes several moments of aching silence before he nods shortly. "Fine. I won't tell them. *Only* until Light The Way."

"Only until Light The Way," I agree and wish it didn't feel like a death sentence.

PART THREE

And now that I left it all behind me
I'm flying high, I'm flying high

—Stray Kids, "Levanter"

41

BASIC INSTINCT—THE ACID

Things are incredibly awkward at the next band practice.

Mohammed is being *beyond* obvious that he's pissed off at me, and I'm dutifully ignoring him to no avail. Even Ethan has picked up on it and keeps staring between us with a question in his gaze.

"Mohammed," I say slowly. "It's simple. Just do the dance moves on beat."

Mohammed glares at me. "We're not dancers. Why should we have to dance?"

I pinch the bridge of my nose. "No one is asking you to be a professional dancer. This is *simple*. Everyone else has it down except for you."

"No one is going to become our fan because we do some stupid dance and upload it online," Mohammed says coldly.

I grit my teeth and try to hold in my frustration. He's mad. He's allowed to be mad. But God, all I'm trying to do is *help*.

"It's worked for other artists in the past," I say before gesturing at the others. "If you're having a hard time learning the dance, I'm sure someone will be happy to walk you through it."

Mohammed gives me a look full of disdain. "Fine."

He walks over to Sky, who's frowning at both of us, but immediately caters to Mohammed, putting a hand on his shoulder. "Yeah, I'll walk you through it."

Ethan sidles up to me and doesn't say anything, but it's obvious he wants to ask what's going on.

"Don't," I say quietly.

Ethan pouts. "Just tell me. I bet I can fix it."

I smile faintly at him. "Probably not this time. But thank you for wanting to help."

Vincent comes over to stand at Ethan's side, which I should have expected. Unlike Ethan, he doesn't bother asking what's wrong. "Is this going to be a problem?"

"No," I say and hope to God I'm right. "It'll be fine."

Vincent hums like he doesn't believe me, which is fair because *I* don't even fully believe me. But one thing about Vincent is that he knows how to mind his business and doesn't meddle, even as Mohammed continues to hit me with dry remark after dry remark.

I force myself to breathe through my increasing irritation. He knows why I did what I did. I *told* him. Being visibly angry in front of the others isn't going to help anyone or anything.

Eventually, I have to take a break. Unable to tolerate Mohammed's glare any longer, I offer to grab everyone boba and leave before anyone can attempt to join me.

I don't know what I'm supposed to do. I'm afraid to prod at Mohammed in case he decides to go back on his word and tell the others. Then I'll have *four* people who are pissed off and want nothing to do with me rather than just the one.

I'm already cried out after spending the weekend at home moping over my father. He didn't show his face once in that entire time. Sometimes it feels like I'm raising myself. I might as well just be a tenant in his home, given that our relationship feels more contractual than anything else.

I'm just so tired. I hate feeling like this all the time. I hate being whiny and broody and miserable.

When is it my turn to be happy? Will it ever be my turn? Or am I destined to be in this strange limbo state?

There has to be an end to this. But *when*?

My will to live grows weaker by the day. I wish that were a joke. I even called UCLA up the other day, checking to see if there was any way for me to start counseling sooner, all to no avail.

This next month is going to go by excruciatingly slowly.

When I come back with the bubble tea in tow, Riya clicks her tongue at me. "You look terrible."

"Thanks for that," I say caustically.

Riya's eyes widen and she mouths, *"Wow."* I look away, unable to deal with this right now and march back downstairs. Before I push the door open, I force myself to count backward from ten and *chill out*. We don't need two people losing their cool.

When I enter, Mohammed looks a little calmer, Sky's arm around his shoulders.

"Thanks, Liana," Sky says with a smile. Mohammed's expression sours a little, but at least he doesn't say anything as I pass around everyone's cups.

"No worries. Should we try filming that promotional video

again? I can set up the green screen," I say, gesturing to all my supplies in one corner of the room.

Ethan nods eagerly, jumping to his feet to help me. "Yeah, sounds good!"

Once everything is set up, I motion for them to all get in front of the tripod. "Okay, let's do this!"

Sky tugs Mohammed along with him, and the four of them get in front of the camera, following my instructions from earlier. At first, it seems like everything is going perfectly, but then Mohammed falters and forgets his move. He remembers a beat later, but it's too late, and I sigh, pausing the video.

"Mohammed, I really need you to get this timing right or it'll have a ripple effect and mess with everyone else's part."

"It'll have a *ripple* effect?" Mohammed repeats, but there's an entirely wrong emphasis on the sentence.

"Mohammed," I say, biting the inside of my cheek to keep myself in check. "Please, just run it again."

"I will," Mohammed says, but now there's a wolflike smile on his face that I don't like one bit. "You know why? Because I love this band more than anything. No matter how many stupid hoops you force me to jump through, I'll do it every time. Because of *them*."

A muscle in my cheek is twitching. "I'm also doing this for the band. I'm asking you to redo it because I want to make sure you have the best possible content. Mediocre is less than Third Eye deserves."

Mohammed scoffs and breaks away from the others. I try not to bury my face in my hands.

"Less than we deserve? You know what we deserve? We deserve to not *have* to do this. We shouldn't be in this position."

I grimace. "I agree with you, Mohammed. That's why I'm doing my best to help."

"You know, you're really not any better than any of us. You're *younger* than Sky and me, for that matter. Why is it you always talk down to us? Who died and made you boss?"

"I don't talk down to you," I say in disbelief. "And I never claimed to be better than any of you. Obviously, you all know more about music than I ever could, and I'd never deny that. But marketing is my *thing*. So I know a few things you might not, yeah, but that's because it's my literal area of expertise."

"Yeah? Based on what? You're not even in college yet. You think an internship is enough for you to advise us on our careers? Really?" Mohammed asks, and I can *see* the challenge in his eyes, daring me to admit who my father is and why I know as much as I do.

"It's better than nothing," I say sharply.

Mohammed sneers. "Is it, though?"

"I've doubled Third Eye's following on Instagram, your YouTube channel's subscribers are through the *roof*, your hashtag on Twitter is used regularly, and the turnout at your last show at Cannon Club was *packed*. So yeah, I think so," I say, matching his expression, my mouth curling.

"You think that any of that shit means anything?" Mohammed asks, and he takes a step closer to me, which seems to be Sky's last straw because he slips between us, shaking his head.

"Mo, calm down," he whispers before shooting me an apologetic glance. "We'll be right back."

He takes Mohammed's hand and pulls him out of the practice room without another word. When the door closes behind them, I slump, my knees buckling beneath me.

"Whoa! Whoa!" Vincent swoops in, grabbing my arm to keep me from falling to my knees. "Are you okay?"

"Sorry, I'm—" I shake my head as if to clear it. "Yeah, I'm okay."

Ethan comes up on my other side, wrapping an arm around my waist and helping me straighten up. "Doesn't seem like it, Lia."

"It's just..." I sigh and lean my weight against them, allowing them to support me. "I just want to help. You guys know that, right? I don't mean to come on too strong or too demanding."

"We don't think that," Ethan says, squeezing my waist before giving Vincent a pointed look. "Right, Vinny?"

Vincent grimaces but nods. "We know you're doing your best to help us. Sky wouldn't have let you in the room otherwise."

"Mohammed is just being silly," Ethan says as he leads me toward the couch. Vincent clears off Sky's sheet music, making room for me to sit down. "He must've woken up on the wrong side of the bed today. Don't mind him. I'm sure Sky will figure out a way to help him feel better."

I melt into the couch, covering my face with my hands. "I hope so, Ethan."

Sky has a way with his band members that I've never seen before. He knows exactly how to soothe them, how to placate them, how to cheer them up. He's perfectly attuned to their behavior, and if anyone can calm Mohammed down, it's him.

And if he can't, then I'm really fucked. There's no way I'll get through the rest of this summer with my secret intact if Mohammed keeps this up.

I put my faith in Sky's leadership qualities and hope for the best.

42

WONDERWALL—OASIS

Later, Mohammed has a shift at work, and Vincent and Ethan head out for what isn't a date but might as well be a date, leaving only me and Sky behind.

Sky sees Mohammed off to the door, and when he comes back, he's staring at me with a pointed expression.

"So do you want to explain what all that was about?" he asks.

"Not quite," I say, picking at the carpet threads. I've since moved from the couch, wanting to be out of the way. The rest of the day was left for actual band practice, all publicity set aside for the sake of some peace.

At this point, I'm running out of records to organize. With the exception of a few boxes, the entire basement has been cleaned out. I don't really have any business sticking around outside of when I'm helping them, but I find myself gravitating here anyway.

Something about this group feels comforting, even when

one of them is harboring intense dislike toward me. I don't know if that makes me crazy, but it's true.

I've never had a friend group quite like this before. I don't know if I ever will again.

Skyler sighs and sits down across from me. There are loose pages of sheet music around us, some crumpled, some whole. Sky's been cycling through them, testing out different melody and lyric combinations. I've done my best to leave him to it, even though my curiosity gets the best of me sometimes. All his lyrics are good, even the ones he throws away.

"Mohammed won't tell me what's going on, either," Sky says, frowning. "Do you know why that might be?"

At least there's that. A part of me was terrified Mohammed might just give in and tell Sky the truth, so it's a relief to hear that he kept his word and kept my secret.

"It's just—it's between us," I say, and shrug. "I don't really wanna talk about it."

Sky makes a disapproving noise. His eyes are dark but somehow still manage to shine under the basement lights, reminding me of tapioca pearls.

"Is it…" Sky starts and then immediately stops, biting his lip and considering his words. "Do you…"

"Spit it out," I say, nudging his foot with mine.

"Do you like him?" Sky says in a rush, barely coherent.

I blink. "Do I like Mohammed? I mean, yeah. Of course. He's being a dickhead right now, but yeah, I like him." Sky looks stricken and I frown at him. "I like all of you. Surely, you know that by now?"

"Oh." Sky's expression eases somewhat, but there's still tension in his facial muscles. "No, I mean…do you *like* like him?"

"*Like* like? Are you five years old?" I ask in disbelief. "Yeah, no. I definitely do not *like* like Mohammed." Then I huff a laugh in surprise. "Oh my God, did you think this was a couple fight? Sky, *no*."

Sky throws his hands up, but he looks a lot more at peace. I find myself smiling without really meaning to. He's so stupid. "How was I supposed to know?"

"Mohammed *definitely* would have told you that," I say with a rueful grin. "You're so dumb."

"Yeah, well." He shrugs, but as usual, the tips of his ears give him away, bright red. "Okay, fine, I won't get involved. But work it out, will you? It's cramping the vibe."

I roll my eyes. "I'll try, Sky. I'm not really enjoying it, either."

Sky sticks his tongue out, and I try not to have a heart attack at the sight of a piercing there. Oh my God, since *when* does Skyler have a tongue piercing?

I look away before I can incriminate myself staring at his mouth. What the fuck? That has to be new. Unless he had a clear one this entire time and finally switched it out for silver? But what—?

I cut off that line of thinking immediately. I don't need to know the background details of his tongue piercing. That is so far from my business.

"Dollar for your thoughts?" Sky asks.

"Real funny," I say, but when I turn toward him again, he's holding out a dollar. Something shifts and slides between my ribs, and I ignore it for the sake of my sanity. I take the bill, tucking it in my pocket. I still have the other one on my bedside table, and this one will join it. "What was the first song you ever learned on guitar?"

Sky's brows knit together. "*That* is what you were thinking about?"

"Yes," I say without missing a beat. It's a better alternative than saying *I was thinking about your tongue for reasons I cannot begin to explain.* "So what was it?"

"'Wonderwall' by Oasis, of course," Sky says, and it makes perfect sense. I can imagine his younger self strumming already. "I was six years old. My mom taught me."

For a moment, I want to ask more. I want to *know* more. About his mother, about his love for music, about everything there is to him, until I painfully rein it back in.

I don't need to know all of that. There's no reason to know all of that.

Especially if this is going to end in flames anyway.

"Can I ask you something, too?" Sky asks, pulling me away from my thoughts. I look over at him and nod without thinking but before biting the inside of my cheek when I realize I've given him a free pass. "When did your mom die? How long has it been?"

Right for the jugular. Clearly, Sky doesn't share my same reservations.

"You don't pull your punches," I say dryly but then I sigh, sinking to the floor. "Three years. What about you?"

Sky lies down beside me, his fingers brushing lightly against mine. The ceiling has random wet stains and is painted two different shades of white, but it's easier to look at than Sky right now.

"She died seven years ago," Sky says, his voice quiet. "It

feels like it's been forever but it also feels like it happened yesterday."

I let out a low laugh. "No, I get it. I'm starting to forget what her voice used to sound like, but I also can't really talk about her without wanting to bawl."

Skyler intertwines our hands, squeezing mine gently. "Sometimes it's good to let it all out."

"I can't afford to mess up my makeup," I say easily but then falter, realizing what I'm doing. I've taken to evading the topic of Ma when it comes up in conversation with others, even though I hate when Baba does the same thing to me. Talking about my mother is hard, but maybe with Sky, who *understands*, it'll be okay. "I miss her. A lot."

"Yeah, me, too," Sky says with a sigh. "But every now and then I get irrationally mad at her, too. And I know that's not fair to her. It's not like she *chose* to have a stroke. But she's still gone and I'm still here, you know? And I have to keep going, even when I don't want to."

There's a thick lump in the back of my throat. "I know what you mean. I—" I let out a long breath. "I feel bad even saying this, but I'm so angry with her sometimes. She left me alone with my dad, and he's…barely there."

"Grief does weird things to people," Sky says, brushing his thumb against my knuckles. "Not that it's an excuse. I'm sorry he isn't present more often."

"I've gotten used to it," I say with a thin smile. "It's nice to have this, though. Something to distract me from it all."

"No one really talks about how grieving doesn't have an end date," he murmurs. "I thought it would be over after a while, but I still feel heavy with it even now. I think I always will."

"Probably," I say, matching his volume. "And we'll spend the rest of our lives getting those weird, sympathetic, strained looks from other people every time we mention our mothers."

Sky snorts. "I can't stand it, honestly. For a while, I stopped bringing my mom up at all so I wouldn't have to deal with people pitying me."

I bite my lip, considering my words carefully, before finally saying, "I used to live in New York. That's where I'm from. But after Ma died, we moved here. I felt like I was going crazy back there, having everyone look at me so differently."

"Did a clean break help?"

"In some ways. But sometimes I remember my new house is completely untouched by my mother, and I feel sick at the thought I'm living somewhere she never will."

"She's still with you here," Sky says, using his free hand to tap my chest, right above my heart. "We're touching the world for them."

I release a shaky breath. "Yeah, I guess so. I suppose all we can do is keep living another day on their behalf. Even when it feels really, really hard."

Sky turns his head toward me. "It always feels hard."

"I know." The words feel more raw than they should, a little too honest. I sit up, pulling my knees to my chest. "Will you play 'Wonderwall' for me?"

He tilts his head quizzically but nods. He sits and leans over to stretch his arms out and grab at his guitar. His tank top rides up, revealing the strip of skin above his waistband, and I tear my gaze away.

Everything about this is getting too real. I don't know if I'm prepared to deal with any of it.

Skyler returns a moment later, guitar in hand, which is a small mercy. He starts strumming, and I close my eyes, basking in the sound of the music.

I don't expect him to start singing, but when he does, it's natural to join in. Baba was the one to show me this song, on a road trip from New York to Boston. Me, him, and Ma sang along way too loudly, the car's windows rolled down, and everything felt right in the world.

And here with Sky, it feels kind of like that, too.

43

HEAVEN IN HIDING—HALSEY

The audition for Light The Way requires an online submission. Third Eye is as ready as I can make them, so now it's all up to them and their music.

I place the tripods and check for stray wires or anything that might throw them off. Each of their phones is set up on an individual tripod to get angles of each of them while my phone is recording in the front to get a wide shot. Once I'm sure everything is ready, I motion for them to go ahead.

They're all dressed cohesively, in dark reds and blacks. Mohammed is wearing a leather jacket on top of a maroon shirt, tied together with black wide-flared jeans. Ethan is wearing a black shirt with slits down the side of his ribs and burgundy slacks. Vincent is wearing a red and black plaid shirt, the top button loose, tucked into a pair of black pants. And Sky, naturally, is wearing a cherry-colored tank top and black ripped jeans.

They look good. Put together.

Like a team.

Then I notice Sky's eyeliner is smudged, and not in the artful way he likes.

"Come here," I say, gesturing for him to come back. "Let me fix your makeup."

Sky sets down his guitar and walks back over to me. "What's wrong with my makeup?"

"Have you been rubbing your eyes?" I ask, and the guilty look on his face is answer enough. "Come on, I have some eyeliner in my purse."

He follows me to the couch, sitting down while I sift through my bag, trying to find where my makeup bag is. I don't wear it all that often, but I refuse to leave the house without it just in case. It's coming in handy now so I feel validated in that decision.

Once I finally find my liquid eyeliner and some makeup remover, I give it a little shake and gesture Sky closer as I sit down beside him. "Alright, stay still, okay?"

I wipe his eye first, making sure to get all traces of the smudge around the corners of his eyelid.

"Perfect," I say, checking over my work. "Now do *not* move. I don't wanna fuck it up a second time."

Sky nods at me in understanding, and I lean in, trying to figure out his eye shape. I frown, shifting back and forth in attempt to get the right angle before adjusting my posture, kneeling instead of sitting.

I move to do the upper lid first, but I can't get my arm to lie flat.

"Fuck," I say under my breath before leaning back. "Do you mind if I get closer?"

Sky blinks his eyes open. "Closer?"

If I think about this too much, I'm going to back out. I just have to do it and deal with the consequences later. Determinedly, I throw one of my legs over his lap and settle in between his knees. "Is this okay?"

His lips part in surprise but he nods, and his hands come to bracket either side of my hips, steadying me. "Yeah. 'Course."

I give him a stiff smile. "Okay, close your eyes."

Leaning in, I trace over the shape of his eye with one hand and hold his jaw still with the other. My tongue sticks out in concentration as I move to do the wing, smaller than I would do on myself but still noticeable enough to show up on camera.

Once I'm done with his upper lid, I shift slightly to do his under eye. It's lighter, more of a shadow, but it rounds out the look perfectly.

"There," I say, satisfied. "You're set."

Sky opens his eyes, and it hits me how close we are. His breath is cool and minty against my cheek, and my fingers are still pressing against his face.

I drop my hand immediately before slipping off his lap. Only now do I notice Ethan and Vincent snickering at us, and Mohammed watching with a frown.

"Right. Did you wanna check it over?" I ask, reaching for my bag to see if I have a compact mirror.

Sky stops me, gently placing a hand on my arm. "No, it's fine. I trust you."

I trust you.

I wish those three words didn't make me want to scream. I somehow smile past the nausea and follow him back to the others.

I walk around, clicking Record on each of their phones

after checking the angle is still good. I figure we can cut off the beginning where they're still adjusting, especially since I can't start all five phones at once.

"Okay, whenever you're ready," I say, circling back to the front and flashing them a thumbs-up.

Sky smiles at me before looking at the rest of his band. "Three, two, one, let's go!"

They start playing one of their new songs, "Lighter," and I bop my head along dutifully, having heard them rehearse it for the last week in preparation for the audition video.

It's easy to relate the idea of wanting to burn everything to the ground instead of dealing with it. I think the judges will agree, too.

It's also a fun song, easy to sing along to. Sky and Vincent sing the second verse into the same mic—though they each have their own—and grin the closer their faces get to each other.

I keep my snort to myself, not wanting to be caught on camera. We can't afford to have even a small slipup, not when so much is at stake.

I want them to win so badly it hurts.

The more they perform, the more obvious it gets. I've known it from the beginning. As good as their music is, as good together as they look, it's their chemistry that's going to open doors for them. The way they look at each other isn't something companies can fabricate, no matter how much they might want to.

It's hard to believe Thomas could leave this all behind.

44

HOPE UR OK—OLIVIA RODRIGO

Ethan has been avoiding spending time alone with me since the Fourth of July party last month. In group settings, we've been right as rain, but the moment I try to talk to him one-on-one, he goes running for the hills.

It's obvious that he doesn't want to talk about his songwriting or his relationship with Vincent, but I'm determined to sit him down and talk sense into him before Light The Way.

Especially since he might not want to ever talk to me again afterward.

One August evening, after my morning shift at the record shop is finished, I corner him on his way to the bathroom. It's a little devious, but I never claimed to play fair.

"Lia! What are you doing?" Ethan protests, scrambling to lock the door when I make a move to follow him inside.

"You and I need to talk," I say, narrowing my eyes, pushing my weight against the door to keep it open.

"Right *now*?" Ethan asks, high-pitched.

I shrug. "Up to you. Will you actually talk to me after you use the bathroom?"

Ethan pouts at me, but when I don't move, he finally nods. "Fine."

I ease up on my weight, making him take an uneven step back, door in hand. "Okay, great. I'll wait outside!"

He grumbles under his breath and I blow him a kiss, skipping over to the opposite wall to lean against while I wait for him.

Ethan loudly closes the door, but I'm unbothered.

When he finally comes back out, he refuses to meet my gaze. I sigh. I wish he would tell Sky, because I know Sky would give a *much* better pep talk than I'm about to.

"Come on, let's talk in the break room," I say, grabbing his hand.

"They're going to wonder where we are," Ethan says in an awful attempt to distract me.

"It's funny how I don't care," I say with a beatific shrug. Once we're finally on our own, I sit down across from him and meet his gaze evenly. "Have you talked to Sky about wanting to write songs yet?"

"Lia," Ethan whines, tugging at his shirt collar. "Can't you just leave this alone?"

"Nope," I say, popping the *p*. "You need to show him the song."

"What if he thinks it's bad?" he asks, and it's the same argument he made before, but this time, his voice cracks hopelessly on the last word.

And suddenly, whatever confidence I had coming into this discussion disappears. Ethan is *scared*.

"Ethan," I say softly, reaching out to take his hand in mine. "Sky loves you. He would never think something you put hard work and effort into is bad."

He shakes his head, blue eyes wide. "You don't know that."

"But I do," I say, squeezing his hand. "And so do you, if you let yourself think about it for more than five seconds. Imagine if Vincent or Mohammed wrote a song and showed it to you. Would you think it's bad off the bat?"

"No!" Ethan says, looking appalled. "Of course not."

"Then why do you think Skyler would do that to you?" I ask quietly. "You have to give him more credit than that."

Ethan bites his lip instead of answering, but his grip is tight on my hands.

"And I know you don't want to talk about this, but—you should consider telling Sky about you and Vincent, too."

"He'll want us to do what makes us happy," Ethan says, shaking his head. "No matter what it might cost the band."

I sigh. "I can't promise it won't cost you anything, but you have to consider that it might be a price the band is willing to pay. You can't decide for them."

"I don't want them to sacrifice anything for me," Ethan whispers.

"Maybe they don't want you to sacrifice anything for them, either," I say, matching my tone to his. "Talk to Sky, please."

Ethan lets go of my hand to rub at his eyes. His blond lashes are wet with tears.

There's a knock on the door and both of us look up in alarm. Before either of us can scramble to hide, someone pushes the door open.

"What's the hold-up—?" Vincent cuts off immediately at

the sight of Ethan, and his face crumples. In a second, he's on his knees in front of Ethan, reaching up to brush away his tears. "Hey, what's wrong?"

"Liana thinks we should tell Sky…about us," Ethan says, and the words are choked.

Vincent looks at me for only half a second before turning back at Ethan. "But why are you crying, sweetheart?"

"I can't—you know we can't tell Sky. He'll throw away the entire band for our happiness. And that's not fair. Thomas already tried to ruin everything. We can't—after everything Sky has done for us, we can't—" He hides his face behind his hands, shoulders shaking with quiet sobs.

Vincent pulls him into a hug, whispering something in his ear that I can't hear. Our eyes meet over Ethan's shoulder and I give him a pleading look, holding my hands together. Maybe he can talk some sense into Ethan.

"Hey," Vincent says, pulling back and gently pressing a kiss below Ethan's eye. "I know we agreed to keep our distance for the sake of the band, but I don't—I think Liana might have a point."

Ethan startles, peering up at Vincent with wide blue eyes. "What? But…but we agreed."

"We did," Vincent says, placing another soft kiss beneath Ethan's other eye. "But we agreed right after Thomas left, when things were fresh and painful. Maybe it's possible we both jumped to the worst conclusion?"

"You want to tell Sky?" Ethan whispers. "You really want to?"

Vincent smiles sadly at him. "If even *Liana* thinks we

should, I think it's fair to say it's worth at least talking about with him."

I blink. "Why'd you say my name like that?"

Vincent glances at me. "I didn't mean anything bad by it. Just that you're so obsessed with all the image and brand stuff, you know? So if we have your seal of approval, talking to Sky doesn't seem like that bad of an idea."

"Right," I say, and do my best to ignore how terrible the words make me feel. "Totally."

Vincent returns his attention to Ethan, resting his forehead against the younger boy's. "Let's go talk to Sky, yeah?"

Ethan swallows, his Adam's apple bobbing nervously, before he nods. "Okay. Let's go talk to him."

They leave with their fingers intertwined, and I don't follow them, waving them off and saying it's a conversation for the band.

Only after they're gone do I let myself linger on Vincent's words. Does he think I'd choose marketing over my *morals*? Is that what they all think? I chose this career to help people, to help them show off the best version of themselves. How could he even say something like that?

And then I think about what I'm doing—lying to them to help win this competition—and feel slightly ill.

Maybe he's not wrong. Maybe this is who I am.

It's a sickening thought.

45

DON'T DWELL.—BARNACLE BOI

Sky loves Ethan's song. It comes as a surprise to no one except Ethan, who is slack-jawed at Sky's praise.

It's also *achingly* obvious the song is about Vincent, especially now that they're officially dating.

Mohammed pretends to gag, but even he's grinning widely as he looks at the lyrics over Sky's shoulder.

I sit on the couch and don't contribute much to the conversation, busy filtering through the Instagram Q&A I'm holding on the official Third Eye band account. It's been getting a good amount of traction, over forty questions so far, though one of them is from *Sky* asking me if I'll go on a date with him because he's nothing if not insufferable.

"Vincent, how many cats do you have?" I ask, lifting the phone to take a candid photo of him.

He blinks at the camera. "Two."

"Great, thanks," I say, and turn back to my phone without another word. The follower count is slowly climbing as I answer more and more questions.

Things have been *slightly* better between Mohammed and me, mostly because we're avoiding each other. But when it comes to things like this, I can't exactly afford to ignore him.

With an internal sigh, I say, "Mohammed, what's your favorite dessert?"

"Gulab jamun," he says, and I nod. His voice is terse, but at least he's answering.

"Thank you," I say and take a picture of him sprawled across Sky's back. "What's everyone's star signs?"

They all look at me blankly, and I remember they're teenage boys.

"Okay, when is everyone's birthday?" I amend, switching to the notes app to make sure I don't lose track.

"I'm February second, Mo is April twenty-ninth, Vinny is December seventeenth, and Ethan is September sixth," Sky rattles off without pause. All of the other members look at him with so much affection that it overflows into the room around us, thick and palpable.

"Aquarius, Taurus, Sagittarius, and Virgo. Got it," I say, typing it all down. "Thank you."

"When's your birthday?" Sky asks, and when I look up, he's watching me with a small smile.

"August sixteenth," I say. "I'm a Leo."

"That's so soon!" Ethan says, bouncing in his seat. "Less than two weeks away!"

His joy is infectious. I find myself smiling without meaning to. "Yours is close, too," I say. "Next month, yeah?"

Ethan grins. "One year closer to legally drinking."

"You're ridiculous," I say, laughing. "Go back to focusing on your song."

Ethan shrugs, but does as he's told. I make a note-to-self to buy Ethan alcohol for his next birthday as I lie down on the couch. I scroll through my notes app, passing by my copy of Mohammed's schedule for the month. Then I slowly scroll back up.

I glance at the time and scramble to sit up. "Mo, don't you have a shift right now?"

Mohammed gives me a bemused look before understanding dawns and he jumps to his feet. "Oh shit. Yeah, thanks, I—" Then he remembers he's talking to me and his expression darkens. "Right, I'm gonna go. I'll see you guys later."

The others nod and watch him go with a wave. I frown after him. How am I keeping better track of his schedule than he is?

That night, when Sky shows up at the counter, dangling his car keys in front of me, I shake my head. Our late night drives have slowly become somewhat of a ritual, but I have something more pressing to take care of tonight. "Could you drop me off at Mo's restaurant?"

Sky tilts his head. "That's in the opposite direction of your home."

"I know," I say but when Sky doesn't say anything else, I backtrack. "If you can't, I'm sure Riya Apu will take me. Don't worry about it, sorry I asked."

"No, no, of course I'll do it," Sky says immediately, eyes wide. "I was just—why do you need to see Mohammed?"

I tug at a lock of hair and shrug. "It's about our...fight. I think I need to clear the air."

Sky's eyebrows furrow. "You two still haven't sorted it out?"

I shake my head. "It's kind of a…situation."

"…Right," Sky says but walks to the front door, holding it open for me. "Better get to it, then."

The drive is quiet aside from my playlist of the day.

for when the thoughts get a little too intrusive:

Anti-Hero—Taylor Swift
Rescue—James Bay
Grow As We Go—Ben Platt
Exhale—Sabrina Carpenter
Take on the World—You Me At Six
Beggin For Thread—Banks
Lonely St.—Stray Kids
When I Watch The World Burn All I Think About Is You—Bastille
Darlin—Avril Lavigne
A Little Braver—New Empire

When Sky pulls up in front of the restaurant, I force myself to take a deep breath. I'm not looking forward to this one bit, but what choice do I have?

"Thank you, Sky," I say, touching a hand to his wrist. "I'll see you tomorrow."

"Are you sure you don't want me to wait?" Sky asks, glancing at the restaurant with a frown. There are a few stragglers inside, but it's closing up soon, which is good timing for me.

"Nah, I'll grab an Uber home when I'm done here," I say, and give Sky an earnest smile. "Thank you. Really."

I unplug my phone and hop out of the car, bracing myself for this conversation. I can do this.

46

I CAN'T STOP ME—TWICE

The second Mohammed and I lock eyes, I realize how badly I do *not* want to do this.

"Are you here to put in an order?" Mohammed asks, but his posture is defensive, like he already knows the answer.

"I'll put one in," I agree and force the next few words out, "but I'm here to talk to you. Do you have any time?"

Mohammed grimaces. "What would you like to order?"

I give him an exasperated look. "Two chicken biryanis. Mo, please, just ten minutes."

He doesn't say anything, clicking buttons on the screen, before holding his hand out. I give him a twenty-dollar bill and wait for him to *look* at me.

Finally, he hands me back my receipt and meets my eyes. "Sit at the corner table next to the sunflower painting. I'll be there in a few minutes."

I release a relieved breath. "Sounds good. Thank you."

There are no other customers on my side of the restaurant,

which is probably why Mohammed said to sit here in the first place. I take a seat and absentmindedly watch the candle in front of me, the flame flickering.

As promised, a few minutes later, Mohammed slides into the seat across from me, apron thrown over his shoulder. "What is it?"

"I wanted to talk about my dad," I say and he blinks at me, taken aback. All my words feel thick and syrupy, reluctant to leave my mouth, but there's no other way to establish an understanding with Mohammed aside from the truth.

"What about your dad?" Mohammed asks slowly.

"The only reason I'm telling you any of this is because I'm trusting you to get it," I say slowly. "I don't want to hear some stupid white-savior-type lecture."

Mohammed rolls his eyes. "Get on with it, Liana."

"To put it bluntly, he's not a good father," I say and ignore the stab of guilt that comes with those words. "Ever since my mom died, he's been AWOL and doesn't give a shit about what I do unless it's related to his career. And you know what his job is."

Mohammed's mouth presses into a thin line. "Okay…"

"So I've been breaking my back to follow in his footsteps," I say and cringe at the words. "Sue me, but I want someone in my family to give a shit about me, and he's all I have."

"I don't know why you're telling me this," Mohammed says, but he's starting to look less annoyed and more uncomfortable. Of course, he's the type that can't handle any show of emotion. Teenage boys are so *ridiculous*. Still, uncomfortable is the better option of the two. "What about Ayesha?"

"Ayesha is great, but you know that's not what I meant," I say, matching his use of Riya's bhalo nam. "Your parents love you. You've said it over and over. I don't know if my dad loves me. I think he did once, when my mom was still alive, but those days are long gone, and I don't know if he ever will again. But a stupid part of me wants him to, so I try every day to be the daughter he wants me to be. I'm telling you because I need you to understand why I did what I did."

Mohammed's discomfort has spread to the rest of his body. His hands are playing with the tablecloth and his shoulders are hunched. "Okay…"

"So I can't tell him the truth about Thomas' demo. I can't disappoint him like that. The same way you can't disappoint your parents by dropping out of college to run off and be in Third Eye."

Mohammed shakes his head. "That's not the same."

"Yes, it quite *literally* is," I say. "And I know, I *know* how much you love Third Eye. But it doesn't matter, does it? If you had to choose, you know which you would pick."

"That's not—" Mohammed's mouth pinches.

"Isn't it?" I ask. "What would you do if I walked into the kitchen right now and told your parents what you do with all your free time?"

His eyes widen. "You can't do that."

"I know. I don't have any intention of doing that," I say. "But it scares you that I could, doesn't it? That you could disappoint them? They actually love you unconditionally, and you're still scared of letting them down. I'm right, aren't I? Be honest."

Mohammed doesn't answer, which is an answer in and of itself.

"So, yeah, I lied to you guys," I say, leaning back in my seat. "But that doesn't mean I don't care. And it doesn't mean I'm not trying to fix it."

"Two biryani!" a man calls from the counter. Then he spots me and Mohammed and raises his brows. "Mo, is this a friend of yours?"

I stare at Mohammed, waiting to hear his answer. Mohammed looks down at his hands and lets out a loud sigh. "Yeah, Baba. This is Liana."

Mohammed's dad's face brightens. "Is this your order? Consider it on the house."

I shake my head. "No, that's okay, really, I already paid."

"Next time, then," his dad says, and some part of me aches at the warm way he looks at Mohammed. "Mo, you should've told us one of your friends was coming!"

"Sorry, Baba. She's leaving now, but I'll tell you when she stops by again," Mohammed says, giving his dad an apologetic look.

His dad waves him off. "No worries, batcha. I'll see you around, Liana, yes?"

I manage a smile. "Yes, sir."

Mohammed's dad grins before disappearing into the kitchen.

I turn back to Mohammed, giving him an uncertain look. "So are we good? Can we stop fighting?"

"I guess," Mohammed mutters. "You swear you'll tell them after Light The Way?"

I nod. "I swear."

Mohammed nods, and something in my heart eases.

I stand to grab my order off the counter but wait for a beat. "For what it's worth, I don't think you'd disappoint them if you told them the truth. Or even if you asked for less shifts."

"Yeah," Mohammed says, "Well."

I smile sadly. "Yeah. Well."

47

THE MOMENT I KNEW—TAYLOR SWIFT

My dad forgets my birthday.

I ring it in at midnight on the phone with Evie, who promises my gift should arrive by the late afternoon but refuses to tell me what it is no matter how many times I pester her.

Once we finally hang up, I leave my room to wander the house. I didn't hear my dad come in, but he must have at some point since his shoes are near the front door.

I tiptoe through the kitchen, dining room, living room, and study, but there's no sight of him anywhere on the first floor. I frown and go back upstairs, Willow following me.

The door to his room is closed, the lights off.

I swallow past the sudden lump in my throat. Maybe he'll wish me happy birthday in the morning.

If nothing else, we've always celebrated this day together. When Ma was alive, we would go to an amusement park and ride all the roller coasters together. In the years since she passed away, my father and I have opted for a more chill day eating In-N-Out and sitting by the beach in Malibu.

Baba hasn't said anything to me about our plans, but I have to believe he remembers.

I don't see Baba before he leaves for work. He doesn't say a word to me, whether in person or over text. I try not to sulk about it.

Maybe he's waiting until the time I was born, at four in the afternoon. That has to be it. He'll come pick me up and we'll head to Malibu together then.

I go to the record shop like usual, clocking in for my 10:00 a.m. shift. Riya greets me at the door with a bright grin. "Happy birthday," she says, pulling me into a hug. "I've got your gift in the back room."

A small smile graces my lips. "Thanks, Riya Apu. I'll check after work."

I slide behind the counter and turn on my customer voice just as someone comes up to me, asking about the latest Kendrick Lamar album.

By the time 4:00 p.m. rolls around, my shift is done, and I have not had a single text from my father. "He forgot."

Riya frowns at me. "I'm sure he didn't forget, Bibi."

"He did," I say, certain of it. "He hasn't said anything to me all day."

"Maybe he's just busy," she says, squeezing my shoulder. "He still has the rest of the day, doesn't he?"

"He's always busy," I say and wish my voice didn't tremble. Riya sighs, pulling me into my second hug of the day. "Ma never forgot."

"Bibi, sweetie," Riya murmurs, smoothing a hand down my hair. "I'm sorry."

I suck in a deep breath and force myself to get it together. I'm at work. I can't have a mental breakdown here, even if Riya is my boss and wouldn't care either way.

I pull away, wiping at my face and fanning my eyes until I'm sure I won't tear up again. "It's fine. No big deal. I can have In-N-Out any day."

Riya gives me a sad look. "Bibi…"

I paste a smile on my face. "No, I'm good. See?"

She crosses her arms, leaning her hip against the counter. "Really, Bibi?"

"Really," I say and take off my name tag. "I'm gonna go downstairs and see what the boys are up to."

Riya's forehead wrinkles. "They're not here. I didn't see them come in this morning."

I blink. "What do you mean? Where are they?"

She shrugs a shoulder. "They didn't say anything to me. I thought you knew."

"No, I didn't," I say and it's just another thing to add to the list of things going wrong today. "I… Okay. I'm going to grab your gift from the back and then head home, then."

Riya's expression is heavy with pity, and I can't look at it for too long. I make my way to the back room and rip open the neat wrapping around my gift.

"New headphones," I say, holding them close to my chest. At least someone in California cares enough to get me a gift. "Thank you, Riya Apu."

"Yeah, of course, Bibi," she says and pulls me into my third, and probably final, hug of the day. "Happy birthday again."

★ ★ ★

When my Lyft pulls up in front of my house, I hesitate long enough that the driver turns to look at me in confusion.

I get out quickly and watch him drive away before glancing back at my house. There's no car in the driveway, so Baba isn't home, not that I expected him to be.

At least Willow will be there. And maybe if Evie isn't busy, I can FaceTime her again. If she is, I'll find some way to occupy myself. It'll probably involve DoorDashing a cake from Paris Baguette and crying, but that's neither here nor there.

I sigh. Might as well accept my fate.

I walk up my driveway, pulling my keys out of my bag, but then fall short at the sight of rose petals in front of my door. They lead away from the door, past the garden, and down the side of my house, toward the backyard.

My pulse picks up. Did Baba remember? Maybe he wanted to change things up this year?

I start following the path slowly, still not believing the rose petals are really there until I pick one up and it's soft to the touch.

With a gentle shove, I push open the gate to the backyard.

"Surprise!" and confetti explodes into the air.

I jump, startled by all the noise. When I finally gather my bearings, I realize Third Eye is standing in front of me holding a massive cake.

"What—?" I say, but before I can finish my sentence, they start singing, harmonies and all. Vincent even goes full falsetto at the end.

"Happy birthday to you! Happy birthday to you! Happy birthday, dear Liana! Happy birthday to you!"

"You guys," I say and promptly burst into tears.

"Oh God, she's crying," Ethan says, eyes wide in alarm. "Did we do something wrong?"

"Just hug her, idiot," Mohammed says as he moves to set down the cake.

"Oh!" Ethan charges toward me, arms open, and I don't even try to dodge him. "Happy birthday, Lia!"

The others join the hug immediately afterward, smothering me on all sides while I cry helplessly.

"Happy birthday, Liana," they all say, squeezing me tighter than I've ever been squeezed before. I nearly whimper. Sky reaches up between all of our bodies to gently wipe away my tears.

I hiccup on a sob, and he strokes his thumb across my cheekbone.

"Did you think we forgot?" Sky asks quietly. "Of course, we didn't."

"We would never," Ethan adds, squeezing his arms around my shoulders for emphasis.

"Thank you," I say, the words choked.

Vincent knocks his head into mine lightly. "You're welcome."

"It's the least we could do," Mohammed adds, tugging on a lock of my hair. "Now stop crying, will you?"

I sniffle and try to put an end to my tears, but it's harder than expected. "I'm s-sorry, I don't—" My voice trembles too much for me to finish the sentence.

"Oh, darling," Sky says and leans down to brush a kiss against my forehead. "Happy birthday."

48

HOME
—EDWARD SHARPE & THE MAGNETIC ZEROS

Once I've calmed down, I realize they've decorated my entire backyard for the occasion. There are poles set up on either side, holding up a huge banner that says *HAPPY BIRTHDAY, LIANA!* and the birthday cake is set up on a foldable table in the middle of my yard. There are also snacks and drinks, and four separate gifts bags waiting for me.

On top of that, they're all wearing silly birthday hats, and they strap one to my chin the moment I stop hiccupping so badly.

"I can't believe you thought we would forget," Ethan says, shaking his head. "We don't miss birthdays around here."

I smile wetly at him. "Thank you, Ethan."

"Come on, cut the cake," Mohammed says, leading me to the table. "It's red velvet."

I wipe my tears with the back of my hand and nod. I can't

believe they put in all this effort. It feels like some kind of hallucination, or a dream that I've yet to wake up from.

"You guys didn't have to do all this," I say, looking at the eighteen candles circling the outline of the cake.

"Yes, we did," Vincent says, handing me a plastic knife. "Go on."

"Don't forget to make a wish," Sky says, coming to stand by my side and squeeze my hand. "Or eighteen wishes, even."

Do I even have eighteen things I want in life?

Right now, all I want is to live in this moment forever. This moment where people who care about me are surrounding me, staring at me with warmth. But I can't wish for that—not when I already know there's an expiration date.

But then what? What do I wish for?

Whatever it is, it should be worth eighteen wishes.

I wish for happiness, I decide, *in whatever form it might be.*

I lean down and blow out the candles, making sure to get each single one.

"Yay!" Ethan cheers, and I finally allow myself to release the tension brewing inside me. "Happy birthday!"

"Thank you," I say again and finally cut into the cake.

Mohammed takes over a second later, cutting up five slices with a practiced ease that can only come from working at a restaurant. He carefully places them into the plastic bowls Vincent gives him, and Ethan adds utensils before passing them around.

"I can't believe you did all this," I say when everyone takes a seat at the table, Mohammed and Sky dragging up some of the lawn chairs on the back patio. "You guys are supposed to be practicing."

"Fuck practicing," Vincent says easily. "Your birthday comes once a year. We can afford a day off."

"But still," I say, my cheeks flushing with something akin to joy. "A surprise party is a lot of work."

"And we were happy to do it," Mohammed says, which means a lot coming from him. He must know because he shoots me a tentative smile. "Really, it was nothing."

"The neighbors could have called the cops on you," I say after a moment, amusement bubbling up in me. "I can't believe you broke into my backyard."

"You don't exactly have intensive security," Vincent says, pointedly glancing at the gate. Only a hook keeps it in place. "We asked your friend before we did anything, anyway."

"My friend?" I repeat.

"Evie," Ethan says with a sheepish grin. "We swapped numbers during the Fourth of July, so I sent her a text to make sure this would be alright."

Immediately, I grab my phone. Predictably, there's a dozen texts from Evie revealing her part in this. Oh my God, I should have known when she refused to tell me what my gift was yesterday.

"I can't believe this," I say honestly. "I've never had a surprise birthday party before."

"There's a first for everything," Mohammed says, holding out a plastic cup filled with apple juice. "Here's to another year around the sun."

We all raise our glasses, clinking against his, and warmth settles comfortably between my ribs. They really didn't have to do this for me, but they *wanted* to. It's obvious in the way pride puffs out all their chests.

"Let me see the gifts," I say, setting down my bowl to make grabby hands at the bags farther down the table.

Vincent stands and snags them, depositing them in front of me before sitting down. "Open them in rainbow order," he says, which is a weird thing to say, but I roll with it.

Pulling the red bag closer, I reach inside to take out a wrapped box. "Whose is this?"

Vincent raises his hand, which explains his instructions. I roll my eyes fondly but rip into the gift, which turns out to be a bunch of cat toys.

"So you got my cat birthday gifts instead of me," I say with a grin.

"Yes," he says but then he shrugs, looking a little embarrassed. "You mentioned your cat a few times, so I thought it might come in handy. I never have enough toys for mine, because they somehow *always* get lost, so… But let me know if you want a gift receipt."

"Are you kidding? No, I love it," I say, giving the toys a pat for good measure. "Thank you, Vinny."

He waves me off, and my grin widens.

I reach for the green bag next, since the other two are blue and pink.

"That would be mine," Ethan says, leaning closer to see my reaction.

Inside is another box, but this one is wrapped a *lot* worse. When I finally manage to rip it off, it reveals a perfume set.

"Is this your way of telling me I smell?" I ask with raised brows.

"Yes," he says before bursting into giggles, unable to maintain the lie for more than a few seconds. "Sorry. No, of course not, Lia. I don't have sisters or anything, so I googled some gift ideas. Is it alright?"

"It's perfect," I say, reaching across the table to squeeze his hand. "Thank you, Ethan."

"Blue is mine," Mohammed says preemptively, gesturing to the smallest bag on the table. "Try not to pass out from how incredible it is."

I snort. "Setting the standard high, huh?"

I reach inside the bag to find an envelope and nothing else. I pull it out, brows furrowed. "Is it just money?"

"Open it," Mohammed says, rolling his eyes.

With a nail, I rip open the side of the envelope and pull out the contents. It's a thick stack of paper, but not money. Coupons.

For Dear Paneer.

My lips part in surprise when I realize they're all for free meals. "Mohammed…"

"You're welcome," he says, trying to appear indifferent, but his eyes are tracking my facial movements.

I shake my head fondly. He knows how often I order from his restaurant. "Thank you. Really."

He shrugs. "No big deal."

Finally, I pull the pink bag closer to me. Sky doesn't bother announcing it's his. Process of elimination makes it obvious, but even if it didn't, his hopeful gaze would be impossible to miss.

"Be careful," he says when I move to unwrap the thin package inside.

I raise my brows but take extra caution when I slowly peel

off the wrapping, realizing what's inside is made of some sort of glass.

With a tug, the rest of the wrapping comes off, revealing a glass plaque. It looks like a screenshot off Spotify and written across in bold white font is:

LIANA AHMED
THIRD EYE

Above the words, it's a picture of all five of us. It was taken a few weeks ago, when Ethan pulled me into the shot and set it on a self-timer. Vincent is on Sky's back, Ethan is clinging onto me like a baby koala, and Mohammed has one arm wrapped around Ethan's neck and the other around Skyler's, pulling us all together while we burst into laughter.

I stare at the last name on the plaque for a beat too long. This gift is for Liana Ahmed, a girl who doesn't exist.

"Scan it," Sky says, gesturing to the QR code right underneath the photo of us.

Almost robotically, I take out my phone and scan the code. It opens up Spotify, leading to the song "Home" by Edward Sharpe & The Magnetic Zeros.

"I set it to a specific time," Sky says, his eyes sparkling. "I bought it, but it's really a gift from all of us. We chose it together."

I drag the cursor until 0:35 on "Home" and press Play, and then immediately will myself not to cry *again*.

"If we had a song called Liana Ahmed, it would probably sound a lot like this," Sky says softly. I wish it didn't hurt as much as it does. *Liana Sarkar*, I want to say, but I can't.

"Thank you," I whisper before looking up at all of them, lashes wet. "Can I have a hug?"

In less than a moment, all four of them are surrounding me, squeezing me so tightly I can barely breathe.

And it feels a lot like home.

49

WRONG—EDEN

A few days later, all five of us gather around my laptop, waiting anxiously for 3:00 p.m. to hit. I refresh the Light The Way music competition website again, even though there's still two minutes to go.

"I just want to know already," Mohammed groans, burying his face against Sky's arm. "Couldn't they have told us *last* week? Why would they wait until there's only a week left before the competition to announce who's competing?"

"To build tension," I say, but there's a frown on my face. "If they announce it too early, the hype could fade."

"Stop being so logical," Vincent says, his head on Ethan's lap.

I reach over to flick his forehead. "I'm just explaining their side of things."

Vincent rolls his eyes and I roll mine right back.

"Catfight," Ethan teases.

Vincent and I both immediately simmer down. I offer

Ethan a sheepish smile while Vincent presses a kiss to Ethan's wrist bone in apology.

I turn back to the screen and refresh again. One minute left.

Sky is biting his lip so hard I'm afraid he's going to break through the skin. His hands are on my shoulders, tapping out an anxious beat that's far too relatable.

"God, *how* is a minute this long?" Mohammed says, dragging his fingers down his face. "I feel like I'm gonna die."

"You'll be okay," Sky says, his voice as steady as ever, even with the visible tension in his frame. "It's not the end of the world if we don't get in."

"It might be!" Mohammed says.

"Shhh," I say, holding a finger to my lips. I'm anxious as well, but I have a lot more practice at hiding the fact my nerves feel like a live wire. "Thirty seconds."

We all watch my screen with bated breath, and when the clock finally strikes three, I hit refresh again. The page turns white, loading and loading and *loading*.

Finally, it loads.

I scroll immediately, ignoring all the unfamiliar faces in favor of finding the photo of Third Eye I submitted weeks ago.

As I move further down the page, Thomas' face passes by, and Sky's hands stiffen on my shoulders. No one says anything, but the tension in the room skyrockets.

Just as I approach the bottom, I spot the picture I took of all four of them, immediately followed by *THIRD EYE*, and I exhale in relief.

Thank *God*.

"You made it!" I say and let out a loud whoop in celebration. "Guys, you made it!"

"Holy shit!" Ethan yells, jostling Vincent in his lap, though he doesn't seem to mind. "We're in!"

"We're in!" Mohammed shouts, jumping up and down in disbelief, clapping his hands. "We're gonna compete in Light The Way!"

"I can't believe it," Vincent says, eyes wide with shock. He only breaks out of it when Ethan plants a chaste kiss on his mouth in celebration.

I lean my head all the way back so I can look at Sky above me. He's staring at the screen with the widest smile I've ever seen, his hands clasped to his chest.

"You made it," I say again, softer this time. "Congratulations."

Sky looks down at me, and I match his smile without even trying. He's so beautiful when he's happy. I'm finding it harder and harder to deny that I'm growing feelings for him. "I can't believe it," he says.

"Well, you better," I reply, reaching up to tap his nose, right on the beauty mark. "We should decide what songs you're going to have on the set list, and which outfits—"

"Oh my God, Liana, some time to celebrate, *please*," Vincent says with a laugh, finally sitting up and pulling Ethan to his side.

"If it's possible, turn off the PR brain for like two seconds," Mohammed agrees, sliding in beside Ethan.

I furrow my brows. "No, I wasn't... Of course, you should celebrate. But the competition is only a week away, we need to start thinking about—"

"Stop thinking," Ethan says, leaning over Vincent to gently clap a hand over my mouth. "Let's just enjoy."

"Okay," I say, the word muffled. I wish I could say I can't *afford* to stop thinking. After this week, I might not be able to ever help them again.

Ethan grins and Sky tucks himself into the space beside Mohammed, all of them falling into an enthusiastic cuddle pile.

And in the midst of all the excitement, I grapple with the fact that in just a few days, I'm going to have to tell them the truth about who I am and what I did.

Chills run up my spine at the thought.

When I finish my closing shift, I realize Sky hasn't come upstairs yet. He's usually on time these days. It's rare for me to have to grab him out of the basement.

"Riya Apu, I'm going downstairs!" I call.

"Tell lover boy I said hello!" Riya says back, because of course she does. Her and Evie have joined forces to convince me Sky has feelings for me, my birthday being the proverbial nail in the coffin.

"I will not," I say sweetly, and make my way downstairs.

When I push the door to the practice room open, I find Sky lying on the ground, his journal splayed open in front of him. At the sound of my entrance, he scrambles up, shoving it behind him.

I raise my brows. "Hiding something?"

"No," Sky says unconvincingly.

I hum and come to sit in front of him. "All of you really

do need intensive media training. I've yet to believe a single lie you tell me."

The words make Skyler pause.

"What?" I ask, when the silence extends beyond comfort. "Is something wrong?"

"No, it's just…" Sky fiddles with the rings on his fingers. "Why do you always do that?"

"Do what?" I ask, replaying the last few minutes in my head. "Interrupt you?"

Sky's eyes widen. "No, of course not. You can always interrupt me." Then he turns bright red, as if he didn't mean to say that. "Sorry, what I meant is—" He laughs nervously.

"Out with it," I say, making a circular gesture. The longer this goes on, the more my anxiety builds in the back of my throat.

Sky sighs. "Don't take this the wrong way, okay?"

"A great way to start," I say dryly.

"Sorry," he says, reaching over to squeeze my hand. It settles me somewhat, but not entirely. "Me and the boys…we've noticed you're really focused on business and strategizing— maybe to a slightly concerning degree?"

My nose wrinkles. This again? "That's the only way to win, Sky."

"No, I know that, but—" Sky exhales loudly "—to be very honest, I don't care if we win or not, Lia."

I gape at him. "How can you not care if you win or not? Isn't that what this is all about? Why you've been working your ass off?"

"Winning would be great, don't get me wrong." He's staring at me with something like pity. It makes my stomach twist and turn uncomfortably. "But it's not the end of the world."

"But—what about Thomas? You can't let him get away with this. You have to win," I say, almost desperate.

"I don't care about Thomas," Skyler says quietly. "He left, and I have to live with that. But there are still three other people in this band who are counting on me. And yeah, what Thomas did sets us back, but at the end of the day, I want this band to thrive because of our love for each other and our love for music. Not because we were mad at someone who doesn't even care about us."

"He stole your work," I say helplessly.

"I know," he says, brushing his thumb over my knuckles. "But it doesn't matter. All that matters to me is that we're proud of the music we're making and we gave it our best shot."

"Then what am I even doing here?" I ask, pulling my hand away from him. "I—I don't understand."

Skyler stares at his empty hand before letting it drop to the ground. "Don't get me wrong, Lia. I'm grateful for everything you've done for us. I genuinely am. I don't think we would have made it this far without you. You've worked so hard and you helped us grow and become better artists."

It's obvious there's more to it than that. "But?"

"But... I think maybe I lost myself a little bit. And for better or worse, I dragged you into it with me. With time, I'm realizing that all of this—" Sky gestures widely to the green screen hanging on the wall and the various tripods still set up around the room "—doesn't matter as much as other things do. I don't want to be a sellout like him, Liana. I want my friends and my music to always come first. I can't put my career over the things I love."

The words hit me like a ton of bricks. Who else do I know that puts their career first, no matter what it might cost those around them?

Bile rises to the back of my throat. I don't want to be anything like my father.

"Oh my God," I say and have to press my fingers against my mouth in a physical attempt to stop myself from throwing up.

"It's not your fault," Sky says quickly, catching the expression on my face. "I enabled it. I led you down this rabbit hole when I should've been the bigger person."

I bite the inside of my cheek to keep from screaming.

"I just…" Sky's nostrils flare and he looks up at the ceiling. "I forgot why I did all this. I got lost in it. My mom was the first person who encouraged my music, you know? Funnily enough, Eomma was also the one who suggested I start a band with Thomas. And it wasn't to become famous or a star or whatever—it was because I loved making music with my friends."

"Our moms would have gotten along," I say, the words coming unbidden from my mouth. "Ma was the same way. Music was our thing, but it was never about—all this shit. It made me happy and gave me an outlet and it was a way for my family to share joy and…"

Somehow, Baba and I lost sight of that. I thought it was just him, but now, thinking back on these last few months with Third Eye, I wonder if I didn't take following in his footsteps too far. I looked at the band like it was a project rather than realizing these boys are human beings with dreams that are not defined by fame and arbitrary levels of success. I wanted to make up for my mistake, but maybe I just created a bigger problem.

"Eomma used to tell me that as long as I stay with my heart, I'll know where to go," Sky says quietly, touching his chest absentmindedly. "And she was right. I lost my way and I have to find it again. Maybe we both do?"

How could I have lost sight about what this was really about? Music has always been an emotional touchstone, something to bring me back to myself, something to share with others and delight in.

Not everything has to be about work, about success. Sometimes it's just about music and love and community.

I often find myself thinking my father is too buried in his career to see what's right in front of him. He's blind to what really matters.

It seems I take after him more than I thought.

Maybe I've been letting his praise from the beginning of the summer cloud my judgment. I wanted to connect with Baba—not become him.

"Hey, what's going on up here?" Skyler asks, tapping my forehead gently and bringing me back to our conversation.

I shake my head. "I don't—I don't know what to say," I confess. "I'm sorry."

"Don't apologize," he says immediately. "It was my fault, too. I—I should've been a better leader."

"That's not true! You're the best leader, Sky, please don't blame yourself for this. I should have never come to you with this stupid plan, and I should have never—"

I stand up, turning away from him to stave off the tears forming in the corners of my eyes. Why do I keep *crying*?

I want to tell him the truth. I want to be honest.

But how can I? How can I tell him what an absolute awful human being I am?

Maybe my father will finally be proud of me—for all the wrong reasons.

"Liana," Skyler says, pulling on my arm. I resist, not wanting him to see my face, but he eventually manages to spin me around. "Let's forgive ourselves, okay? Thomas got in our heads, but it doesn't have to stay this way. We can do better."

"There's no reason for me to be here," I say, and the words are shaky. "I'm not a part of the band. Me being here has just made things complicated and I can't—"

Sky pulls me into his arms, one hand cradling my head and the other around my waist. "Liana, as kindly as possible, shut up."

My mouth closes and I stand there stiffly, not knowing what to do. Eventually, my hands slide around him, resting against his back.

"We want you here," Sky murmurs. "It doesn't matter if you're a part of the band."

"I'm going to ruin everything if I stay," I say, and it's the most honest I've been with him yet. "You should cut me loose while you still can."

Sky's arms tighten around me. "Not a fan of that plan. What's my other option?"

"There is no other option," I say, wishing with my entire heart it wasn't the truth.

He pulls back to look at me, his gaze determined. "Then I'll make one."

I resist the urge to whimper. I don't deserve his kindness or his conviction in me.

"Lia, I..." Sky takes a step closer, his gaze dropping to my mouth. I move away without thinking. I can't let him kiss me, no matter how much I might want him to. He's going to find out the truth sooner or later, and the least I can do is spare him this betrayal, too.

"You don't have to run," he says, and when he reaches for me, I stumble backward desperately—only to crash into Mohammed's keyboard setup.

It collapses under my weight and I hit the ground with a painful thud. Sky is staring at me with wide eyes, and I can't—I can't handle this. I jump to my feet, trying my best to set Mohammed's keyboard up again. I don't want to imagine him arriving tomorrow morning and seeing it on the ground.

Skyler crouches beside me to help and I jerk back. He looks at me in surprise, and it's *hurt* that spreads across his face.

"I'm so sorry," I whisper and flee the room without another word.

50

FOR MY FRIENDS—KING PRINCESS

Skyler and I don't talk about it the next day. In fact, I don't go to rehearsal at all. When Ethan comes upstairs to ask if I'm going to join them soon, I jerk a thumb at Riya and shake my head. "Sorry, work is really busy today. But text me if you need anything, okay?"

Ethan looks confused but shrugs it off, giving my ponytail a light tug before he disappears.

Riya stares at me with narrowed eyes. "Work is not *really busy* today."

"Just leave it, please," I say. I must sound pitiful because she actually lets it go, but not without frowning.

I also don't go to rehearsal the next day. Or the next. Or the next.

Part of it is shame. The other part of it is being stuck in the throes of a depressive episode. I have no motivation to leave my bed. All I want to do is lie here and pretend I don't exist for the next few days.

Still, when Vincent texts me asking about outfit sugges-
tions, I respond. When Mohammed texts me asking about the
set list, I respond. When Ethan texts me asking about posting
about the competition on Instagram, I respond.

When Sky texts me asking about our usual late night drive,
I pretend not to see it.

I still go to work and my internship, still do what I have
to and maintain my responsibilities, but it all feels useless. At
one point, I go into the bathroom at Ripple Records and just
cry and cry and cry. There's no specific reason for it, but it
happens all the same. I don't even feel better afterward—no, I
somehow feel worse. Tired and wrung out and sick of myself.

It wasn't supposed to be like this.

I wasn't supposed to like Sky. That was never part of the
plan. This was supposed to be a simple project, in and out,
no one any wiser about my involvement.

That, in and of itself, is the problem. These are real people
with real feelings, and I somehow convinced myself it was
okay to play God. What's wrong with me?

And it's worse now, because this band means something to
me. Skyler Moon means something to me.

And none of it matters because I sabotaged it before I ever
stepped foot into their rehearsal space.

"Bibi, can I talk to you?" Riya asks, poking her head out
from the back room.

"Yeah, give me a minute!"

I finish dusting the country music shelves, running my
finger along it to make sure nothing remains. Once I'm satisfied, I make my way over to where Riya is.

"What's up?" I ask, leaning in the doorway. I've been pretty decent at keeping my game face on at work, even though I feel like shit.

"You start college next month," Riya says slowly, like that's supposed to mean something to me.

"Yeah, I know. We already talked about lessening my shifts, remember?" I ask, raising a brow. "I know you're twenty-five now, but that's too early for memory loss, isn't it?"

"Real funny," Riya says, swatting my arm. "I wasn't talking about your shifts."

"Okay," I say, bemused. "So what are we talking about?"

Riya frowns and her eyes glance in the direction of the stairs leading to the basement. I shift uncomfortably. That doesn't bode well.

"What?" I ask again.

"So you know how Third Eye have been practicing in the basement," she says after a beat.

"Yes," I say, giving her a weird look. "It's been a thing for three months now."

"Right," Riya says before sighing. "Alright, I'm just gonna come right out and say it."

"I wish you would," I mutter, fixing my bangs.

"Someone has to cover the fee for the rehearsal space," Riya says. It doesn't click at first, what she's talking about, and by the time it does, she's talking again. "I've been taking it out of your paycheck like you asked me to, but since you'll only be working every other weekend when you're at UCLA, it won't be enough to cover the fee. And you should have spending money in college, Bibi, so…"

"Shit," I say, running my hands through my hair. "I didn't even think of that. *Shit*."

"You don't have to figure it out right now," Riya says, putting a hand on my shoulder. "But I thought I'd bring it up sooner rather than later. Maybe you could tell them? I'm sure they can find a way to pay. I'll even give them a discounted rate for you."

I shake my head. "I don't know. I… I'll circle back, okay? Shit. I can't believe this slipped my mind."

"You've had a lot going on," she says, tucking a lock of hair behind my ear before reaching up to smack a kiss against my forehead. "Let me know when you can."

I nod and leave the room before she can, wanting to bang my head against the wall. I pride myself so much on strategizing, and yet the simple matter of the band's *rehearsal space* slipped my mind.

Before I can go back to the storefront, someone wraps a hand around my elbow and pulls me into the hallway.

"Hey, what—?" When I see it's Sky, I fall silent.

Then I realize he's staring at me incredulously, his eyes sharp like daggers. "You're paying for us to use this rehearsal space?"

Oh dear God.

I shuffle deeper into the hallway, moving toward the emergency exit. Sky follows me, still holding my arm, even as I push the door open and come out the side of the building.

"Liana, *explain*," Sky says, letting go of me only to grab at his own hair, disbelief painting his movements. "Your cousin emailed Ethan and said the space was free for us to use. Why would she—?"

I clench my eyes shut. The lies are starting to unravel already, and I have no idea how to begin explaining this.

"Look at me," he says. "Lia, *look* at me."

Painstakingly, I blink my eyes open. I can see the suspicion growing on his face, the heat climbing into his cheeks and the glint in his eyes.

"How much have you been paying? How long has this been going on? Why didn't you *tell me*?"

"I'm sorry," I say, unable to meet his gaze. "I don't know what to tell you."

"Why would you do this?" Sky asks, shaking his head. "You didn't even know us—you shouldn't have... Was it pity?"

I bite my lip to keep from responding. There isn't a right answer here. No matter what I say, it's going to be *bad*.

"Did you think I couldn't pay it?" Sky asks. He sounds almost insulted. "If you had told me, I would've found a way to make it work. This shouldn't have been your responsibility! I'm the leader of this band, I should be the one who—"

That turns my head. "Stop it. Why do you always do that?"

"What?" Sky's expression is wary.

"Maybe other people want to help you!" I say, throwing my hands up. "Why do you always have to shoulder so much weight? Why can't you share your burdens with others? We all know how stressed you are, how you're worried about the band's future, so why can't you just *tell us*?"

"That has nothing to do with this," Sky snaps.

"But it does. Of course, it does. You don't have to be so selfless all the time, Sky! It's okay to look out for yourself. It's *okay* to ask for help." I gesture widely at the store. "The rest of the band would bend over backward if you asked them. Why don't you let them?"

Sky laughs in disbelief. "Are you kidding? Why would I do that? I'm the *leader* of this band. I accepted that responsibility—they didn't. They shouldn't have to worry about any of this. Not when it's my literal job, Liana! Why would I stress them out over stupid shit like this?"

"It's not stupid shit," I say, shaking my head and pointing a finger at his chest to emphasize my point. "It's *important*, and you don't deserve to be stressed out over all of this, either. I know for a fact they'd be happy to lend a hand if you'd just give them the chance!"

"That's not why I asked them to join the band!" Sky says, grabbing my hand and holding it still between us.

"It doesn't matter!" I say, snatching it back. "Stop thinking about everyone else and think about yourself for once!"

"No! They're my *family*," Sky says, voice cracking. We both wince. "I'd do anything for them."

"You're hopeless," I say, taking two steps back and moving for the door that leads inside. "One of these days, you're going to realize that everyone has always wanted to help you but you were too blind and stubborn to see it."

"And why are *you* helping us?" Sky asks sharply as I turn the handle to the door. "Am I too blind to figure that out as well?"

My hand pauses. "I'd do anything for my family, too," I say, and slip inside the store without another word.

51

ROOM—JIHYO

Evie frowns at me over FaceTime. She's tucked away somewhere at LaGuardia Airport, waiting for her flight to California to board, but when I texted her with SOS and flashing red sirens, she immediately called.

"What are you going to do?" she asks. We both ignore the baby wailing in the background.

"I don't know," I say as I pace the length of my room. "Light The Way is *tomorrow*. I have to be there, I can't miss it. But—Baba is going to be there, and if he sees me…"

Evie winces. "You have to tell them, Liana."

"But I can't," I say and pull my fingers down my face to keep from screaming. "It'll throw off their performance. They've worked so hard for this. *I've* worked so hard for this. Even if they don't win, they deserve to put on a performance they're proud of. I can't ruin that."

My best friend looks at me like I'm an idiot.

"Mohammed understood eventually, didn't he? The rest of them will, too," Evie says, her voice soothing.

"We don't know that," I say, my teeth pressing into my bottom lip until it starts to ache. "And even then, it took Mohammed *ages.*"

"You're full-on spiraling," Evie says to me, shaking her head. "Just take a deep breath, okay?"

I do as instructed, breathing in, *3, 2, 1,* breathing out *3, 2, 1.*

"Is that better?" Evie asks.

"Not really," I say and starfish onto my bed. "Maybe a meteor will hit the Earth before tomorrow. I'd really appreciate that to be honest."

"Good lord, Li," Evie says, touching her fingers to her temples. "Alright, new game plan. I'll see you in less than twenty-four hours. My mom said she'll drive me to the theater first thing in the morning. After Light The Way, let's grab some food from Jack in the Box and figure out what you should do, okay? Just make it until then."

"No promises," I say, staring at the Pink Floyd poster on my ceiling. David Gilmour provides me absolutely no answer, but he's a comforting face all the same.

If nothing else, at least I'll always have my music.

Hurray.

For once, Baba comes home early. I'm in the living room, shoving forkfuls of Dear Paneer's chicken biryani in my mouth when I hear the front door unlock. Willow runs to the door and I immediately set aside my food to chase after her.

She always forgets she's an *indoor* cat.

Thankfully, Baba shuts the door before Willow can run out onto the street, but then it just leaves the two of us staring at each other awkwardly across the foyer.

"Should you put her on a leash or something?" my dad asks after a moment, toeing his shoes off.

I squint at him. "Well, she's not a dog, so...no?"

"Okay," Baba says with a shrug and then moves to go upstairs without asking anything else.

"So tomorrow is the Light The Way music competition, right?" I ask, stopping him at the base of the staircase.

He shoots me a disconcerted look over his shoulder. "...Yes. I didn't realize you were keeping track. That's good that you're paying close attention to our company calendar."

At the beginning of the summer, a compliment like that would've brightened my entire day. Worse, it would've given me false hope that things could be alright with us one day. Now it falls flat. I'm sad and I'm tired and I'm over it—I don't know what else I can do to make him *see me.*

I might as well tell Baba the truth. Just get it right out into the open. Maybe I could have Thomas eliminated from the contest completely from the get-go.

But when I open my mouth to say it, I can't bring myself to form the words. *Coward.*

"Was there something else?" my dad asks, when I keep standing behind him.

"No, I... No." I mess with my bangs. "I was thinking I might go to competition tomorrow. Riya Apu said she'd cover my shift at the record shop."

Baba blinks at me. "That's nice, Bibi. Hopefully you'll learn something. Let me know what you think next time we're in the office, yeah?"

"Yeah," I say, biting my bottom lip. Before I even know what I'm doing, I ask, "Did Ma ever go to these with you?"

My dad's face changes entirely, becoming eerily blank. "Let's talk about this another time. I'm exhausted and need to get some rest before tomorrow."

"But when?" I ask and wish I didn't sound so pathetic. "You never talk to me."

"I'm talking to you right now," Baba says slowly, like I'm stupid.

"That's not—that's not the same thing," I say. "We never talk about anything that really matters. We barely see each other outside of work. You only ever spend time with me when you *have* to."

"Not this again, Bibi," my dad says, waving me off, turning his attention to his phone. "We've been through this already."

"You're not even looking at me right now," I say, scoffing, but it comes out wet and choked and awful. "Unless it's about work, everything I say to you goes in one ear and out the other. Can you—I'm trying to have a conversation with you, Baba!"

"You're shouting for no reason," Baba says derisively. "Cool off and get your head on straight. I have business to attend to."

"I don't want to *cool off*, Baba! You're not listening to me!" I say, and I force myself to take a deep breath before I start hyperventilating. "You never do."

My dad looks up from his phone to frown at me. "What is that supposed to mean?"

"You didn't even wish me happy *birthday*," I say, my voice

cracking. There are tears forming in my eyes, and I blink them back forcibly. "When was the last time you asked me about my day? When was the last time you showed *any* interest in me? Ever since Ma died, you've acted like I don't exist! All you care about is your job! The only time you give a shit about what I do is when I contribute to your career. God, why can't you just *love me*?"

"You're being ridiculous," Baba says, which isn't a denial. It hurts worse than if he'd stabbed me in the chest.

"You're still not listening to me." I laugh bitterly. What's the point in any of this? "You know what? Fine. If it's going to be like this, don't even call yourself my father. I don't want a relationship with you if you can't even take two minutes to listen to me when I talk to you. Should I start paying rent to live in your house? Go ahead, tell me what I should do. You're just my landlord at this point, right?"

My dad is shocked into silence, staring at me in wide-eyed disbelief.

"Aren't you going to say anything? Should I move out? I guess I might as well. It's not like our house has felt like a home since Ma died." I smile nonsensically, trying to keep from breaking down in tears. "She would be so proud of us, wouldn't she?"

"Bibi, stop," my dad breathes, more air than words.

Something wet slides down my cheek and I wipe at it hastily. "Whatever, Baba. Forget I said anything."

I push past him and run up the stairs, all the while wondering, hoping, *praying*, he'll call me back and apologize. *I'm sorry. I do love you.*

His voice never comes.

Willow curls around my feet as I grip the banister to hold myself steady at the top of the stairs.

Maybe the relationship between Baba and me is unsalvageable. Maybe this is it.

I painstakingly peel myself off the stairs and go into my room, Willow following after me. I scrub at my face, wiping away any stray tears. I can't afford to think about my and Baba's problems right now. The competition is tomorrow and that's what matters. Everything else that comes afterward is secondary.

Still, before I go to sleep, I find myself sending Baba a text. One last lifeline for him to use to bridge this gap between us. Good luck tomorrow.

Then I send the same text to my group chat with Third Eye, for entirely different reasons.

By the time I wake up in the morning, there's no response from my dad. In comparison, Ethan sent back an enthusiastic array of nervous and excited emoji, Vincent thumbs-up'd the message, and Mohammed replied with LET'S GET ITTTT. Even Skyler sent back a heart, despite the fact we aren't really talking to each other right now.

I take a deep breath. It's time to get this over with.

52

LOVE AND WAR—FLEURIE

"Liana! You made it!" Ethan says, running over to envelop me in a hug.

Despite everything, I manage a smile at the sight of him. "Of course. I wouldn't miss it for the world."

The four members of Third Eye are all dressed and ready to perform, wearing black and blues today, coordinating perfectly. Pride swells in my chest at the sight of them.

Vincent and Mohammed are grinning at me from across the stage, but Sky is staring at me like I'm an alien, something strange and foreign he's never encountered before.

I pointedly ignore him, going over to hug the other two, Ethan still clinging onto my arm. "Hey! How are you guys feeling?"

"Nervous," Mohammed says, tugging at the fringe on his new leather jacket. "And it's only stage rehearsals."

"It'll go great," I say, squeezing his shoulder. "You could not be more prepared."

Even Vincent looks spooked as he looks out at the empty crowd. The auditorium isn't meant for more than a thousand people, but even that number is intimidating. It's probably the biggest venue they've ever played.

"I've seen you work your ass off all summer for this," I say, grabbing Vincent's hand. He looks at me in surprise, but his fingers are warm as they clasp around mine. "All four of you."

Sky scrutinizes me for a moment. When our eyes meet, he sighs and visibly softens. Something in my chest loosens at the sight of his familiar gaze. "She's right, guys. We've made it this far, right? Let's make it all the way to the end."

With my free hand, I reach out and grab Skyler's. He intertwines our fingers without any hesitation. The other boys join in, all of them interlocking hands until we form a small circle.

"We can do this," Sky says, looking at each of them one by one. His eyes are determined, fierce. He's never been more beautiful. "One for all, all for one."

"One for all, all for one," we cheer, throwing our hands up.

Someone behind us claps slowly.

We all turn as a unit to see Thomas standing there, his eyebrows raised as he continues his sardonic applause.

"This is a real nice setup you've got here," Thomas says, the words dripping with venom.

I immediately hide behind Sky's frame, praying Thomas didn't see me.

"What's your problem?" Mohammed sneers, taking a step forward. Vincent immediately grabs his hand, holding it tightly between both of his.

"I don't have a problem," Thomas says, brushing an invisible piece of lint off his jacket. "I was paying you a compliment."

"Leave us alone," Ethan says, his tone darker than I've ever heard it before.

"I can't wish my old group *good luck*?" Thomas harrumphs dramatically. "I'm surprised you made it this far. I guess you clean up better than I thought."

I grab two fistfuls of Sky's shirt when he starts to move forward. "Don't," I whisper.

Sky startles but listens to me anyway, one of his hands coming behind his back to wrap around my wrist gently.

"You're a shame to the music industry," Mohammed says, his face ripe with disgust. "You're really going to get onstage and sing our songs? Don't you have any shame?"

"*My* songs," Thomas corrects. "Don't spread such awful rumors, Mo. It's unbecoming."

Vincent lets go of Mohammed's hand to slip his arms around Mohammed's waist instead. It would look like a hug if not for the fact I can see how much energy Vincent is exerting to hold his bandmate back.

Similarly, Sky's back muscles are tense under my hands, where they're still buried in the fabric of his tank top.

"Anyhow, I hear you four have a publicist now?" Thomas says, tapping a finger against his chin. "When I recommended we should get one, all of you ignored me."

"Can you just go?" Ethan asks, pointing toward the backstage area. "Or should we?"

"Touchy, touchy," Thomas says, chuckling under his breath. "I guess I should have expected this immature behavior from you guys."

That seems to be Sky's last straw because he marches forward, taking me with him. "Leave them alone, Thomas. This is between you and me."

"And whoever is behind your back?" Thomas asks, and I don't have a chance to react before he walks around Sky to catch sight of me. "And who are—*Liana*?"

"Don't talk to me," I say sharply, letting go of Sky's shirt so I can go stand behind the others, wanting to be *far*, far away from this dude.

Thomas' eyes widen in disbelief when both Mohammed and Vincent step forward, shifting closer to shield me from his view.

"No way," he says in shock, his eyes darting between the band and me. "This is your little publicist? She's the one who's been rebranding Third Eye? *Her?*"

"You heard what she said," Sky says, his tone icy. "Don't talk to her."

Thomas scoffs. "You can't be serious. You're going to settle for my leftovers?"

"*Excuse me?*" Vincent asks, and this time Ethan is the one who has to hold him back, though he looks just as pissed off.

Blood rushes to my cheeks, burning hot and humiliating.

"Don't talk about her, either," Sky says darkly. "Especially not like that."

"Wow," Thomas says, meeting my eyes again. There's anger in his gaze, bright and fiery. "You have them all wrapped around your finger, huh? Do they even know what you did?"

My heart drops to my stomach. *No.* Not like this.

"Stop," I say, taking an uneven step backward. I need an escape, but I also can't leave him here with Third Eye.

"They don't," Thomas says, awful glee in his voice. "They have no idea."

"Haven't you done enough?" I ask, shaking my head. "Can't you just fuck off?"

"I'll fuck off," Thomas says agreeably, but he's smiling a truly terrible grin. "After I tell them the truth about you."

"You don't know shit about me," I hiss, ignoring the acid burning in my stomach. "Just shut up, Thomas."

"I know enough," Thomas says, shrugging. "More than them, at any rate."

"I don't know what the hell you're talking about and I don't care, frankly," Sky says, stepping in between me and Thomas. "Leave all of us alone."

"Haven't you been wondering how Jhilmil Sarkar and I got in contact?" Thomas asks sweetly.

In front of me, Mohammed freezes.

"I don't give a shit," Sky says before turning around, herding us like sheep. "Let's go. It's obvious he's not going to be the one to leave."

I turn on my heel, ready to *run*, when Thomas says, "His daughter gave my demo to him. You might know her? Liana Sarkar."

The following silence is deafening aside from Thomas' smug laughter.

"Don't worry, I was just leaving," he says, and though I can't see him anymore, I hear his footsteps walk away, a cheerful whistle following it. "Bye, Liana!"

I close my eyes and pray for death.

53

WISH I WAS BETTER—KINA, YAEOW

Vincent is the first to get his bearings, walking over to tug my arm and spin me around. "What's he talking about? I thought your name was Liana Ahmed?"

I don't respond, even as he shakes my arm more urgently.

Ethan is the next to come to my side, his blue eyes wide with shock and hurt. "It's not true, is it?"

I suck my bottom lip into my mouth instead of answering. Horror slowly dawns on both Ethan's and Vincent's faces. Behind them, Mohammed is holding his head in his hands.

I can't even bear to look at Sky. I'm terrified of what his reaction will be.

"Liana, come on," Ethan says, his voice trembling. "Your dad isn't Jhilmil Sarkar, right? Thomas is lying like he always does."

"Say something," Vincent says, giving my arm one last shake. *"Say something."*

Sky finally comes into view. His expression is blank, but

his eyes are on *fire*. "Do you know what Thomas is talking about?"

Something inside me breaks and he must see it on my face because he takes a step backward, aghast.

"I was trying to fix it," I whisper.

Ethan inhales sharply and Vincent's entire face closes off.

"You've been lying to us this entire time," Sky says in disbelief. "You gave your dad his *demo*?"

I shake my head, trying to find the right words or even *any* words. "I didn't know. I'm sorry, I didn't *know*. I would have never—" I let out an uneven breath. "I've been trying to fix it."

"We didn't even know your real name." Sky is staring at me like I'm a stranger. Maybe to him, I am. "This entire summer has been a lie."

"That's not true," I say desperately. "I've been trying so hard to make up for what I did, I never meant for—"

"We trusted you," Skyler says, his voice small. "*I* trusted you."

"You're not listening to me," I say, and when I take a step closer to him, he takes a step back. It feels like a slap in the face. "I had no idea what Thomas did, I would've never knowingly—"

"How are you any better than him?" Sky asks, and the words rip through me like a knife. "We thought you were our friend. We let you into our *family*."

"I made a mistake," I say and reach for him with a shaking hand. "I didn't do it on purpose. Thomas lied to me, he told me—"

"Yeah, but *you* lied to us," Sky says and he lets out a pained laugh. "I should have known. It was too good to be true."

"Sky," Mohammed says, coming up behind him. There's sweat pooling on his forehead and a muscle in his jaw is twitching, but his next words are steady. "Maybe we should let her explain."

Vincent's expression shifts minutely, his gaze sharp on Mohammed's face. "Why aren't you upset?"

Mohammed's eyes widen, far too obvious. A litany of swear words run though my head. "I am upset."

"Not enough," Vincent says, his nostrils flaring as he glances between us. Then he blanches, grabbing Ethan's arm for support. "You knew. You *knew*?"

Mohammed makes a pained noise. "Vinny, this isn't about me."

Sky's face crumples at Mohammed's unintentional confirmation, and my heart feels like it's bleeding out.

"Last month, when you—that's why you were so mad at her," Ethan says, his mouth falling open. "You've known for a *month*?"

"Give her a chance to explain," Mohammed says instead of defending himself. "You said it yourself, I was furious, but I'm not anymore, and I think if you take a second to listen—"

"How is she going to explain this?" Vincent asks coldly. "It's obvious she hasn't told her father the truth about Thomas' demo yet, otherwise he wouldn't *be* here!"

Mohammed opens his mouth to defend me again but I shake my head, pushing past him so I can stand in front of the others instead. This isn't his hit to take.

I did this. I knew it would come to this. And while I wish

it weren't right *now*, it was inevitably going to happen sooner or later.

"I made a mistake. I know that. I should've been more careful, I should've paid more attention, I should've done ten million things differently, but I can't go back in time and change what happened. So I'm trying to own it and make amends. That's what I've been trying to do *all* summer." For the umpteenth time this month, my eyes start to water. "I wanted to tell you sooner, but I was afraid you wouldn't let me help you if I did."

"So you went behind our backs instead," Sky says, the words choked and wet with unshed tears.

"What was I supposed to do?" I ask, ignoring the growing ache in my chest. "I told Thomas who I was and he *used* me, Sky! I trusted him and he threw it right back in my face, just like he did to you! Do you think I wanted this? I thought—he told me the four of you were *awful* to him, and I believed him. Was I supposed to somehow know he was lying to me? You, of all people, know how easy it is to buy into his whole act."

Sky doesn't say anything, but he's blinking rapidly, as if that'll stop his tears from existing.

"So, yeah, I lied to you, but I'm *telling* you how sorry I am. I shouldn't have given my dad Thomas' demo, but I thought those were his songs! That's what he told me! He seemed so hopeless and insecure about his place in the band, and I didn't know any better, so I tried to help him. Maybe I'm stupid, maybe I'm naive, I don't know. I regret it *every fucking day*, Sky. I've been covering the cost of you rehearsing in the record shop, I've been snooping around Ripple Records for anything that might help you win this competition, I've been trying to build your brand so that even when I'm gone, there will be *something* to show for all my efforts." I shove my fingers against my mouth to stifle the sob building in my throat. "I've been trying to fix it. I don't know what else to say."

No one speaks, all of them looking at me with varying expressions. Ethan is staring at me with sorrow, Vincent is staring at me in disappointment, Mohammed is staring at me with pity, and Sky is staring at me in anguish.

"I'm sorry," I say in a whisper. "I'm so sorry."

Sky turns around and walks off without another word, and I watch him go with a heavy heart.

54

SILVER SPRINGS—FLEETWOOD MAC

An entire hour passes. Third Eye's stage rehearsal goes ahead without Sky, and the lack of guitar is painfully obvious in the song. Thomas smirks at me when I pass him in the hallway, and I glare at him.

"Don't fucking look at me," I say, shoving my shoulder into his harder than I need to.

Thomas makes a noise of pain that's as fake as the rest of him. "Ow, Liana."

I scoff and stretch on my tiptoes to look him in the eye. "Go anywhere near Third Eye again," I say, "and I will fucking ruin your career. I don't care if I take myself down in the process."

Something like fear flashes in Thomas' gaze before he quickly collects himself. "You won't say anything. You would've already done it if you were going to."

I smile darkly. "See, the thing is you're counting on my silence because you think I'm afraid of telling my dad the truth. But I don't care anymore. I have nothing left to lose. You made sure of that."

Thomas rolls his eyes. "You're not going to do anything."

"Stay away from them," I say, and my smile stretches so wide my cheeks hurt. "I'm not going to give you another warning."

"I'm so scared," Thomas says sarcastically. "You're nothing but a coward, Liana."

The urge to slap him rises in me, but I tamp it down. I'm not going to do anything else to jeopardize Third Eye's performance.

"Go to hell," I say and leave before he can get a word in edgewise.

As soon as I turn the corner, I lean against the wall and slide down until I hit the ground. A shadow approaches almost immediately, and when I look up, Vincent is frowning down at me.

"What?" I ask tiredly. I don't think I have it in me to keep defending myself. This entire day has been a nightmare.

All I want is to call Evie and have a breakdown, but her connecting flight was delayed last night and she's thousands of feet in the air right now, on her way to this train wreck of a competition.

"You just threatened Thomas for us," Vincent says, and there's a question in his voice.

"Yeah, well, I fucking hate that guy," I mutter, burying my face in my knees. "He can choke for all I care."

Vincent sits beside me, his warmth familiar and comforting when it has no right to be. "You could have told us the truth, Lia. We would've understood."

"Could've, would've, should've," I say, the words pressed into the fabric of my jeans. "There were a lot of things I could have done. Even more things that I should have done."

Vincent sighs, and I startle when his hand rests on my back, gently rubbing up and down. I've never known him to initiate physical affection.

"I can't say I'm not pissed at you," Vincent says, "but I get why you did it. I might have done the same thing in your shoes. Sky is—he's stubborn when it comes to accepting help. He doesn't like to lean on others. If he had known..."

I don't reply, but I turn my head so my cheek is resting against my knees instead and I can see his face.

"I'm not forgiving you," Vincent says, meeting my gaze evenly. "But I will. Maybe in a week or something. Let's circle back?"

That's more than I thought I'd be afforded. More than I dared to hope for.

"Yeah," I say hoarsely. "Let's circle back."

Vincent squeezes the back of my neck before dropping his arm to his side. "I guess it doesn't matter now," he says, his forehead wrinkled. "The competition starts in an hour and Sky is nowhere to be seen."

"Still?" I ask, sitting up straight. "Have you tried calling him?"

Vincent gives me a flat look. "No, why didn't I think of that?"

"Don't be sarcastic right now, I'm sensitive," I say, bumping my shoulder into his.

"Yeah, yeah," Vincent says, waving me off. "Yes, we've called him, texted him, searched this place up and down.

Ethan and Mo are still trying to find him, but it's not looking good."

I worry my bottom lip between my teeth in hesitation. Vincent sees the expression on my face and sighs. "Go on, then. Maybe you'll actually find him."

"I'll let you know if I do." I press a quick kiss to Vincent's cheek before launching into a jog down the hall.

If Ethan and Mo are looking for him in the building, then I'll cover our bases and check outside.

Vinny Alvarez: ok we're going sixth apparently

Vinny Alvarez: so we should have at least an extra half an hour to find him

Vinny Alvarez: any luck anyone ???

Ethan Mitchell: nothing in the basement :(

Mo Anwar: nothing on the roof

Me: nothing in the parking lot

Vinny Alvarez: jfc

Sky's car is missing from the parking lot as well, which isn't great. I should probably tell the others, but I have a feeling that's not going to help anyone's stress levels.

I walk back and forth a few times, checking license plates, but nowhere do I spot his car.

I don't even know what I'd do if I did find Sky. Would he listen to me? Would he run away at the sight of me?

I know how committed he is to this band, that there's no way he would miss this performance. I believe that if nothing else.

But where is he?

Finally, I venture onto the nearby streets, glancing through the shop windows to see if maybe he decided to go somewhere close. But what about his *car*?

I finally give up in front of a cupcake shop, wiping sweat off my forehead with the back of my hand. I probably just messed up my bangs but who cares at this point?

"This is all my fault," I say to myself. "Good going, Liana."

As if on cue, a black Toyota Corolla pulls up to the curb, the windows rolled down.

"Get inside," Sky says, and I don't even think before I do.

55

WOULD YOU—PINK SWEAT$

The song playing in the car is "Leave Me Before I Love You" by ASTN. That makes me feel a thousand times worse.

Skyler hasn't looked at me since I got in the car, his gaze focused on the road ahead. He doesn't seem angry, he doesn't seem sad, he doesn't seem much of *anything*. Just blank. Empty. Devoid of any and all emotion.

And we both know it's my fault.

"You're performing in thirty minutes," I say for lack of anything better.

Sky taps his phone, upholstered to the car dashboard. "So I've heard."

The tension in the car grows and grows and grows until I can't take it anymore. "I can walk, Sky."

That seems to break through to him because a wrinkle appears between his brows. "You're already in the car."

"I know, but you—you're mad at me. I get it. I deserve

it. Just let me out and I'll walk, okay?" I say, fidgeting with my seat belt.

Sky presses his lips together, and instead of stopping the car so I can get out, he reaches over to his phone and switches the song.

The first few notes aren't familiar so I glance at the screen. "Would You" by Pink Sweat$.

"So you're not going to drop me off, then," I say, even though the answer is obvious.

Again, Sky doesn't answer.

Well. If we have to sit here, I'm not going to do it in silence.

"If you're not going to kick me out of the car, I'm going to go ahead and talk, yeah?" I take in a deep breath and remind myself the worst of the damage has already been done. There's nowhere to go from here but up. "I'm pretty sure my dad doesn't love me."

Sky's hands tighten on the steering wheel, the veins in his forearms growing more prominent.

"That sounds random without context," I say with a half-hearted laugh. "I don't know. I hope it was different for you when your mom died, but when mine passed away, my dad just…shut down. It was like he didn't have any emotions anymore. All he cared about was work. It didn't matter to him what I did or didn't do."

Though he's trying to be inconspicuous, it's obvious Sky is staring at me from the corner of his eye. He doesn't ask, but there's a silent nudge in the air.

"It got worse when we moved to LA. The only way I could get him to pay attention to me, to care even a *little* bit was to show an interest in music. Maybe because it was the thing that Ma loved most in the world." I shrug, crossing my arms across my chest. "I don't know. It's all a little silly, chasing after my dad's affection like this. But it's all I've known these last few years, and I don't know how to break out of it. Maybe college will help. Maybe it won't."

"Liana," Sky says slowly.

"No, let me finish," I interrupt, shaking my head. "All of this is to say that when I gave my dad Thomas' demo, he was impressed. He told me he was *proud* of me. I don't even remember the last time that happened. I don't know if it'll ever happen again."

"How could he not be proud of you?" Sky asks. He sounds pained. He sounds familiar.

"You'd be surprised," I say, more bitter than I intend. "When I realized Thomas had used me, I panicked. If I told my dad the truth…he would never look at me the same. And he already barely looks at me as it is." I close my eyes. "I think his eyes glaze past me. Sometimes, I think he pretends I died when Ma did. And sometimes, I wish I did."

Sky hits the brakes and my eyes blink open in alarm. Then I realize we're back in the parking lot of the theater hosting Light The Way, near the far side where no cars are in immediate danger of hitting us.

"Be careful," I say, adjusting my seat. "Can you at least park before we have the rest of this conversation?"

Skyler sucks in a harsh breath between his teeth but hits the gas pedal again, steering us into an empty spot. Once he's settled, he turns his entire body to face me.

"How can you say that?" he asks, wide-eyed. "Do you really want to…?"

"No," I say but it comes out funny. My nose wrinkles, and I clarify, "I mean... I have before. In the middle of night, when I'm miserable and alone with my thoughts, you know? But I have reasons to live. I'm going to *college* soon. I have an incredible job. And I have people who care enough about me to throw me silly birthday parties and take me on late night drives, even if that doesn't include my dad. It's not so bad. In fact, it could be a lot worse."

Sky looks heartbroken, which is the opposite of what I want.

"Don't feel bad for me," I say. "That's not—I just wanted to explain why I did what I did. No matter what, it was cowardly and it was wrong. I'm so sorry. I really have been doing my best to make up for it. But... I still lied, and it's not something I can be forgiven for overnight, if at all. If you want nothing to do with me, I understand. But you have to go out there and perform, okay? Not for me and not to win. For you, and for your band."

Music continues to play softly in the background as Sky looks at me beseechingly. I don't know what he's hoping to find.

"Can I ask you something?" Sky asks.

"Anything," I say. "I'm done lying to you. It won't ever happen again."

"Do you even like music?" His voice is soft. "Not like— just enjoy it as a casual listener. But does it actually bring you joy? Are you going to study music management in college because you genuinely enjoy it or because...because you feel like you have to?"

I shake my head. "I don't—of course, I like it. How could I not?"

Sky frowns, tilting his head to one side. "Why? Why do you like music?"

I stare at him, trying to make sense of the question. Why do I like music?

"Because I do," I say, at a loss for how else to explain it.

"Not because of your dad?"

Oh. *Oh.*

I sit back in my seat. Do I like music because of my dad? The simple answer is yes. He introduced me to music. Ma and Baba both constantly had something playing in the background. Some of my earliest memories are of attending concerts and music festivals. I can't think of my parents *without* thinking of music.

But do I *like* music because of my dad? I don't know.

I don't know to what degree I'm doing all of this because of my dad, and to what degree I'm doing all of this for myself. The lines are a little blurry.

But I love music. I *know* that. It's like the air I breathe. I can't think of anything better.

And I want to help people. I want to advocate for them and promote them and help them accomplish their dreams. But maybe there are better ways to go about it—maybe my views on the industry got a little warped along the way, but I can unlearn it and find what music means to *me* rather than what I've been told.

"I forgive you, by the way," Sky says, jarring me out of my thoughts.

"That easily?" I ask in disbelief.

"How can I be mad at you for trying to help my band?" He reaches over to take my hand, squeezing it in his. "Yeah, you shouldn't have lied. And to be honest, I am upset about it. But I can also recognize that you're right. I wouldn't have let you anywhere near them if I knew the truth. And all you wanted to do was help us. You didn't have to. You could have left us to rot. But you didn't, because you're a good person, because you *care*."

I stare at our hands, our fingers interlaced. "I'm sorry," I say, because even with his acceptance, it doesn't feel like I've said it enough.

"Hey," Sky says, tapping my chin with his free hand. His gaze is tender and honest. "Remember what I said before? We deserve to forgive ourselves."

Then with one last squeeze, he lets go. "Now come on, I've got a performance to get to, and we're running behind schedule. My publicist would have a fit if she knew I was sitting around in the parking lot, trying to make a beautiful girl smile, instead of getting ready for the stage."

I laugh despite myself. "Then we'd better hurry."

56

HALL OF FAME—STRAY KIDS

We're *almost* late to the performance.

As soon as we enter the auditorium, Sky immediately heads for the backstage area, giving my hand one last squeeze before he leaves.

With a quiet grunt, I scuttle past the people sitting in one of the first few rows of the auditorium and try not to make eye contact with anyone in the process.

Once Sky disappears from sight behind one of the stage side doors, I sit up straighter and crane my head, looking for my dad. It takes a while, but I finally find him in the front row of a small upper balcony section. Oliver Andrews is beside him, along with the rest of the judging panel. Baba looks bored, staring at his phone rather than the performance happening right now.

I frown at the sight, remembering the conversation I had with Sky just a few minutes ago.

What does music mean for me without my dad in the picture? Would I still be so devoted to it?

Is *he* even devoted to it anymore or is it just a way to distract him from his grief?

Baba feels like such a stranger to me. I know him, in the way all kids know their parents, but I don't think I know him as a person. I don't think he wants me to.

I turn back to the stage, mulling that over. Is this the relationship Baba and I are going to have for the rest of our lives? And am I going to let that define my future?

The host of the show comes back out on stage as the current performance ends. "How was that? Let's hear it for The Stepping Stones!"

Everyone in the audience bursts into a round of applause as the curtains go down so the next act—Third Eye—can set up. I clap along slowly, but there's a swarm of butterflies in my rib cage, flapping incessantly. This is what they—*we*—have worked for all summer long, and it's finally happening. I don't even know what songs they ended up choosing, too cowardly to ask when I was actively avoiding Sky.

Before the curtains rise, I send Baba a text.

I'm at Light The Way too. Please watch the next performance. They're incredible and I think they deserve your full attention…

I flip my phone over instead of waiting for his response. I have to believe he'll listen to me this once.

The curtains rise, and I exhale slowly. This is it.

My stomach twists with nerves as the band comes into view under the bright lights—Ethan on the drums, Mohammed on the keyboard, Sky on his guitar, and Vinny on bass, though he's temporarily gripping the mic stand in front of him like he's about to start fighting for his life.

I expect them to launch right into the music, but Sky taps one of the microphones before chuckling softly at the sound of the feedback.

"Hi, everyone! I'm Skyler Moon, and we're Third Eye. Before we start, I wanted to explain some of the context for our first song." He smiles, and I have no idea whether anyone else can tell, but there's a hint of tension in the corner of his mouth. He's nervous. Of course, he is.

"When I was younger, I always dreamed of performing onstage. At the time, I had no idea how hard it would be to make it as far as I was hoping to go, but now I have a better grasp on the situation. And it's *hard*, but what's kept me going is my love for music and these boys behind me. I've never felt more at home than when I'm performing with them, on- or offstage. They make me a better musician just by existing. We push each other to follow through on our ambitions, no matter how difficult things might get. They believe in me—and I believe in them."

Vinny wanders over to ruffle Sky's hair and Sky pushes him away half-heartedly, a real smile replacing his tense one.

"Anyway, all this to say, I couldn't do any of this without them. A few years back, my mom passed away, and I think she sent the members of Third Eye to be my guardian angels, so they could watch over me for her. She knew I'd need them. So this song is for her, and for my boys. I couldn't make music without you."

Pride bursts in my chest at the words. Ethan, Mohammed,

and Vinny are staring at Sky with such unadulterated love in their eyes.

"This is 'Guardian Angel' by Third Eye," Sky says, and the entire room seems to vibrate as they dive headfirst into the song.

I can't believe Thomas left this all behind. I'm not even in the band, but I can't ever imagine willingly abandoning these boys.

But this isn't about Thomas. Sky made that undoubtedly clear with his speech and this song. This is about love that perseveres, even in the face of pain and heartbreak.

You're my guardian angel
Though I don't think you know
You picked me up when I fell
I could scrape my knee, break my arm, free-fall through the sky
End up in hell
And through it all,
I'm certain you'd be there

Vincent's vocals are strong, heady, and when Sky leans over to sing into the mic with him, goose bumps rise on my skin.

I've heard them practice this before, but it's never felt as visceral as it does tonight. I swear I can feel my heart matching the beat of Ethan's drums, my blood rushing to the same tempo as Mohammed's piano notes.

And I wonder to myself if maybe the lyrics apply to me, too—I don't know if Ma sent these boys to me, but I'm certain she'd love them.

It's impossible not to.

57

PERFECT HARMONY
—MADISON REYES & CHARLES GILLESPIE

"Bear with us, we have one more song," Sky says, beaming wide at the crowd. They absolutely killed the first performance. There's sweat dripping down the side of his face, and he's so beautiful it physically hurts.

The entire room is on their feet, cheering loudly and giving them a standing ovation. Some girls near the front are screaming at such a high pitch I fear they're going to ruin their vocal cords.

"Do you want to explain what the next song is about?" Vinny asks into the mic, smirking at Sky. "Since you wrote it all by yourself."

Heat rises into Sky's cheeks, but he doesn't lose his smile. "Of course, Vinny. Why not?"

Mohammed snorts loud enough for his microphone to catch it. Ethan is shaking his head, his eyes bright with mirth.

"Go on, then," Vinny says, gesturing with his hand. "The crowd is waiting."

Sky laughs nervously, rubbing the back of his neck. "Okay. Uh, so…this next song is called 'Late Night' and…"

"And?" Ethan asks into his microphone with a giggle. They're teasing Sky, and I have no idea why, because the song title doesn't sound familiar in the slightest.

I cock my head in confusion as Skyler somehow turns even *more* red.

"I wrote it in the last few weeks," Sky says, licking his lips. He's scanning the crowd now, searching for someone or something. When our eyes meet, he finally pauses, holding my gaze. "I've been having a little bit of writer's block, so someone suggested that going on a few late night drives might help. So I did—with them. And suddenly, I was always looking forward to the end of the day. Without meaning to, I found a new muse. I don't think she realized how much of an effect she was having on me. I still don't think she knows. So I thought I'd write a song to tell her."

My mouth falls open. He can't mean he wrote a song for me. But who *else* would he be talking about?

"This one's for you. You know who you are," Sky says before winking at me.

My jaw dips even lower as Vincent starts singing and it becomes immediately obvious this is a love song. A *confession*, even.

Late night driving
Small talk and smiling
I'm slowly learning

Every road leads me back to you
No matter what I do
The wind in your hair
The flush in your cheeks
My God, it's bad for me
I roll down the windows
And toss away my sorry excuse for a heart
How do I hit the brakes?
I'm afraid to tell you
I hope we never end this drive
I'm afraid to tell you
You make me feel so alive
I'm afraid to tell you
I'm afraid to tell you
I'm afraid to tell you
If I was braver
I'd kiss you tonight

My eyes are the size of saucers. There's no way this is a real song. There's no way Sky is singing *these* lyrics and looking right at me.

"This is so romantic," a girl two seats away from me whispers to her friend, hands clasped against her chest.

Her friend nods, starry-eyed as she stares at Sky. "Whoever she is, she's beyond lucky."

I simultaneously want to float into the air and sink into the ground. I can't believe Sky wrote this song and all of Third Eye managed to hide it from me. When did they even practice this? Did they only rehearse it when I was working my shifts?

When the final chorus starts, Vinny stops singing, leaving only Sky's vocals to shine.

And maybe I want to tell you
I hope we never end this drive
And maybe I want to tell you
You make me feel so alive
And maybe I want to tell you
And maybe I want to tell you
And maybe I want to tell you
I'm braver by your side
Please kiss me tonight

A sappy smile is breaking across my face despite my best attempt to hide it. Sky's eyes crinkle in the corners at the sight of it.

I shake my head and blow him a kiss.

He grabs it out of the air and places two fingers against his lips right as the song comes to end, Mohammed playing the last few notes on the piano.

The audience breaks into thunderous applause. I get to my feet, and the girls beside me follow shortly afterward. Soon the entire place is giving Third Eye a standing ovation, and when I look to the balcony, I see that my dad is standing, too, clapping slowly. Beside him is Oliver Andrews, applauding a lot more vigorously.

"Thank you, Light The Way!" Mohammed says into the mic, a wild grin on his face.

"Thank you!" Ethan, Vinny, and Sky echo.

All four of them come together at the front of the stage,

clasping hands with each other. Even if I didn't know them, I would be able to tell this is where they belong—onstage with each other.

They take a bow, once, twice, and a third time. "Thank you!" they all say again as the host comes onto the stage.

"And that was Third Eye!" he says.

The audience keeps cheering, so loud that my ears ring. The curtain starts to descend and the boys wave at the crowd one last time. Ethan is jumping up and down, holding onto Vinny's arm and Mohammed is leaning down to touch the hands of people in the front row. Sky's eyes catch mine again, and he's the one who blows me a kiss this time.

I catch it and tuck it into my pocket. Skyler bursts into laughter and the curtains finally fall.

I don't stick around to watch the rest of the performances. I don't care to watch Thomas sing Third Eye's stolen songs.

I make my way backstage in time to see Third Eye in a group huddle, their arms wrapped around each other.

I can't hear what they're saying to each other, but I can imagine the gist of it.

When they finally break apart, Ethan catches sight of me first. I'm not sure how he's going to react—we haven't had a chance to talk one-on-one since they found out the truth about my dad, and Ethan was the first one to take me in with open arms when this all started.

Neither of us react at first but then Ethan says, "Fuck it," and runs to capture me in a hug. "How were we?"

"Amazing," I say, squeezing my arms around him, mostly

to keep my grasp on reality because I feel a little weak in the knees at his easy forgiveness. "So good, honestly."

The other three members join in on the hug. I can barely breathe, but I'm not complaining. This may very well be my favorite place on the Earth.

"I'm so proud of all of you," I say, my voice muffled in the crush of bodies. "You absolutely killed it. Whether you win or not, it won't take away how absolutely *incredible* you were."

They let go of me, and it's obvious how hyped up they are on adrenaline, all of them grinning at me despite the sweat sliding down their skin.

Sky leans in again for a second hug and I indulge him without hesitating, wrapping my arms around his neck and squeaking in surprise when he lifts me off the ground, spinning me around.

"Put me down!" I say, but I'm giggling so much it's hard to speak.

"Okay, okay," Sky says and sets me down on my feet. We sway for a moment and he uses it as an excuse to sneak a kiss to my cheek and then quickly shift away before I can so much as squawk in protest. Not that I would have.

I'm ready to admit to myself how much I like him. There's no denying how much affection I hold for him—it threatens to burst out of me constantly.

"I want to do it all over again," Vinny says, ignoring us playfully flicking each other. He turns to look at the stage longingly. "How do we reverse time?"

Mohammed nods in agreement. "What if we stage an accident and Thomas can't go on, so we do an encore?"

Sky turns away from me to lightly smack the back of Mohammed's head, but there's immeasurable fondness in his gaze. "Don't say things like that, Mo."

"You never let me commit violence," Mohammed says with a pout.

"And for good reason," Sky says, rolling his eyes. "Forget Thomas, anyway. This isn't about him, yeah?"

"Yeah," Mohammed says, softer. "This is about us."

"Exactly," Sky says and pulls Mohammed into a one-armed hug. I burst into laughter again when we all get wrapped in another group hug.

Even though the results of the competition haven't been announced yet, it feels a lot like we've won already.

58

BRAVADO—LORDE

"And in first place, we have…Third Eye! You've won a record deal with Ripple Records!"

For a moment, my brain isn't able to process the words. Then Ethan lets out an earth-shattering screech, running onto the stage, and Vincent follows after him, whooping. Sky is staring with wide eyes, and Mohammed has to physically drag him onto the stage to accept their award.

"Oh my God," Sky gasps into the microphone, completely stunned. *"Oh my God."*

"Say something!" Vinny shouts.

"Oh—I—" Sky shakes his head, eyes brighter than the stage lights. "Thank you so much! Thank you, thank you, thank you. Thank you, Ripple Records! To everyone who's supported our band in any way, shape, or form, we couldn't have done this without you. To our families, sitting somewhere in the crowd. To our friends, who helped make us who we are.

To our ten fans, I can't believe you exist but I'm unbelievably grateful you do."

I'm going to have to lecture Sky about that later. Third Eye does not have *ten* fans. They have nine thousand on Instagram alone, as of this morning. I didn't quite hit my goal of ten thousand followers by Light The Way, but I have a feeling I will soon. Their engagement is climbing rapidly, and it feels *good* to see the product of my hard work mixed with their talent.

Sky turns to look at the other members of Third Eye, a proud smile on his face. "To Vinny, for singing your heart out every single time. To Ethan, for bringing sunshine and joy to our lives. To Mohammed, for being the rock and holding us together."

Mohammed grabs the mic from Sky. "To Sky, for being the best leader we could ever have. Thank you for being the heart of Third Eye."

Sky grins and pulls the boys into a hug, and they all start jumping, moving in an excited circle while the audience cheers.

"This is bullshit!" a familiar voice says somewhere behind me.

I glance over my shoulder to see Thomas throwing his sweat towel on the floor in a nonsensical fit.

"Grow up," I say dryly.

Thomas looks up at me with an unhinged gaze. "*You*. You did this! How could you—?"

"What? Help the people *you* screwed over? You're so pathetic," I say, nauseated with myself for ever liking him. "Take the loss with grace."

"Bibi?"

I stiffen, but slowly turn to face my father. The other judges are standing at the side of the stage, applauding Third Eye, but my father is staring right at me.

"Baba," I say with a thin smile. "I told you I'd be here."

"I thought you said you were in the crowd," he says, brows furrowed. "What are you doing backstage?"

"Yeah, what are you doing?" Thomas asks with a sneer.

Baba glances to the side, recognizing Thomas. The confusion on his face grows.

"You are playing with fire," I tell Thomas darkly. "I already told you I have nothing to lose."

I turn back to my dad and come to a decision. I can't live my life hoping for Baba's approval. I love music for *me*. Not for him.

I can't keep doing this.

Third Eye deserves for my father to know the truth.

"Baba, I made a mistake," I say, forcing my voice to remain steady. "Thomas is a liar. He didn't write the songs from his demo. Third Eye did. He used to be in a band with them, but he wanted to go solo, so he stole their songs and passed them off as his own."

"*What?*" Baba asks in disbelief.

"What the fuck is wrong with you?" Thomas asks at the same time, his eyes wide and panicked. "Shut up!"

"He's a liar," I repeat firmly. "He used me, Baba. He knew you were my father, so he manipulated me into giving you his demo. He's not worth your time."

"Fuck," Thomas hisses and makes a run for it, inadvertently confirming everything I've said. Idiot.

Baba's face shutters, and I wish his frustration weren't visceral. It feels like I've been slapped in the face. "Bibi, how could you let this happen?"

"I didn't find out until it was too late," I say and blow out a harsh breath. "And when I did find out, I was afraid to tell you. You barely talk to me as is."

My dad is silent, staring at me with a blank expression. Why did I expect anything different?

"But you can't work with him, Baba. He's a liar and a cheater and a fraud," I say after a beat. Even if my dad can't understand why I did what I did, he needs to at least stay away from Thomas.

Baba shakes his head, his mouth curled in disgust. "I have no intention of working with that boy ever again."

"That's good…" I tug at my bangs and clear my throat. But I can't leave it at that. I need to say something now or I never will. Music is for me. For *me*. "For Third Eye, I—since I'm interning at Ripple Records through the fall, I'd like to work with them. I think they have what it takes to make it big, and I—"

"No," Baba says before I can finish. He looks so disappointed in me that it physically aches. "Absolutely not. After what happened with Thomas? I can't justify letting you work with them."

And this is exactly what I was afraid of.

"You wouldn't have even paid attention to this competition if I didn't text you," I say, but I'm losing some of my patience. "I would've told you sooner about Thomas if I didn't think you'd hate me for it."

"I don't hate you," Baba says dismissively.

"Yeah, maybe," I say, and my voice is thin, reedy. "But you don't love me, either."

"You're going to do this in front of everybody?" Baba asks, casting a look around. No one is paying any attention to us, everyone focused on the stage where Third Eye is still celebrating.

I can't help but scoff, more out of hurt than anger. It feels like there's a bruise in my heart, steadily spreading outward. "So that's it then? That's how it's going to be? Okay. How much is rent? How much should I pay?"

"Bibi, stop it," my dad says darkly.

"No, give me a number," I say, matching his tone. I've never felt this sick in my life, but I force myself to get the words out. "I'll get another job. Maybe my next boss will take pity on me. I'm an orphan now, did you hear?"

Baba inhales sharply. "Don't say things like that."

"Forget paying rent, then. I'll just move out," I say, offering him an awful smile despite my blurry gaze. "Right in time for college! Isn't that perfect? And when I leave, you can truly pretend I died when Ma did. Maybe you'll finally be happy then."

"*Bibi.*"

"What?" I ask, the too-wide smile stretching my cheeks painfully. "*What?* Are you going to deny it? You don't care about me, Baba. If you did, we wouldn't be here!"

"You can work with Third Eye," Baba says, looking away from me. "I'll make sure you're on assignment with them."

All the fight drains out of me. It's what I wanted, but it feels like a hollow victory. Even after all this, he still can't tell me he loves me.

"Thanks," I say weakly. Behind him, Sky catches my eye as Third Eye finally come off stage. "Baba…"

"What, Bibi?"

I sigh, dragging a hand down my face. "I lost sight of why I loved music because of you. But I think you lost sight of why you loved music first. I hope one of these days you can remember why you started loving it. Maybe that's the day you'll remember how to love me again."

Without another word, I walk past him, toward the people who actually feel like my family.

59

BLINDED—EMMIT FENN

As we're gathering our stuff to leave and grab ice cream at Dacu Creamery to celebrate, Thomas appears.

I don't have the energy to deal with him, so I tug on Vinny's arm, since he's the closest to me. "Ex-bandmate alert."

Vincent follows my gaze to where Thomas is lingering, staring at all of Third Eye with a strange look in his eye.

"Fantastic," Vinny says, sounding as tired as I feel. I hate that Thomas can suck the joy out of all of them so easily. "You distract Mo and Ethan, I'll grab Sky."

I nod and move across the dressing room to take Ethan's hand. He looks up from where he was admiring their first-place trophy with a curious smile.

I don't bother distracting Mohammed. He's talking to his family, holding a bouquet of flowers they brought for him. I'm surprised he told them about the performance at all.

I guess now he won't have anything left to hide from them. A record deal is nothing to scoff at. As long as Third Eye negotiates with Ripple Records well, they'll be financially set for a while. He can provide for his family without feeling guilty.

But he was right. It's obvious they love him. Even now, they're looking at him with nothing but pride. It's a far cry from the way my father looks at me, but this isn't about me—I'm glad that *someone* has a family that supports them whole-heartedly.

"I haven't gotten a chance to talk to you alone yet," I say to Ethan, looping my arm with his. "I wanted to say I'm sorry for lying about everything. You put a lot of trust in me. I don't know that any of them would've given me a chance if you didn't first."

Ethan knocks his head against mine lightly. "Once I took a minute to think about it, I understood why you did it. Even if you did lie to us about the circumstances, it doesn't mean our friendship was a lie."

"You're way too mature for your age," I say with a fond shake of my head. "I'm still sorry. I promise it won't happen again."

Ethan offers me a sweet smile. "I know it won't."

Mohammed comes up to us a moment later, his grin so wide it must hurt his cheekbones. "What's going on here?"

"I'm sorry I got you in trouble earlier," I say instead of answering his question. "Thank you for trying to stick up for me."

He blinks at me in surprise. "Oh. I mean…yeah. Of course. You're part of our tiny family now, aren't you?"

My heart swells. "I'd like to think so."

Mohammed tweaks my nose, but then his gaze catches on

something over my shoulder, and his grin slips off his face. "Why is he here?"

Ethan spins around to see what's undoubtedly Sky and Vinny talking to Thomas.

With a sigh, I turn, too. Thomas appears to be close to *tears* for some reason beyond me. Vindictively, I take pleasure in it. *Asshole.*

Vincent seems beyond over it, but Sky is listening to Thomas with a serious expression.

"Liana!" someone calls.

My head turns again, but this time I nearly vibrate with excitement when I realize who it is.

"Evie!" I shout, waving her over. I use two fingers to point at my eyes before turning them toward Ethan and Mohammed, pinning them with my gaze. "I'm watching you. Don't fight with Thomas. I'll be right back."

And then I run full speed at my best friend who easily catches me, swinging me around in delight.

"You made it!" I say, squeezing my arms around her waist. "Did you get to catch Third Eye's performance?"

"I absolutely did," Evie says, beaming. "And I saw them win, too. That's amazing."

"I still can't believe it," I say, shaking my head. And then I hug her again. "I've missed you beyond words. I have to fill you in on so much."

"I was barely out of commission for a day," Evie says, looking baffled. "Why didn't you text me?"

"It was one day too many and I don't think this is something I could explain in a *text*," I say, and then in a quick rush, "Third Eye knows who my dad is and miraculously don't want me dead for lying, my dad knows about Thomas being a fraud and we kind of had a fight but I think I got some closure, *maybe*, and also the second song in Third Eye's set was about me, so Sky might have a crush on me, and do *not* say I told you so because I will kill you, and also I've had like four separate mental breakdowns. Okay, yeah. There we go."

Evie blinks at me. "Okay. You're right, that's…a lot to process."

"Tell me about it," I say with a sheepish smile. "Oh, and Sky and Vinny are fighting with Thomas right now. I think." I glance at them again, and naturally, Ethan and Mohammed have joined them despite my warning. "Oh, maybe they're all fighting with him. I don't know."

"Well, I'm nosy, so let's go find out," Evie says, grabbing my arm and pulling me toward them. Then she pauses halfway there. "Also, I told you so."

I shove my shoulder into hers and she laughs, dragging me over to Third Eye again.

"…you've caused too much damage," Sky says quietly. "There's no coming back from that."

"But Sky, I thought—you said we'd always be there for each other," Thomas says, shuffling his feet. "I made a mistake, I know that now."

I trade an incredulous look with Evie.

"You could've killed someone and I would've helped you bury the body," Sky says, and the words are filled with intense regret. "But you stabbed all of us in the back. And that's not something I can forgive. I'm sorry."

"Sky, *please*," Thomas says desperately.

"I'm sorry," Sky says again. He looks pained by his own words. "I'm sorry."

Vincent steps in between Skyler and Thomas. Unlike Sky, he doesn't appear to have any sympathy for whatever plight Thomas is going through.

"You need to let this go," Vincent says. "Sky is too good of a person and loves you too much, so he won't say it, but I will. You did an unforgivable thing, and you need to live with it."

Behind him, Mohammed and Ethan nod in solidarity.

Thomas looks at Sky again, but Vincent moves closer to Thomas, placing a firm hand on his shoulder. "Leave," Vincent says. "Now. Before I lose the little patience I have left."

Thomas keeps standing there, waiting for *something*, but Sky doesn't lift his gaze from where he's staring at his feet.

"Fine," Thomas says after a moment. "But I am sorry, Sky. Really."

"Go," Mohammed says, pointing in the opposite direction. "I'm not going to be as nice as Vinny."

With a frustrated grunt, Thomas leaves. He passes Evie and I on the way, and we flip him off simultaneously.

"What an asshole," I say, not bothering to be quiet about it.

Evie nods in agreement. "Thank God you upgraded."

"Shut up," I hiss, flicking her arm.

"Have you kissed yet?" she whispers back, because my best friend is nothing if not a menace.

I shush her and move closer to the other boys, nudging Vincent with my shoulder. "You did a good job."

"Yeah, well." Vincent runs a hand through his hair. "Someone had to do it."

Sky sighs, leaning against the wall. "I wish things could have been different."

All of his boys move as one to surround him in a show of support. "I know," Ethan says softly. "But you have us. And we're not going anywhere."

Skyler smiles at them, though it's a wistful thing. "I know. My guardian angels."

"Always," Mohammed says, squeezing Sky's shoulder.

"You couldn't get rid of us if you tried," Vinny adds.

Ethan holds his pinky out. Immediately, Sky, Vincent, and Mohammed add their pinkies. When Ethan looks at me pointedly, I step closer, adding my pinky to the mix. It doesn't really work, too many fingers in the mix, but I don't think any of us really care.

"Pinky promise?" Ethan asks.

"Pinky promise," everyone says, and it feels like an oath.

60

LOVE AGAIN—DUA LIPA

Eventually, we split into separate groups to get ice cream. Evie announces she'll be going in Vincent's car with a not-so-subtle wink at Skyler.

I glare at her and she only laughs in return. "What? It's a gays-only car. I can't help you."

Vincent chokes on air while Ethan snorts.

Mohammed frowns, holding his keys out pointedly like that'll change Evie's mind. "This feels like a hate crime somehow."

"It's not," Evie says with a derisive pat on the head. "Now everybody get in their respective vehicles before I start swinging."

"I still don't like her," Mohammed announces. Sky huffs a quiet laugh.

"It makes so much sense that you two are best friends," Vincent says, looking between Evie and me with exasperation.

"I think she's great," Ethan says with a shrug. "And she's right. Let's go, I want ice cream and I want it now!"

And as everyone knows, when Ethan wants something, he

gets it. Vincent starts the engine of his Jeep while Moham-med reluctantly slides into his own beat-up car. I'm hyper-aware of the fact that I'm alone with Sky for the first time since the showcase ended.

"So," I say, tugging uselessly at my bangs as we start walk-ing to his car.

"So," Sky says, a smile on his face. He's playing with his keys, flipping them between his fingers.

There's something in the air between us that neither of us is willing to put into words. A flush rises on my cheeks when I catch him staring at me.

The tips of Skyler's ears turn red, but he doesn't look away. We hold each other's gazes for one beat, two beats, three beats, until I finally break the silence.

"I made you a playlist," I say, holding out my phone.

He raises his eyebrows but takes it, glancing down at the screen.

(s)orta (k)inda (y)ours:
Scary Love—The Neighborhood
Blinded—Emmit Fenn
Spectrum—Florence and the Machine
Trust—Alina Baraz
Songbird—Fleetwood Mac
Magic—Coldplay
Work Song—Hozier
Heavenly—Cigarettes After Sex
Atlas: Two—Sleeping At Last
Nobody but Us—Noah Mac
It's Nice To Have A Friend—Taylor Swift

"Sorta kinda yours?" Sky asks, his lips settling into a crooked grin as he hands me back my phone.

"Sorta kinda," I agree, the corners of my mouth lifting in response to how bright his face is.

"You like me," he says, bumping shoulders with me. "You *like* like me."

"Debatable," I say but there's so much affection in my voice that I'm not fooling anyone, much less him. "I think you *like* like me. You wrote me a song or whatever?"

Sky taps his chin, pursing his lips. "I don't recall doing that."

"No?" I ask and stop walking to put my hands on my hips. "So what was 'Late Night' about?"

"My secret love affair with Mohammed," Sky says without missing a beat.

"Wrong sibling," I say and Skyler gives me a scandalized look. I burst into laughter. "Sorry."

"You're a menace to society, Liana," he says but his eyes are so, so warm.

I don't think I've ever liked someone this much. There's a rush in my blood and a flutter in my rib cage and kick in my heart. I have no idea how I let Skyler Moon of all people do this to me.

Except that I do, and I don't regret it at all.

I go to mess with my bangs again when he stops me, brushing them gently off my forehead.

"Dollar for your thoughts?" he asks.

"The price went up," I say lightly. "Inflation."

Sky gives me an exasperated look but enables me anyway because he's a sweetheart. "Two dollars for your thoughts?"

I hold my hand out, wiggling my fingers.

He looks skyward, as if asking a higher being for help, but

reaches into his back pocket all the same, pulling out his wallet. When he sifts through, all he finds is a twenty-dollar bill.

"I don't have change," he says with a frown.

I let out a dramatic sigh. "I suppose I'll have to start a tab for you."

"You're too kind," Sky says dryly, putting his wallet back. "Go on, then."

I stick my tongue out at him. "I was thinking you're ridiculous and I have no idea why I like you as much as I do."

It's heart-wrenching how quickly Skyler's face lights up at the words. "So you do like me."

"You knew that," I say, rolling my eyes and walking ahead of him, toward his car. At this rate, the others are going to get there eons before us.

"I like hearing it," Sky says, jogging to catch up with me. "Don't walk so fast, Lia."

"Walk faster, old man," I say over my shoulder.

"I'm only six months older than you," he says, distraught.

When I reach the passenger door, he slips in front of me, stopping me from opening it.

"Yes, Skyler?" I ask, tilting my head back to look at him. When our eyes meet, my heart skips a beat for absolutely no reason.

He tucks my hair behind my ear before cupping my face. "I want to be brave, Liana," he says quietly.

"Is this your way of asking to kiss me?" I ask, peering up at him through my lashes.

"Sorta kinda," he says, brushing his thumb against my cheekbone. "Is this your way of saying yes?"

"Sorta kinda," I say, and it's more than answer enough.

Skyler smiles and leans in.

61

EPILOGUE—JUSTIN HURWITZ

The clock in my therapist's office is two minutes slow. I've had weekly appointments for the last eight months, and it's the first time I've noticed it.

"Are you looking forward to something?" Helen asks, pulling my attention back to her. She's smiling at me warmly, her thin wire glasses perched on her nose.

"Sorry, what?" I ask.

"You keep checking the clock," she says, a knowing look in her eyes. "You usually linger even after our sessions end, but today, you seem to be in a rush."

"Oh." I flush, leaning back in my seat and fiddling with one of the fidget toys Helen keeps in her office. It's a nice, comforting environment, with earth-toned walls and bookshelves filled with cute little knickknacks. "No, sorry, I'm good. It's just—my boyfriend is picking me up today."

Helen's eyes light up. "Skyler, right? How is he?"

Even though it's been months since I started seeing her, it

still warms my chest to know she remembers the names of people I mention to her. I know it's her job, but it's nice to feel listened to. "Yeah, Sky. He's good! Him and his band have been recording their first album, so he's been a little busy. I scaled back my days at Ripple Records to focus on finals, so I haven't seen him since last week."

Helen nods, jotting something on her notepad. Her note-taking made me anxious the first few weeks, but when I told her, she offered to show me what she was writing. It was mostly to keep track of everything I was saying, to make sure she did her job properly and didn't slip up. Since then, I haven't thought much of it.

"Speaking of finals," Helen continues, "they're coming up pretty soon. How are you feeling about them?"

"Stressed," I admit, putting down the fidget toy to mess with my bangs. They're getting a little too long, in need of a trim. "But it's my own fault. I've been putting off studying and leaving my final papers to the last minute."

Helen hums. "Any particular reason why?"

She probably already knows why, but she asked a question, so I answer. "The end of the semester already feels too real. If I actually start gearing up for finals, it means my freshman year is over…and I don't want to think about going home."

"To your father," Helen says, kind but blunt. "Have the two of you spoken much lately?"

"Only at work," I say, chewing on my bottom lip. Ever since our fight last summer, the two of us have been walking on eggshells with each other, even more so than usual. I still technically live at my father's house, though I dorm for most of the year. After college… Well… I'll cross that bridge when I get to it.

Helen raises her brows. "Earlier, you said you scaled your internship days back in preparation for finals. But just now, you mentioned that you've been procrastinating. Is there any other reason you might be scaling back your days?"

I smile ruefully. "You're a little too good at your job."

Helen returns the smile but doesn't say anything, waiting for me to speak.

"Fine. My mom's birthday is coming up, and I don't really want to be around my dad for it," I say with a sigh. I can only imagine how suffocating it'll be if we spend the day together. Both of us drowning in grief, but refusing to talk about it with each other. "Are you happy now?"

"Are *you* happy?" Helen asks instead, which feels like an unexpected sucker punch to the chest.

I blink slowly, considering the question for longer than is probably necessary. Helen doesn't rush me, content to wait for me to gather my thoughts. "I don't know," I finally say. "I think I'm getting there."

"That's good," Helen says softly. "What makes you happy these days?"

I shrug. "I don't know. My classes? They're pretty fun. I like learning new things. Um, my suite mates? We're having a movie night this weekend. It's my turn to pick, and I think I'll probably go with that new Emmitt Ramos movie. Evie, always. I'm not looking forward to the summer, but I am looking forward to seeing her again. Spring break wasn't long enough. There's my boyfriend, obviously, and the rest of Third Eye. They're like a second family to me. I guess all things considered, I have it pretty good."

"But…?"

"…But I'm still sad sometimes. I'm still exhausted by life sometimes. It's weird, knowing you should be happy, but not quite feeling it?"

Helen makes a noise of understanding. "Have you been writing to your mom like we discussed in your last session?"

I nod. I left the leather journal back in my dorm, but I've been using it diligently. "Yeah, I write in it every night. I usually just recount my days, but that's fine, right?"

"Of course! What you write in your journal is up to you," Helen says, making another note. "Have you found that thinking about her is a little easier nowadays?"

I tap my fingers against the arm of my chair. I don't register it at first, but it's to the beat of one of Third Eye's new songs. "What do you mean?"

"You mentioned a few sessions back that sometimes even talking about your mother can be triggering for you. But now you write to your mother every day. Has it helped when it comes to thinking about her? Or do thoughts of her still cause you to spiral?" Helen asks, as patient as ever when it comes to my questions.

I take another long moment to think about it, searching through my recent memories. "It's…been a while since it's bothered me," I say, slightly surprised. "I guess thinking about her has become kind of normal for me?"

Helen smiles widely. "Okay. Let me know if there are any further changes on that front. Grief isn't a linear path, but you know that already."

"Yeah, I do," I say, brushing my bangs away from my face. "You know, my dad could probably benefit from therapy, too."

"He definitely could," Helen says, a little bit of derision slipping into her voice, and I press my lips together to keep from laughing. For the most part, Helen tries to stay neutral, but it's obvious she doesn't like Baba.

I don't know much about Helen's background, but she's also a woman of color, being Filipino, so she understands a lot of the weird, tricky dynamics between me and my dad that I don't have the energy to explain to white people. It's nice to be able to speak freely and trust that she'll get it.

"Maybe in another lifetime," I say, rolling my eyes. "In this one, he's too stubborn to accept help."

"But you're not, which is what matters. I know you're not looking forward to spending the next few months at home, and I don't blame you. However, I did ask around about our school policy, and we should be able to continue our sessions through the summer, so hopefully that'll provide a safe space for you to express yourself," Helen says, and I sit up straight, my eyes wide. She must see the excitement on my face because she chuckles. "Will you be able to make the necessary travel accommodations?"

"Yes," I say, nodding rapidly. If Sky can't drive me, I'll take an Uber. The campus isn't too far from my dad's house, anyway. "I'll be here."

"I'm glad," Helen says warmly. "Now let's talk about cognitive distortions. Last time, we were discussing..."

The rest of the session goes by quickly, though my eyes do

drift to the clock now and then. Helen doesn't call me out on it again, but I'm sure she notices.

When I'm heading toward the door, Helen calls, "Have fun with Sky!" and I feel my chest flood with warmth.

"Thank you," I say, flashing her one last smile.

As far as therapy sessions go, this was one of our more relaxed ones. The first few were brutal, recounting all kinds of past trauma and forcing myself to reconcile with the fact that neglect is still abuse. Nowadays, it's a little easier, since Helen already knows the worst of it.

I knew going to therapy would help, but I didn't realize just how much. When things get bad, I know there's a light at the end of the tunnel, someone to tell who will know how to help me, and it makes all the difference in the world.

Once I've packed my things for the weekend, I make my way to the parking lot near my dorm.

Within seconds, I spot Skyler. He's leaning against his car, thumbs tucked into his jean pockets, and my stomach bursts into butterflies for no reason at all. He's been growing his hair out a little recently, the front strands falling into his face in a way that's awfully attractive.

When he sees me skipping toward him, he grins, dimples pressing into his cheeks. "Hi, Lia."

"Hi, Sky," I say and throw my arms around his neck once I reach him. He immediately slips his hands under my thighs to pick me up, spinning me around for good measure while I laugh into his neck, pressing a kiss to one of the beauty marks there.

He sets me down eventually, but not without leaning in and capturing my lips in a brief kiss. "It's been too long."

I roll my eyes good-naturedly. "It's been a week."

"Too long," he says very seriously, and then walks around the car to open the passenger door for me.

It shouldn't make me as happy as it does, but I'm just so glad to see him. He's right. It has been too long.

Once we're settled into the car, I pull out my phone, a playlist already prepared for our drive.

I dreamed of you:

Electric—Alina Baraz (feat. Khalid)
Waking Up Slow (Piano Version)—Gabrielle Aplin
Call It What You Want—Taylor Swift
bad—wave to earth
Words Will Never Do—Sarah Close
Nonsense—Sabrina Carpenter
Love Poem—IU
Beautiful Mess—LOS LEO
Mirrors—Justin Timberlake
Bravery—Summer Ali

Before I can grab the aux cord, Sky stops me, his fingers circling around my wrist gently. I stare at his hand in confusion, focused on his rings like they'll give me an answer.

"What? Should I pick a different playlist?" I ask when he doesn't say anything.

Still silence.

I glance up at him in question. He looks...nervous?

"Oh God, what did Mo do?" My head thunks against the headrest. "Or was it Vinny and Ethan? Whose mess am I cleaning up?"

My words startle Sky into laughter, easing the wrinkles by his forehead. "No, there's no mess. Not that I'm aware of, at least." He shrugs, smiling slightly. "You never know with them."

"I can't believe you're leaving them unsupervised for the whole day," I say, grinning. "Who knows what havoc they'll wreak?"

"They promised they'd be on their best behavior," Sky says, and the nervous tension melts entirely off his face, replaced by fondness. "I want to show you something."

"Oh?"

He nods, reaching into the back seat for his bag. I lean forward, intrigued. I figured he'd show me a new song on his phone maybe. What could possibly be inside his bag?

"Close your eyes," he says after a moment, shoving whatever it is deeper in between the flaps to maintain the surprise.

I raise my eyebrows. "Seriously?"

"Seriously," he says, and when I don't immediately do it, he pouts at me. "Lia, come on. Just for ten seconds."

My nose wrinkles in protest, but the longer he works his beautiful brown eyes on me, the harder it becomes to refuse him.

"Fine," I grumble and cover my eyes with my hands. "There."

Sky leans in, pressing a quick kiss to the back of my hand, and my blood rushes to my cheeks. I don't know how he still manages to fluster me this much. "Thank you."

There's a bit of rustling, and finally he taps my hands lightly. "Open."

It takes a moment for me to process what Sky is holding, but when I do, I inhale sharply. "Is that—?"

"Yeah," Sky says, beaming at me. "Our first album."

I gape and snatch it out of his hands. He laughs, letting go easily so I can look at it.

Across the front, in bold gold lettering:

THIRD EYE
FAMILIAR

"Holy shit," I breathe, my fingers ghosting over the picture of the band in their usual spots—Ethan on drums, Mo behind his piano, Vinny and Sky in front with their respective guitars. They're dressed in black-and-white coordinating outfits we picked together with the design team. They wanted to shoot the cover in the music studio, simple and unassuming.

Familiar, like the album title promises.

"Holy shit, Sky," I say again, eyes wide. "I'm so proud of you. This is incredible!"

Sky's cheeks are bright pink with pleasure. "Thanks, Lia. We couldn't have done it without you. *I* couldn't have done it without you."

"You could have, but I'm glad to be a part of the journey," I say, bumping my shoulder against his across the console. "This is amazing, really. I can't believe I'm holding your first album right now!"

I flip to the back, looking at the track list. Instead of an EP, they're going all in with a full album that has twelve tracks, all of which I've heard before…except now that I'm looking at it, there's one I don't recognize.

$$$ For Your Thoughts?

"Which one is this?" I ask, but a part of me already knows, buzzing with giddy anticipation. "I don't think I've heard it."

Sky laughs quietly. "Why don't we play it and find out?"

I tilt my head to the side. "Skyler Moon, did you write another song about me?"

"Aren't you awfully full of yourself?" Sky asks, but he's teasing, his eyes warm and full of stars. "Play the song, Liana Sarkar."

"You wrote another song about me," I say, sure of it now. He's so ridiculous, and I'm so unbelievably smitten. "Wasn't one enough?"

Sky takes the CD out of its case, slipping it into the stereo. The first few notes start playing, beautiful and vibrant, just like him. I relax into my seat, letting the music wash over me.

"I could write a million songs about you," Skyler says, "and it still wouldn't be enough."

★ ★ ★ ★ ★

ACKNOWLEDGMENTS

In honor of Liana, I'd like to start off by thanking the people that music and fandom and community brought to me—Fari Cannon, Kristina Urbanova, Pietra Ibrisimovic, Z. Ahmadi, Holly Hughes, Juliana Ogarrio, and Nina Petropoulos. Thank God we all decided to love the exact same musician at the exact same time. Kind of the equivalent of being at the same gig, isn't it? Siri, play "Fireproof" by One Direction...

Aside from that, there are so many people to thank for allowing me to bring this story to life. Thank you to the publishing team that made this possible, starting with my wonderful, incredible agent, JL Stermer, who deserves all the pretzels in the world. Thank you to my editor, Claire Stetzer, who helped the heart of this story shine through. Thank you to the entire crew at Inkyard Press, including the wonderful Bess Braswell, Brittany Mitchell, and Kamille Carreras Pereira. And thank you to Alex Niit and Karmen Loh for creating the book cover of my dreams!

Thank you to my most beloved Chloe Gong, the person this book is dedicated to. Though music isn't what brought us together, it feels a little like Taylor Swift had a hand in it. I'm certain that Liana has definitely sent Evie the same unhinged texts I send you every time we lose a surprise song on the Eras Tour. (Still mourning the loss of "You Are In Love." A Brutal Hit.) I'm so grateful for your existence in my life, and I truly don't know how I would cope with how dire the publishing industry is without you by my side. Here's to a few less standing-side-by-side emojis and to a few more WIMZ! Thank you to the rest of my dear D.A.C.U., Christina Li, Racquel Marie, and Zoe Hana Mikuta. Thank you to my loves, LinLi Wan, Rachel Koltsov, Kadeen Griffiths, Hannah Vitton, Genesis Mendoza, Lorena Valenzuela, Kaitlyn Findley, Sofia Tulachan, Anam Sattar, Dustin Thao, Leah Jordain, Page Powars and Helen Urena. Thank you to my family, Zareen Khan, Fabia Mahmud, and Shannon Ali. Thank you to my cat, Zuko "Zucchini" Bhuiyan.

Thank you to my Dadu, wherever you are now. I promise you'll always live on in my stories.

Thank you to every single musician mentioned in this book. Your art inspires my art, and I'm so grateful for it. I hope you all continue to create music forever.

Finally, thank you to Stray Kids and 3RACHA for allowing me to use your lyrics to help tell Liana's story. I hold the song "Levanter" close to my heart for a number of reasons, and this is another one to add to the list.